SEATTLE NOIR

SEATTLE NOIR

EDITED BY CURT COLBERT

AKASHIC BOOKS
NEW YORK

Published by Akashic Books
©2009 Akashic Books

Series concept by Tim McLoughlin and Johnny Temple
Seattle map by Sohrab Habibion

ISBN-13: 978-1-933354-80-4
Library of Congress Control Number: 2008937353

First printing

Akashic Books
PO Box 1456
New York, NY 10009
info@akashicbooks.com
www.akashicbooks.com

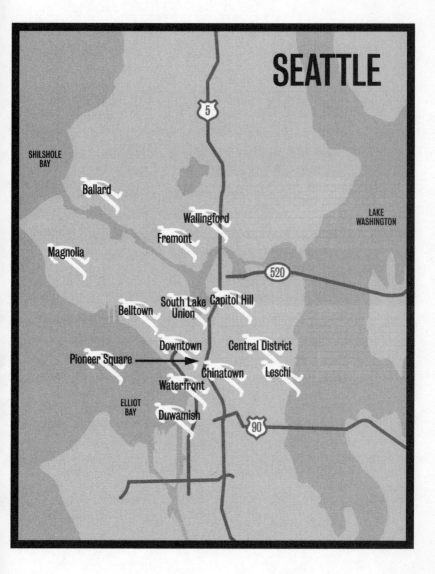

TABLE OF CONTENTS

PART III: LOVE IS A FOUR-LETTER WORD

PART IV: TO THE LIMITS

INTRODUCTION

E arly Seattle was a hardscrabble seaport filled with merchant sailors, longshoremen, lumberjacks, rowdy saloons, and a rough-and-tumble police force not immune to corruption and graft.

Among the more notorious crimes in the city's early history was the case of Seattle Mayor Corliss P. Stone. A businessman and former member of the city council, Mayor Stone's term was cut short in 1873 when he got caught embezzling $15,000 from his firm, Stone & Burnett. He promptly fled to San Francisco with another man's wife.

In 1909, members of the Chamber of Commerce decided that a totem pole would be the perfect finishing touch to the downtown business core known as Pioneer Square. They saw nothing wrong with taking a steamer up the coast to Fort Tongass, Alaska, and stealing one from a Tlingit Indian village. Apparently, neither did the citizenry of Seattle, who gathered in great numbers for the totem pole's unveiling, cheering and celebrating not only the grand new symbol, but also the initiative taken in securing it for the city.

Prostitution flourished in early Seattle, the first brothel opening in 1861. By the time of the Klondike Gold Rush in 1897, it was a thriving trade. The city leaders felt they should be getting a cut of the action. But how could this be done? Taxation and license fees came to mind, but what would they call this new source of revenue? They couldn't very well call it a whore tax or prostitute levy. Then somebody came up with a brilliant plan: henceforth, the city would officially designate all prostitutes as "seamstresses" and license and tax them as such. (Outsiders would have been amazed to find that Seattle had more "seamstresses" per capita than any other city in the nation.)

Seattle was also one of the rum-running capitals of America during Prohibition. There were many bootleggers, but the most famous and prolific was a former Seattle police lieutenant named Roy Olmstead. Olmstead was fired from the police department after being busted while unloading a hundred cases of smuggled Canadian whiskey from a boat in Edmonds, Washington, just north of Seattle. After paying a fine, he devoted himself full time to building the largest bootlegging operation in the area and became known in Seattle newspapers as "The King of the Puget Sound Bootleggers." He bought a mansion and lived high on the hog until he was finally taken down in 1924 through the use of federal wiretaps.

By the '50s, Seattle had added Boeing to its claim to fame, but was still a mostly blue-collar burg that was once described as an "aesthetic dustbin" by Sir Thomas Beecham, a short-term conductor of the Seattle Symphony Orchestra. Present-day Seattle has become a pricey, cosmopolitan center, home to Microsoft and legions of Starbucks latte lovers. The city is now famous as the birthplace of grunge music, and possesses a flourishing art, theater, and club scene that many would have thought improbable just a few decades ago. Yet some things never change—crime being one of them.

Seattle's evolution to high finance and high tech has provided even greater opportunity and reward to those who might be ethically, morally, or economically challenged (crooks, in other words). *Seattle Noir* explores the seamy underbelly of this gleaming, modern metropolis known as "The Emerald City."

The stories in the first section of the book, "Gone South," delve into the sinister direction that some people's lives can take. Thomas P. Hopp's "Blood Tide" follows a Native American shaman caught in a web of secrets and tribal allegiances. An East Indian woman's assumptions about friendship and loss, death and rebirth, are reflected by how her garden grows in Bharti Kirchner's "Promised Tulips." Stephan Magcosta's cautionary tale, "Golden Gardens," focuses on the wages of prejudice and the cost of hate. Next, Robert Lopresti's "The Center of the Universe" is set in the city's Fremont neighborhood, the self-proclaimed "center of the universe," where the resolution of the story's violence and strange happenings is, itself, exceedingly strange.

The anthology's second section, "What Comes Around," might best be illuminated by a quote from the greatest pitcher in the old Negro Leagues, and maybe in the history of baseball, Satchel Paige: "And don't look back—something might be gaining on you." "Blue Sunday" by Kathleen Alcalá takes a Latino soldier on leave from the Iraq War and throws him to the mercies of a not-so-friendly cop—a cop who later finds out exactly what comes around. Simon Wood's story, "The Taskmasters," actually takes exception to the rule: that what comes around, in rare instances, can actually be redeeming. Patricia Harrington's "What Price Retribution?" answers its own question with an example of doing what's right, even when it's wrong.

The book's third section, "Love Is a Four-Letter Word," explores some of the alternative four-letter words that love can conjure up. My own historical story, "Till Death Do Us . . ." features a husband and wife whose marriage has gone south, while they've gone east and west. Paul S. Piper's "The Best View in Town" relates the problems faced by a guy who thinks his view is the best around . . . until another person's views collide with his own. In R. Barri Flowers's "The Wrong End of a Gun," a divorced African American father meets a gorgeous woman who takes him on as many twists and turns as the Senegalese twists in her hair.

The authors in the final section of the book take their characters, and the reader, "To the Limits." In Brian Thornton's historical tale, "Paper Son," a newly minted Treasury agent working in Chinatown finds inscrutability to be an unavoidable fact of life. And in Skye Moody's story, "The Magnolia Bluff," a famous dwarf actor finds that his roles begin to shrink as he mysteriously starts growing taller. One of the Moriarity brothers lures Sherlock Holmes to Seattle in Lou Kemp's historical "Sherlock's Opera"—but the trap he's laid with musical precision unexpectedly plays a few sour notes. Concluding the volume, G.M. Ford's "Food for Thought" stars a private eye who finds the case of a delicatessen owner to be less than kosher.

This is *Seattle Noir*. Cozy up in your favorite easy chair and crack the book open. And be sure to turn up the lights—you'll need them for when it gets dark.

Curt Colbert
Seattle, Washington
March 2009

PART I

GONE SOUTH

BLOOD TIDE

BY THOMAS P. HOPP

Duwamish

W hen we arrived at Herring's House Park, the police were clearing off the yellow warning tape and packing their forensics bags and boxes, closing their case of an odd death in a parking lot and moving on. Kay Erwin, epidemiologist at Seattle Public Health Hospital, had declared it shellfish poisoning, and the cops had quickly lost interest. But Peyton McKean was of a different mind. He was getting the lay of what had happened two days before by interrogating a young cop, rapid fire, as the officer rolled up the crime scene tape.

"The body lay here?" McKean asked, drawing an imaginary oblong line around a spot in the middle of the damp gravel.

"Uh huh," answered the officer, stashing tape in a black garbage bag.

"And the victim's pickup, parked here?" said McKean, sawing a transect line from the parking bumpers out into the lot with his long-fingered hands.

"'At's right," said the officer, cinching the bag and pausing to gaze amusedly at McKean, who moved animatedly around the rain-drizzled lot quickly on long legs, marching off distances with his hands tucked behind his back like some intense, gangly schoolteacher. McKean was, I could tell, worried that he'd lack some detail of the circumstances surrounding

Erik Torvald's death, when the last cop who had actually seen Torvald lying facedown in the parking lot was gone and done with the case.

As the officer got in his squad car and prepared to close the door, McKean called somewhat desperately, "Anything else I should know?"

"Nuttin'," said the cop, slamming his door and backing away, making a half-friendly wave at McKean as he left us alone in the lot.

"There's more here than meets the eye, Fin Morton," muttered McKean, lifting his olive-green canvas fedora and scratching in the dark hair of one temple.

"There's nothing here that meets my eye," I replied, zipping up my windbreaker against the drizzle that had begun as soon as we got out of my Mustang. I looked around the otherwise empty quadrangle of gravel, the alder woods that stretched down to the bank of the Duwamish River below the lot, and the mud-puddled gravel footpaths, without much hope of spotting a clue. The park was devoid of people on a wet Thursday afternoon. "Maybe the cops are right. Maybe he just had shellfish poisoning. Don't you think that's possible?"

"Answer: no," said McKean in his pedagogical way. "The levels of red tide poison in him were without precedent, off the scale by any measure. To get the dose Kay Erwin found in his blood, he'd have to have eaten ten buckets of steamers, or a dozen geoducks"—he pronounced the word properly: *gooey ducks*. "And yet," he continued, "my immunoassay tests for shellfish residues in his guts came up strictly negative. He hadn't eaten a bit of shellfish. The police may be satisfied that he poisoned himself, but neither Kay nor I believe it. Foul play is at work here, Fin. Somebody killed him, and I'd like to know who."

"Right now," I said, moving to the door of my midnight-blue Ford Mustang, "I'd like to get out of this drizzle."

McKean took one last look around the park as if wishing there were more to see than bare alder trees against a gloomy gray Seattle sky. Then he acquiesced, lapsing into thoughtful silence as I drove us out onto West Marginal Way and headed north past the Duwamish Tribal Office, an old gray house beside a construction site with a sign that read: *Future Site of the Duwamish Longhouse.*

"Muckleshoot Casino cash finally having an impact," mumbled McKean absentmindedly as I headed for his labs on the downtown waterfront, where I had picked him up earlier. McKean suddenly cried, "Turn right, right here!"

I pulled the wheel hard and we bounded across some railroad tracks and onto a gravel drive that took us to another riverside parking lot, this one with a sign reading, *Terminal 105 Salmon Habitat Restoration Site and Public Access Park.*

"What's here?" I asked, pulling up at a dismal postage stamp of greenery wedged between a scrap yard downriver and a defunct container terminal pier upriver, irked at how easily McKean had yanked my chain.

"It's not *what's* here," he said, opening his door with a cerebral glow in his eyes, "but *who's* here."

At the end of a graveled path an observation platform overlooked the Duwamish River. McKean leaned his lanky frame on the rail and pointed a thin finger out across the expanse of muddy water to where several strings of Day-Glo–red plastic gillnet floats drifted on a slow upstream tide, overshadowed in the distance by the container cranes and skyscrapers of Seattle. A fisherman in a small dingy was at the nets, pulling a big sockeye salmon into his boat. He quickly disengaged the netting from its gills and returned the net to the water. A fine drizzle dappled the brown water and lent a sheen to the fisherman's dark green raincoat and hood. It put a damp chill on the back of my neck.

"Unless I miss my guess," said McKean, "that's my old high school chum, Frank Squalco."

"How can you be sure that's him?"

"I recall Franky Squalco from art class at West Seattle High School," said McKean. "Based on that fisherman's humble stature and his rather square form, I guessed it might be Frank when I saw him as you drove. Furthermore, as you see, he's gillnetting salmon, and only tribal people can use gillnets, so the odds improve. I'd like to get his take on this shellfish poisoning business."

"Why would he know anything about it?"

"Because Erik Torvald was a geoduck fisherman, and Natives hold half the rights to geoduck licenses in this state, by law."

As the fisherman drew in another salmon, our view of him was cut off when an outbound tug came down the shipping channel pulling an immense black barge piled with rusty cargo containers, so stupendously huge and near that it seemed for a dizzy moment that our viewing platform was moving past its black metallic hulk, rather than the other way around. When the barge passed downriver under the gray concrete rainbow of the West Seattle Freeway Bridge, the fisherman was already steering his dingy toward our shore. McKean waited, unaffected by the clammy air or the cold droplets that beaded his olive-green canvas field coat and were getting down the neck of my jogging shell. I knit my arms around myself for warmth and wondered why I never dressed sufficiently for the weather I inevitably encountered when I tagged along on these adventures.

The fisherman throttled the boat down and glided into a

small inlet on our right, helloed up at us absentmindedly, and then paused to take a long second look as his dingy bumped the beach.

"Peyton McKean!" A grin of recognition spread across his broad, brown, forty-ish Northwest Native American face. "I haven't seen you in a while. What you doin' down here where us poor Indians fish?"

"We're investigating a murder."

Squalco's face clouded as he stepped out of his boat and pulled it onto the muddy shore with a bowline, his black rubber rain boots slurping in the muck.

"Torvald?" he said. "Yeah. Too bad. Good geoduck man. But why they got you on the case? You're not a cop. You're a DNA man, so I heard. Pretty famous around here. When the Jihad Virus came, your vaccine saved a lot of lives, they say."

McKean brushed the compliment aside. "Not DNA and not vaccines this time. I'm looking into a case of deliberate red tide poisoning."

Squalco was transferring three big salmon from the bottom of his boat into a large plastic bucket on the shore. At McKean's remark, he paused, the third salmon cradled in his arms, one boot in the boat and one in the mud, stooped over. The pause was just momentary, and then he put the salmon in the bucket and turned and faced us where we stood above him on the observation deck. He swallowed hard but said nothing.

"You know something?" McKean asked encouragingly.

Squalco's eyes shot sideways. "Red tide? Sure," he said. "Puts poison in the clams. State of Washington orders us not to dig 'em then. We usually do anyway. I never got more'n a little buzz or two from it. Maybe threw up once or twice—but that coulda been the booze, y'know." He laughed thinly.

"I meant," McKean persisted, "do you know something about red tide in the murder of Erik Torvald?" At 6'6", McKean had a way of looking imperiously down his long nose at people, and our height above Squalco on the deck amplified this effect until the man flinched. He cast his eyes aside again, and then bent and picked up the bucket with both gloved hands, grunting at its weight. He walked up the mud bank to a dented old blue pickup truck, where he huffed the bucket onto the waiting lowered tailgate, and then said to us, "Gotta go. Got plenty-a hungry mouths to feed." He closed the tailgate, came back in a hurry, tied the boat's bowline to the trunk of a small Douglas fir tree, and turned to go. As he reached his truck door, McKean called to him.

"Interesting case."

Squalco paused before getting in. "Yeah?"

"Massive dose of red tide poison. Died quick. No trace of shellfish in his stomach contents. Any idea why?"

"No," Squalco replied without conviction, his eyebrows high and mouth round.

"Red tide poison," said McKean, "is one of the most toxic substances known; a paralytic toxin. First the tongue and lips tingle, then general paralysis sets in."

"I gotta go," said Squalco.

He got in and slammed his door and drove off spraying gravel. Watching him speed down the driveway and turn south on West Marginal Way, McKean shook his head.

"Oh, Frank," he said with a note of regret. "What has my old pal got himself mixed up in?"

Earlier that morning, I had sat at my computer keyboard in my funky old Pioneer Square writing office, working on a boring piece of medical reporting about a new gene therapy for baldness, when I got the phone call from McKean that put me on this case.

He was at the Seattle Public Health Hospital on Pill Hill. "Kay Erwin's got an interesting case for us," he'd said. "A dead man with all the signs of red tide poisoning, but there are reasons to suspect foul play. Wanna follow this one?"

Like always, I'd said, "Sure," and went to meet him. Writing about the exploits of the brilliant Dr. McKean is how I make my best money these days. I caught up with him at the hospital in epidemiologist Kay Erwin's office.

Kay is another person of interest to me. She's a small, cute, pageboy brunette, about forty-five, a bit too old for me to ask on a date, but she always has some piece of news for the medical journalist side of me. White lab–coated, she sat behind her office desk and motioned me into a guest chair with McKean in the other, then launched into a quick update.

"Torvald," she explained, "was found lying comatose beside his pickup, scarcely breathing. The passerby who found him called for help and Torvald was rushed to our ER, where it became clear he had shellfish poisoning symptoms. They pumped his stomach, worked up a blood sample for toxins, and called me in on the case."

"That's when things got interesting," said McKean.

"Yes," agreed Erwin. "His stomach contents didn't contain shellfish. In fact, they matched what was found in his car: the remnants of a McDonald's Quarter Pounder, fries, and a Coke. But the symptoms and the lab analysis are consistent: a massive dose of saxitoxin."

"Saxitoxin is about a thousand times more toxic than nerve gas," said McKean.

"But the most anomalous thing," said Kay, "is that this case doesn't coincide with an actual red tide. The only red tide on Puget Sound this year was in August, and it's now late October. Something fishy's going on."

"Or rather," said McKean, "something clammy."

After Frank Squalco left, I drove us back to McKean's labs at Immune Corporation, feeling that a long-enough day had already transpired, but McKean was indefatigable. On the way, noting that it was only 4:15 p.m., he called his head technician, Janet Emerson, and barraged her with concepts for a new project. As I chauffeured him back across the West Seattle Bridge, he bubbled to her about red tide microbes and toxins, and ways and means to create a new treatment for paralytic shellfish poisoning.

"Get some saxitoxin and crosslink it to diphtheria toxoid and inject it into some mice and we'll make a therapeutic monoclonal antitoxin. What say?" I couldn't hear Janet's reply, but knowing the two of them as I do, I had no doubt she was bravely shouldering the new burden of lab work. And I had little doubt that a creation of McKean's brilliant scientific mind, even one conceived on a drizzly day while riding in my Mustang, would lead to a medicine of great potential. That's just the way things tend to work out with Peyton McKean.

"I should have started this project long ago," he explained after getting off the phone. "But shellfish poisoning is so rare, and so rarely fatal, that no big pharmaceutical company has an interest in developing the antitoxin. But I'll bet Kay Erwin would gladly test my antibodies someday on a desperate patient."

"Anti what?" I asked, my mind more on a road-raging tailgater than McKean's conceptualizing.

"Antibodies," said McKean. "The body's own natural antitoxin molecules. I've just asked Janet to begin preparing some, by immunizing mice against saxitoxin. It's all pretty straight-forward."

As I drove downtown, he did his best to explain how antibodies could bind saxitoxin molecules and remove them from a victim's circulation. Eventually, I dropped him off at Immune Corporation's waterfront headquarters and headed home to my apartment in Belltown with a head full of wonder at how quickly McKean could get involved in a new science project, and doubts as to how all this could solve the case at hand.

Nothing happened for a week or two, but then on a morning that dawned gray and cold, Peyton McKean summoned me to pick him up at his labs and drive to West Seattle to follow a new lead he was exploring. Back on West Marginal Way, McKean pointed me onto Puget Way, which branched off and snaked up the Puget Creek canyon, a damp, fern-bottomed, tree-choked gorge. Up canyon, McKean directed me onto a small moss-covered alleyway that led to a tree-shrouded homesite. The large old house had brick red–painted cedar shingles on its sides, a few of which had dropped loose, a mossy roof with a blue plastic tarp covering a patch where rain had breached the decaying shingles, and a chimney spewing a lazy stream of wood smoke. The hillside yard was home to a jumble of trash, including black plastic garbage bags tossed in the underbrush and overgrown with blackberry brambles. There was a car behind the house without wheels, held up on wooden blocks, and a chaotic pile of alder cordwood next to the porch.

We got out of my car and climbed the mossy concrete steps, but McKean held up a hand and paused to listen. From inside came a slow Native American drumbeat accompanying a male voice singing in a high pitch—a tremulous wail of indecipherable syllables punctuated now and then by unfamiliar consonants: a "tloo" here, a "t'say" there. McKean nodded in thoughtful recognition.

"Lushootseed," he whispered.

"Lu-what?"

"The local dialect of the Salish language. Beautiful, isn't it?"

I listened a moment, thinking McKean's definition of beautiful and mine might vary by a bit, but enjoying the song until it ended with three strong drumbeats.

McKean rapped three times on the weather-beaten door and soon we were greeted by an old, gray, short, and almost toothless lady whose round wrinkled face broke into a broad gummy grin at the sight of McKean.

"Ah!" she cried in a tiny but vibrant voice. "You! After so much time. Welcome!"

She ushered us into a dim, cluttered front room, where a dilapidated couch was occupied by two mongrel dogs that appeared too tired to lift their heads let alone bark and, leaning forward in an overstuffed chair whose arms were losing their stuffing, Frank Squalco, holding a round tambourine-like drum in one hand and a leather-headed mallet in the other.

"*Hui!*" he said, smiling up at my tall companion, who nodded a hello.

"Peyton McKean," the old woman said. "I was teaching Franky a song to call the salmon home, and instead we called Franky's old friend."

She introduced herself to me as Clara Seaweed, then brought us Cokes on ice and offered McKean a comfortable rocking chair near the fireplace, relegating me to the only other seat available, a corner of the couch next to an almost hairless spotted mongrel. I sank into the mangy-smelling cushion with a set of rusty springs croaking.

"So," said Frank, "what brings you here?"

"I came to discuss red tide poison," replied McKean firmly.

"I know you did," said Frank, his smile fading. He leaned forward with his elbows on his knees, looking nervously from McKean to Clara as if realizing the only words possible in this room were truthful ones. He started without prompting.

"Shamans used to make a kind of potion from red tide."

"How was that done?" asked McKean, perking up like a dog on a scent.

"Don't know."

"But you know something. I could see it on your face the other day."

Frank looked at the floor. "Yeah. I know something." He looked up at McKean and said, "Henry George knows how to make the poison."

"Perhaps he's our murderer," I said, to a resounding silence.

"Naw," said Frank. "He's a harmless old geezer, part Muckleshoot and part Suquamish."

"And all crazy," interjected Clara. "Stays with folks on charity. Been under this roof a few times."

"But he's a real shaman," said Frank. "Knows the old ways. Told me once, when I was a kid, about making red tide poison. I don't remember much except you skim the pink foam off the water, then you make it into poison."

"Where can we find this Henry George?" asked McKean.

"He sometimes stays down along the river in our village."

"Village?" I said. "I didn't see any Indian village down there."

"Our village is gone," said Squalco. "White folks burned

us out in the 1890s—nothin' left standing. Used to be across the street from where they're building the new longhouse."

"Or," said Clara, "try upriver at Terminal 107. Our village was all along there, for a mile or more by the Duwamish river-banks. You look for Henry anywhere in there. A lot of bushes and trees and places to camp."

We left to search for Henry George, but first went to The Spud at Alki Beach on the west side of West Seattle to get some fish and chips and Cokes to go. At Herring's House Park we ate lunch in the car to avoid a drizzle and then got out to find George. After some searching along trails in the wet under-growth that paralleled a meandering loop of the main chan-nel, we checked a culvert through which Puget Creek trickled into the Duwamish River and found the old man camped in a lean-to made of blue tarps.

"Poison?" he said bitterly when McKean explained our interest. "I got white man's poison in me right now. Alcohol. Tide's running against Duwamish people these days. We had it running our way a few years ago when Clinton signed a piece of paper saying Duwamish was a recognized tribe. Then Bush came along and crossed out every order Clinton made. Just like that. Swept us out like trash. A'yahos knows why."

"A'yahos?" I asked, getting out a pen and notepad. "Who's that?"

"The two-headed serpent god, like the river slithering first this way, then that way, with the tide. He brings strong medi-cine from the sea, but he can take away stuff too, like people's lives. He's part of the balance of nature. In, out, back, forth, everything moves in time to the tides. Someday the white man's tide will go out."

McKean scowled, impatient to learn what we'd come to

find out. "Can you tell us," he said, stooping to look George in the eye, "how to make red tide poison?"

The old man stared at McKean for a moment, then picked up a stick and poked at a little smoldering fire. "You take two canoes out on a calm day, towing one behind the other. You find some big eddy lines of the pinkest foam on the water. Then you take your paddle and skim the foam and put it in the second canoe until it's full to the gunnels. Then you paddle somewhere people can't see, like over on Muddy Island, and you mix the foam with sea water and some pieces of whale blubber."

"Who can get whale blubber?" I asked.

"Indian people can get lots of stuff," he said, flashing a gap-toothed grin. "After you soak up enough poison to make the blubber blood-red all the way to the middle, then you put it in a pot and add firewood ashes and heat it till it melts. Then you skim off the grease, and the water's all dark red now. Then you dry it. It's a blackish-red powder. Don't taste like nothing. Don't smell like nothing. Just poisons folks real good. Lotta work, though. Takes all the foam you can get into a boat to make a few doses. Takes a lotta time."

"Assuming you're working alone," said McKean.

"Shamans always work alone. You don't ask your mother to help you gather poison. She'd tell everyone."

McKean questioned George further, but there was little else to be gleaned, especially as the old man sipped wine from a pint flask until his eyelids drooped and he lay down and fell asleep next to his cold fire.

Heading back along the footpath to the parking lot, we found our way blocked by a young Indian man. He was dressed in a long black leather coat, had his black hair braided on each side, wore a scowl on his otherwise handsome dark face, and, ominously, carried a woodsman's hatchet.

"What you white folks want with Henry George?"

McKean said, "We're here about a poisoning. You know anything?"

"Wouldn't tell you if I did. You leave the old man alone."

McKean sized up the young man. "What's your name?"

"Won't tell you that either. Now, you'd best move along." He stepped aside to let us pass, pointing the way with his hatchet. He tailed us back to the lot, keeping his distance.

Nervous about his intentions, I hurried into my car and quickly fired the engine while McKean got in. As I drove away, the young man stopped beside a shiny black Dodge Ram pickup that hadn't been there before, conversing sullenly with its occupant, a tall man silhouetted through a tinted windshield. I turned onto West Marginal Way and headed for downtown, slugging down some Coke to sooth a fear-parched throat. "Now what?" I asked.

McKean tapped his own Coke against mine in a mock toast and took a long pull. "Leave nothing but footprints," he said, "and take nothing but pictures." He held his cell phone so I could see the image on its screen. He'd snapped a photo of the man beside the pickup. "We'll ask Frank to tell us who that is. Oh, and a bonus," he said. "I got their license plate in the shot."

Peyton McKean is, among other things, the inventor of a couple dozen DNA forensic tests, so he is pretty well connected for a man who doesn't carry a detective's badge. As I drove, he called an acquaintance who owed him a favor: Vince Nagumo of the Seattle FBI office. Within minutes, Nagumo had identified the owner of the pickup as Craig Showalter, age thirty, of White Center. McKean asked him to look into the man's background and Nagumo promised to get on it right away. I had another sip of Coke and then set it down in its cup holder.

"Do your lips tingle?" I asked McKean.

"I was hoping it was just the chill air," replied McKean thoughtfully.

Adrenaline ran through me like an electric shock and I pulled to the side of the road. "Have we just been poisoned?" I asked. Without comment, McKean opened his door, put a finger down his throat and vomited. I followed suit, splattering the pavement on my side as well.

"That may be too little prevention, too late," said McKean. "Depending on the dose. Can you drive, Fin?"

"To the hospital?"

"No. Take us to my labs, quickly."

I floored the gas and he got on his phone. "Janet, get all the mouse antiserum together. Get it ready for injection into two patients."

"There's not enough blood in a mouse—" I began, but McKean interrupted.

"You can dilute antisera vastly. A little may go a long way."

Panicky minutes followed as my car roared and McKean described the very symptoms I was experiencing. "Depending upon the toxin dose, the sensation of tingling lips progresses to tingling of fingers and toes—" I felt my fingers tingle as I wrenched the steering wheel and skidded onto the ramp of the West Seattle Bridge; my toes tingled as I floored the accelerator and the tires screamed. "Next," McKean continued as we streaked across the highrise span above the Duwamish River, "you may lose control of your arms and legs—" I struggled to keep in my lane as the Mustang rocketed northbound on the Alaskan Way Viaduct toward downtown. "Some victims experience a sense of floating or vertigo—" My head swam and my vision grew hazy while I fought to keep from driving through the railings and dropping us fifty feet onto the railroad tracks.

"How about going blind?" I gasped. "I'm having trouble seeing the road. It's all going red."

McKean thought a moment. "Blindness is not a part of this syndrome. But seeing red is common when people feel extreme rage or fear."

"I'm feeling both right now."

"Is your heart pounding?"

"Isn't yours?"

"Seeing red occurs when blood pumps so rapidly it floods the retina of the eye until one can actually see it. I suggest you keep cool, Fin."

"Keep—" I tried to protest but gagged on my pounding heartbeat.

My vision grew redder, my hearing roared, and McKean's voice receded as he said, "Finally, the chest muscles become paralyzed and the victim stops breathing."

Just two blocks from the lab, my vision went from red to black.

"Wake up, Fin."

An angelic voice brought me back and I looked around groggily. "Wha—? Where?"

"You're with me, Fin," said Kay Erwin, her pretty face coming into focus above me. "You're at Seattle Public Health Hospital. How do you feel?"

"Better than yesterday," I said, noticing Peyton McKean leaning over her shoulder, observing me like I was a lab rat.

"Better than two days ago," he corrected. "You've been comatose for forty-eight hours. Took one sip more than I did. The antibodies barely pulled you through."

"But your vital signs are great this morning," said Kay. "No permanent damage."

"How'd I get here?" I asked, struggling to remember missing events.

"You managed to get us to the lab, Fin," said McKean, "though it was close. Janet met us at the curbside and injected half the antibodies into each of us, then called an ambulance. Kay tended us through the crisis. We're both well on the way to recovery. My antiserum worked!"

The next day, as Kay signed my release papers, McKean rushed into my room. "I hope you're up for a drive, Fin. Vince Nagumo just called with news. The police are after Craig Showalter. They raided his home and found a methamphetamine lab. Two of his henchmen dead in a gun battle, but Showalter's still on the loose. He hightailed it the evening before, according to his girlfriend."

"So, what next?" I asked.

"Let's go have a powwow."

An hour later, sitting in Clara's living room, McKean showed Frank and Clara his photo of the man by the pickup. Clara gasped, "That's my nephew, Billy Seaweed. He's a good kid."

Frank shook his head. "Got some strange friends, though, like Erik Torvald. For a white guy, he was all right, but still a white man to the bone, because he was using Billy's tribal rights to get geoduck licenses. Used power gear to siphon up half the sea bottom when he took 'em. Not like we used to do:

dig 'em up with a stick and fill in the hole. Still, Torvald was a lot nicer than Billy's new partner."

"Craig Showalter?" asked McKean.

"How'd you know that?"

"I've got connections. Vince Nagumo, FBI."

"Billy's an Internet addict," said Frank. "A kinda Indian Goth. Obsessed with darkness and apocalyptic stuff. But I don't think Billy's a killer."

"Showalter's a bad choice of friends," said McKean. "According to Nagumo, he's got quite a rap sheet: ex-con, home invasion robbery, drug dealer."

The scruffy dog came to its place beside me and began nibbling a bare patch at the base of its tail. I withheld my dismay, but the dog abandoned itself to a frenzy of licking and nibbling, raising a stench that nauseated me. I got up, trying to look nonchalant by wandering to a back window while McKean continued his discussion with Frank and Clara. I gazed at the trees overarching the house but then spotted something on a back drive that sent a chill through me: a black Dodge Ram pickup exactly like the one at the park when we were poisoned. Immediately certain it was Craig Showalter's, I made a small wave to catch McKean's eye, then pointed out the window.

"What is it, Fin?" he asked without the faintest effort to keep my concern a secret. He came to the window, saw what I had seen, and turned to look expectantly at the people in the room. Clara flinched first.

"Oh dear," she moaned, her eyes welling with tears. She fanned her throat, and then quit trying to hide the obvious. "He's here!" she sobbed. "Billy's in the basement. He's been staying here for a couple of days now." She covered her eyes and wept. "Poor Billy!" she gushed between wet hands.

McKean went to her solicitously. "Don't be so sure we're here to get Billy in trouble, Clara. He's unlikely to be the murderer."

A voice came from a back doorway. "I'm just as much to blame as Craig Showalter. I made the poison he used."

We all turned to see Billy Seaweed standing at the top of a stairway that came from the basement. "It's all gonna come out pretty quick," he said. "So why hide anymore?"

He stood in the doorway with one hand braced on the jamb, an odd, faraway look on his face, seeming not to hear anyone's exclamations of concern or questions.

"I was just tryin' out the old man's recipe," he said. "Internet guys were stoked. I thought we'd test it on somebody's dog or something. But Craig talked me into giving him some. When Erik Torvald turned up dead, I knew I was in deep shit. Showalter poisoned Torvald so he could take over his business."

"I figured that," said McKean.

"Showalter was looking for a way to get out of the meth business; go legitimate."

"If you can call it legitimate," I said, "to kill a man for a few geoducks."

"Lotsa money in geoducks these days."

"Was it him who tried to kill us at the park?" asked McKean.

Billy nodded. "We was here at Aunt Clara's the first time you guys came by. We heard what you said to Frank, so we knew you were onto us. Craig jimmied your car door and poisoned your Cokes while I was in the woods yelling at you guys. I didn't know it till later. I was tryin' to protect the old man, but Craig was tryin' to get rid of you for good."

"We were on the right track," said McKean, "but unfortunately you were a step ahead of us."

Billy laughed in an odd, sad way. "I'm still one step ahead."

McKean's dark eyebrows knit. "How's that?"

After a long moment, Billy turned robotically and said, to no one in particular, "C'mon. I've got something to show you."

Frank, McKean, and I followed him down the stairs, leaving Clara weeping in the living room. In the basement day room a TV blared a sequence from *Dancing with the Stars.* At one end of the room was a door through which a sink and toilet could be seen. Through a second we glimpsed a disheveled bed. In a corner of the day room a man appeared to be sleeping in a reclining chair facing the TV, and my pulse shot up when I realized it must be Craig Showalter. McKean went to him and pressed his fingertips to a carotid artery, then straightened and looked from Frank to Billy to me, shaking his head in the negative.

"I killed him with the poison," said Billy, "after we got high on some red wine, so he wouldn't feel it coming on."

"The police are gonna wanna talk to you," said Frank.

Billy shook his head slowly. "No, they won't."

I said, "I don't see how you can stop that."

"I do," said Billy. "I saved enough poison for me. Gettin' a little woozy right now." His eyelids drooped.

McKean called for an ambulance but Billy was nearly gone when it arrived, slumped on the bed in the basement bedroom. He was on death's door as Kay Erwin admitted him to Seattle Public Health Hospital, and although McKean had double-checked with Janet about antiserum while we followed the ambulance, Janet only confirmed that the antiserum had been consumed completely in saving him and me. With no other source of antiserum, Billy's death was a foregone conclusion.

* * *

Several days later, McKean and I went to find the old shaman in his lean-to. He came out to the riverbank with us and we stood listening to a bald eagle crying from a snag tree on a little island. Two more flew overhead and the first flapped off to follow them toward the mouth of the Duwamish, under the gray arch of the freeway bridge.

"That's a fledgling," said Henry George. "Joining Mom and Dad for his first hunt. Going fishing along Alki Beach. Maybe Billy Seaweed's spirit is in that eagle."

"Too bad about Billy," lamented McKean.

"Billy's buried now," said George, "in the white man way. Highpoint Cemetery. Should be over there on Muddy Island, left in a canoe until the birds pick his bones clean. Then you put 'im in a cedarwood box and maybe make a totem. Billy wasn't famous enough for a totem, I suppose."

We stood in silent contemplation until the old man said, "Look at Muddy Island over there. White men cut it in half, shrank it, polluted it, gave it a white man's name, Kellogg Island. Treated it just like they treated the Duwamish people. We're a little polluted island of Indians in a white man's world nowadays. New things like freeway bridges and Microsoft computers and Boeing airplanes and Amazon books go right over our heads."

"I'm sorry," said McKean.

"Oh, don't feel sorry," replied George. "You see, the old ways aren't all dead yet. The river still snakes past here like A'yahos, slithering this way and that with the tide. Billy proved A'yahos's medicine is still strong. And President Bush, he took his pen and wiped us Duwamish people off the map, but we're still here, and now there's a new president. A'yahos knows better than presidents. The tide will turn again."

PROMISED TULIPS

BY BHARTI KIRCHNER

Wallingford

I am floating between dream and wakefulness in my cozy treehouse nestled high in the canopy of a misty rain forest when he murmurs, "You're so beautiful with your hair over your face."

I smile and bid him a *Guten morgen*. Ulrich—I like the full feel of that German name in my mouth, the melodious lilt, and I definitely appreciate the warm masculine body, its sculpted hardness visible beneath the sheets. He stretches an arm toward me, as if about to say or do something intimate, then closes his eyes and allows his arm to drop. I snuggle up against him, savoring the musky sweet skin, on a morning so different from others. Usually I rise at dawn, slip into my greenhouse, and appraise the overnight progress of the seedlings.

If my mother were to peek in at this instant, she would draw a corner of her sari over her mouth to stifle a scream.

"Sin!" she'd say. "My twenty-five-year-old unmarried girl is living in sin!"

Fortunately, she's half a world away in India.

And I'm not in my treehouse, but rather in the bedroom of my bungalow in Wallingford, a.k.a. the Garden District of Seattle.

Next door the Labrador retriever barks. Never before have I invited a man home on the first encounter and I'm unnerved by my daring. If my friends could see me now, they'd exclaim in disbelief, *A shy thing like you?*

The silky, iris-patterned linen sheets are bunched up. He sleeps more messily than I, but for some reason I like the rumpled look. Last night's coupling, with its wild tumbling and thrusting—I wouldn't exactly call it lovemaking—has put me into deep communion with my body, and also taken me a bit out of my zone. My lips are dry and puffy from a surfeit of kissing.

The man beneath the blanket turns his blond head, nuzzles the pillow, regards me with his green eyes, then looks at the clock on the lamp stand. "Eight-thirty?" He throws the blanket aside and bolts from the bed. "*Ach*, I'm supposed to be at work by 7."

An engineer by training, he works in construction, a choice he's made to get away from "wallowing in my head." So, he happily hammers nails all day, fixing roofs, patios, kitchens, and basements. Siegfried, his German shepherd, always goes along.

I point out the bathroom across the hallway. He scrambles in that direction, mumbling to himself in his native tongue. A sliver of sun is visible through a crack in the window draperies. I can tell from its position that the morning has passed its infancy, the galaxy has inched on to a new position, and I've already missed a thing or two.

I hoist myself up from my nest. My toes curl in protest at the first touch of the cold hardwood floor. I stoop to retrieve a pair of soft-soled wool slippers from under the nightstand.

Then I look for my clothes. The long-sleeved print dress I wore last evening—a tantrum of wildflowers—lies on the floor, all tangled up with my bra and panties and Ulrich's charcoal jeans. Crossing the room, I rummage around in the closet, grab a pewter-gray bathrobe, and wrap it around me.

As I fluff the pillows, I hear the sounds of water splashing in the sink, and snatches of a German song. A peek through the draperies reveals a quick change of weather—a bruised, swollen April sky.

The jangling of the telephone startles me. Not fair, this intrusion. If it's Kareena on the line, I'll whisper: *Met a cool Deutsche last night . . . We're just out of bed. I know, I know, but this one is . . . Look, I'll call you back later, okay?*

Tangles of long hair drown my vision; I reach for the receiver. This is what a plant must feel like when it's uprooted.

"Palette of Color. Mitra Basu speaking, how can I help you?" Plants are my refuge, my salvation and, fortuitously, my vocation.

"Veen here." The downturn in her voice doesn't escape me. Vivacious and well-connected, architect by profession, Veenati is an important part of my social circle. "Have you heard from Kareena recently?"

"Not in a week or so. Why? Has something happened to her?"

"She didn't show up for coffee this morning. I called her home. Adi said she's missing."

"Missing? Since when?"

"Since the night before last. I was just checking to see if she'd contacted you. I'm late for work. Let's talk in about an hour."

"Wait—"

Click. Veen has hung up. This is like a dreadful preview of a hyperkinetic action flick. How could Kareena be missing? She's a people person, well respected in our community for her work with abused women. Although we're not related, Kareena is my only "family" in this area, not to mention the closest confidante I've had since leaving home. A word from my youth, *shoee*, friends of the heart, hums inside me. I'm badly in need of explanation to keep my imagination from roaring out of control.

A vase of dried eucalyptus sits on the accent table. Kareena had once admired that fragrant arrangement—she adores all objects of beauty. Now she, a beautiful soul, has been reported missing. Wish I'd pressed her to take the risks of her profession more seriously. Don't use your last name. Take a different route home every day. Always let somebody know where you are.

Ulrich is back. "Everything okay?"

"A friend is missing." I make the statement official-sounding, while glancing at the window, and hope he won't probe further. I'm of the opinion that intimacy has its limits. In the cold clarity of the morning, it discomfits me that I, a private person, have already shared this much with him.

Standing so close to me that I can smell the sweat of the night on his skin, he dresses hurriedly. I linger on his muscles. His large fingers fumble with the buttons of his muted blue shirt and a thin lower lip pouts when he struggles to insert a recalcitrant button in its hole. He wiggles into his jeans and throws on his herringbone jacket. Then he draws me closer with an eager expression and cups my face in his hands. I grow as still as I've ever been. He gives me a short warm kiss which softens my entire midsection. The hum in the air is like static electricity crackling.

Will I ever see him again? Coming from nowhere, the morbid thought slaps me on the forehead, but I recover quickly and my attention stretches back to Kareena. She could have gone somewhere for a breather from the daily battles she fights on her clients' behalf.

"I want to stay here with you," Ulrich says, "but . . ."

Modulated by his accent, the word want, or *vant*, hints at delicious possibilities for another time. I look up at his pale-skinned round face, and I really do have to look up, for he's a good nine inches taller. I struggle with words to convey my feelings, to put a lid on my concerns about Kareena, but stay mute.

"Catch you this evening," he murmurs.

As we walk to the doorway, our arms around each other, a yen to entice him to stay steals into my consciousness. I smother the impulse. Self-mastery is a trait I've inherited from my mother. (She denies herself pleasure of all sorts, refusing chai on a long train journey, and even returns bonus coupons to stores.)

Ulrich gives me one last look followed by another kiss, sustaining the connection, that of a conjurer to a captive audience. As he descends the front steps, his face turns toward my budding tulip patch—an exuberant yellow salutation to the coming spring—and he holds it in sight till the last second. Yellow is Kareena's color and I am growing these tulips for her. She'll shout in pleasure when she sees how gorgeous they are.

A Siamese cat from down the block watches from its customary perch atop a low brick wall as Ulrich lopes toward a steel-gray Saab parked across the street.

I shut the door, pace back to the living room, open the draperies. Ulrich's car is gone. Feeling a nip in the air, I cinch the belt of my bathrobe. Kareena and I bought identical robes at a Nordstrom sale. Despite different sizes—hers a misses medium and mine a petite small—we're like twins or, at least, sisters.

As I look down at my slippers, they too remind me of Kareena. A domestic violence counselor, she'd bought this pair from the boutique of a client who was a victim of spousal abuse. While I function in a universe of color, bounty, growth, and optimism, Kareena deals with "family disturbances." Hers is a world of purple bruises, bloodshot gazes, and shattered hearts huddling in a public shelter.

I look out at the long line of windows across the street. A blue-black Volvo SUV speeds by, marring the symmetry and reminding me of Kareena's husband Adi; a real prize, he is.

I met both Adi (short for Aditya, pronounced *Aditta*) and Kareena for the first time at a party they hosted. Before long, we began discussing where we were each from. Kareena had been raised in Mumbai and New Delhi, whereas Adi, like me, hailed from the state of West Bengal in Eastern India. Even as I greeted him, "*Parichay korte bhalo laglo*" ("How nice to meet you," in our shared Bengali tongue), Adi's name somehow brought to mind another word, *dhurta*: crook. The two words sort of rhyme in Bengali. That little fact I suppressed, but I couldn't ignore the insouciance with which he flicked on his gold cigarette lighter, the jaunty angle of the Marlboro between his lips, the disdainful way he regarded the other guests.

At just over six feet, he looked as out of place in that crowded room as a skyscraper in a valley of mud huts. He obviously believed that the shadow he cast was longer than anyone else's. He informed me in the first ten minutes that his start-up, Guha Software Services, was in the black; that his ancestors had established major manufacturing plants in India; that he'd recently purchased a deluxe beach cottage on the Olympic Peninsula. Then he walked away without even giving me a chance to say what I did for a living.

A chill has hung between us ever since. "Two strong personalities," Kareena has maintained over the years, but there's more to it. I don't know if Adi has a heart, and if he does, whether Kareena is in it. His smirk says he knows I think he's not good enough for her, but that he could care less. And, to be honest, they have interests in common. Both have an abiding love for Indian *ghazal* songs; both excel in table tennis when they can manage the time; both detest green bell pepper in any form. They make what one might call a perfect married couple—young, handsome, successful, socially adept, and with cosmopolitan panache. They look happy together, or, rather, he does. His attention to her is total, as though she's an *objet d'art* that has cost him no small sum. He professes to be "furiously, stormily, achingly" in love with her. *Every millisecond, I dream of you and you only,* he gushed in a birthday card I once saw pinned on a memo board in their kitchen.

Do the purplish contusions I saw on Kareena's arm attest to Adi's undying affection? I grit my teeth now as I did then.

Adi doesn't answer my phone call. I think about ringing another friend, but a peek at the red-eyed digits of the mantle clock stops my hand. Better to postpone the call and shower instead. Better to gauge what actually happened before I get everybody upset.

My nerves are so scrambled that the shower is no more than a surface balm. I towel myself but don't waste time blow-drying my shoulder-length hair.

In the mirror, my bushy eyebrows stand out against my olive skin. My nose is tiny, like an afterthought. Although I'm fit, healthy, and rosy-cheeked and my hair is long and lustrous, I'm not beautiful by either Indian or American standards. Friends say I have kind eyes. It has never occurred to me to hide the cut mark under my left eye caused by a childhood brush with a low-hanging tree branch. I don't like to fuss with makeup.

Dressed in a blue terry knit jacket, matching pants, and sneakers, I drift into the kitchen. Breakfast consists of a tall cool glass of water from the filter tap. I slip into my greenhouse and inhale its forest fragrance. The sun sparkles through the barn-style roof and the glass-paneled walls. I hope the fear signals inside me are wrong.

The plants are screaming for moisture. I pick up a sprayer and mist the trays, dispensing life-giving moisture to the germinating seeds and fragile sprouts poking up through the soil. A honeybee hums over a seed flat.

All around me, the life force is triumphant: surely that'll happen with Kareena too. Whatever the cause, her disappearance will be temporary, explainable, and reversible.

An hour later I call Veen. "According to Adi, Kareena was last seen with a stranger," she says. "They were at Toute La Soirée around 11 a.m. on Friday. A waitress who'd seen them together reported so to the police. I find it odd that Adi sounded a little jealous but not terribly worried over the news about this strange man."

I've been to that café many times. Kareena, who had no special fidelity to any one place, somehow took a fancy to rendezvousing there with me. Could that man have blindfolded Kareena, put a hand over her mouth, and dragged her into a car?

No, on second thought, that's impossible. A spirited person like her couldn't be held captive. Could she have run away with that man because of Adi's abuse? That's more likely. I ask Veen what the man looks like.

"Dark, average height, handsome, and well-dressed. He carried a jute bag on his shoulder."

"Oh, a *jhola*." In India some years back, *jholas* were the fashion among male intellectuals. My scrawny next-door neighbor, who considered himself a man of letters but was actually a film buff, toted books in his *jhola*. He could often be seen running for the bus with the hefty bag dangling from one shoulder and bumping against his hip. Tagore novels? Chekov's story collection? Shelley's poems? The only thing I ever saw him fishing out of the bag was a white box of colorful pastries when he thought no one was looking.

"But 11 is too early for lunch," I say, "and Kareena never takes a mid-morning break. Why would she be there at such an hour?"

"Don't know. And what do you make of this? I was passing by Umberto's last night and spotted Adi with a blonde. They were drinking wine and talking."

"He seems to be taking this awfully easy." I remind Veen that Adi has the typical Asian man's fixation on blond hair. According to Kareena, Adi's assistant is a neatly put-together blonde stationed at a cubicle outside his office. Veen and I discuss if Adi might be having an affair, but don't come to any conclusion.

As I hang up, my glance falls on my cell phone, the mute little accessory on the coffee table in front of the couch. Kareena and I get together most Fridays after work, and she often calls me at the last minute. No cause for concern, I assured myself when I left a message on Kareena's voice mail a few days ago and didn't hear back.

Silently, I replay my last face-to-face with Kareena at Toute La Soirée. On that afternoon two weeks ago, I was waiting for her at a corner table, perusing the *Seattle Globe* and reveling in the aromas of lime, ginger, and mint. It filled me with fury to read a half-page story about a woman in India blamed for her village's crop failures and hunted down as a witch. I would have to share this story with Kareena.

Sensing a rustle in the atmosphere, I looked up. Standing just inside the door, Kareena peered out over the crowd, spotted me, and flashed a smile. She looked casually chic in a maroon pantsuit (maple foliage shade in my vocabulary, Bordeaux in hers) that we'd shopped for together at Nordstrom. Arms swaying long and loose, she weaved her way among the tables. Her left wrist sported a pearl-studded bracelet-cum-watch.

As she drew closer, a woman in chartreuse seated across the aisle from me called out to her. Kareena paused and they exchanged pleasantries. The woman glanced in my direction and asked, "Is that your sister?"

Kareena winked at me. We'd been subjected to the same question countless times, uttered in a similar tone of expectation. Did we really look alike, or had we picked up each other's mannerisms from spending so much time together? At 5'1", I am shorter than her by three inches, and thinner. Our styles of dressing fall at opposite ends of the fashion spectrum. I glanced down at my powder-blue workaday jumper, a practical watch with a black resin band, and walking flats. My attire didn't follow current fashion dictates, but it was low-key and comfy, just right for an outdoors person. Fortunately, Seattle accommodated both our styles.

"*Kemon acho?*" Kareena greeted me with a Bengali pleasantry I'd taught her. "Sorry I'm late. First, I had a gynecologist appointment, then a difficult DV case to wrap up."

I pushed the newspaper to the far side of the table. DV—domestic violence—is an abbreviation that sounds to me more like a fearsome disease, less like a social thorn. Kareena likes to help women who are in abusive relationships and, as yet, unaware of their legal rights. She was named the top DV counselor in her office and has received recognition for her efforts.

"I really think you're overworking." I touched her hand. "Do you really need the money? Do you need to shop so much?"

She ran her fingers over her bracelet. "You don't resent my spending, do you?"

I shook my head, then stopped to ruminate. Well, in truth, there have been times. She likes to shop at Nordstrom, Restoration Hardware, and Williams-Sonoma, places that are beyond my means, but she insists on having my company. I have an eye for quality and she values that.

I got back to the subject at hand. "Was today's case one from our community, another hush-hush?"

"Unfortunately, yes." She mimicked a British accent: "A 'family matter, a kitchen accident.'" She paused. The waiter was hovering by her shoulder. We placed our orders.

Not for the first time, I agonized over the threats Kareena faces due to the nature of her job. Signs have been plentiful. She is frequently called a man hater and, at least once in the last month, has been followed home from work. The spouse of one client even went so far as to publicly question her sexual orientation.

"You're the only one I trust enough to talk about this case," Kareena continued. "She's an H-4 visa holder, so scared that she couldn't even string together a few coherent sentences. I spoke a little Punjabi with her, which loosened her up. Still, it took awhile to draw out her story. Her husband beats her regularly."

I appraised Kareena's face. How she could absorb the despair of so many traumatized souls? Listen to songs that don't finish playing? Lately, her lipstick color had gone from her standard safe pink to a risky red. Brown circles under her eyes spoke of fatigue or, perhaps, stress, and I suspected the brighter lip color was intended to redirect a viewer's attention.

"Did you see bruises on her?" I asked and watched her carefully.

It was still so vivid in my mind, Kareena's last cocktail party a few weeks before and the freshly swollen blue-black marks on her upper arm. In an unguarded moment, her paisley Kashmiri shawl had slid off her shoulders. Through the billowy sheer sleeves of her tan silk top, I glimpsed dark blue, almost black finger marks on an otherwise smooth arm. The swelling extended over a large area, causing me to nearly shriek. Adi must have attacked her. Upon realizing that I'd noticed, she glanced down and repositioned the shawl. Just then, a male friend approached, asked her to dance, took her arm, and they floated away.

"Yes, I did see bruises on her forehead," now Kareena replied. "She'd be in worse trouble if her husband suspected she was out looking for help."

"The law is on her side, isn't it?" I allowed a pause. "You don't have problems at home, by any chance, do you?"

"What are you getting at?"

"Well, I happened to notice bruises on *your* arm at your last party. Who was it?"

I noticed the mauve of shame spreading on her face. "I don't want to talk about it," she said.

"Sorry to barge into your private matters, but if you ever feel like talking—"

Our orders came. Mine was a ginger iced tea and hers an elixir of coconut juice and almond milk. She raised her chin and lifted her glass to clink with mine, her way of accepting my apology.

I took a sip from my beverage; she drained hers with such

hurried gulps that I doubted she fully appreciated the flavors. Typical Kareena; appearances must be maintained. Both of us looked out through the window and took in the sky-colored Ship Canal where a fishing vessel was working its way to the dry docks that lined the north shore of Lake Union. Sooner or later, I thought, I'd have to find out the truth about those bruises.

When the silver waves died down in the canal, Kareena spoke again: "But enough of this depressing stuff! How did things go for you today?"

I filled her in on the most interesting part of my day: consulting with a paraplegic homeowner. "Believe it or not," I said, "the guy wants to do all the weeding and watering himself. It'll be a challenge, but I'll design a garden to suit his requirements."

"You live such a sane life and you have such a healthy glow on your face. Just listening to you, I seem to siphon off some of it. " She gave me a smile. "Come on, Mitra. Let me buy you another drink."

She signaled the waiter. The room was emptier now, the sounds hushed, and a genial breeze blew through a half-open window. We ordered a second round.

"Before the alarm went off this morning," she said after a while, "I got a call from my nephew in New Delhi. He's seven."

"Does he want you to visit him?"

She nodded and mashed her napkin into a ball. I guessed she was undergoing one of those periodic episodes of homesickness for India, the country we'd both left behind. I, too, experience the same longing to visit people missing from my life. Whereas she can afford to go back every year, I can't.

I digressed from this aching topic to a lighter one by pointing out a cartoon clip peeking out from under the glass cover of our table. A tiny boy, craning his neck up, is saying to his glowering father, *Do I dare ask you what day of the week it is before you've had your double tall skinny?*

That got a spontaneous laugh from Kareena which, in turn, raised my spirits. I didn't have a chance to discuss the newspaper story with her. Well, the next time.

I go back to my living room. The airy tranquility has been transformed into a murky emptiness, as though a huge piece of familiar furniture has been cleared out but not replaced. I have an urge to confide in someone, but who could that be? The only person I can think of is the one who's gone away.

I wander into the kitchen, open and close the cupboard, rearrange items in the refrigerator, and fill the tea kettle with water. With a cup of Assam tea and a slice of multigrain toast, I sit at the round table. Bananas protrude from a sunny ceramic bowl within arm's reach. I fiddle with my iPod.

The tea tempers to lukewarm, the toast becomes dense, and the bananas remain untouched. It's difficult for me to stomach much food in the morning, and this news has squelched whatever hunger I might otherwise have. I stare at the *Trees Are Not Trivial* poster on the sea-blue wall. Even the cushioned chair doesn't feel cozy. I itch all over.

Could someone have murdered her?

I peer out through the western window. The Olympic Mountains appear stable, blue, and timeless. Somehow I doubt that Kareena could be the victim of a lethal crime.

How can I help find her? My career focus in art and landscape design—the study of the physiology of new growth, awareness of color and light, and harmony of arrangements—hasn't prepared me to deal with a situation like this.

I walk over to my side yard. Blue bells are pushing up from the winter-hardened ground. I notice a slug, pick it up with a leaf, and deposit it on a safe spot. Once again, spring season is in the balmy air. I look up to the sky, out of a gardener's propensity to check the weather. It helps me see beyond the immediate.

Back to the living room, I sit at my desk, grab a notepad, and begin listing friends and acquaintances who I can call upon. The page fills speedily. The Indian population in the Puget Sound area, described recently by the *Seattle Globe* in a feature story as a "model" community, is some twenty-five thousand strong. The community's academic and professional accomplishments are "as lofty as Mount Rainier," the same article proclaimed. I'm troubled by such laudatory phrases, aware that we have our fair share of warts and blemishes. According to Kareena, the rate of domestic violence among our dignified doctors, elite engineers, and high-powered fund-raisers equals, perhaps even exceeds, the national average.

I consult my watch. It is 10 o'clock, an hour when everyone's up and about, when the disappointments of the day haven't dulled one's spirits. This'll be a good time to ring Adi and draw him out. He loves to talk about himself in his Oxford-accented, popcorn-popping speech, which will give me a chance to tease information out of him, however distasteful the process might be, however potentially dangerous. Kareena is my best friend. When we're together, I'm fully present and my voice is at its freest. Day turns into twilight as we relax over drinks, gabbing, laughing, and trading opinions, oblivious to the time. We don't parse our friendship. It just is. We scatter the gems of our hours freely, then retrieve them richer in value.

* * *

With the phone to my ear, I pace back and forth in front of my living room window. Adi, at the other end, is ignoring the ringing.

The Emperor comes to focus in my mind—an impeccable suit, sockless feet (part of his fashion statement), and eyes red-rimmed with exasperation at some luckless underling behind on a project or the changeable Seattle sky. Adi takes any potential irritant personally. He snatches a ringing phone from its cradle at the last possible moment. The world can wait. It always does for Adi Guha.

The stand-up calendar on the mantel nags me about tomorrow's deadline for a newspaper gardening column. Yet, as I pace the cold floor once again, the phone glued to my ear, it becomes clear that such an assignment is no longer a high priority for me. My missing friend is my main focus now. All else has faded into the background.

Adi comes on the line, gasps when he recognizes my voice. I mention Veen's call, then get straight to the point. "What time did you get home that night?"

"Your core competency is gardening, Mitra. I'm not saying it's menial labor, but neither is it nuclear physics or private investigation. Go back to your garden and leave this situation in more competent hands, like mine."

I ignore the insult. "Do the police have any clues? Did they come to the house?"

"I gave them a photo which they looked at, then began to pepper me with questions. They gave me a song and dance about how many people disappear daily from the city. They assigned a laid-back cop, the only one they could spare. It's obvious they're not interested unless it's a blond heiress and television cameras are everywhere."

"What about the stranger she met at Soirée?"

"I'm not worried about that. She's a big girl. She can take care of herself."

"Have you talked to her gynecologist?"

Adi mumbles a no.

"Do you think she needed a break and decided to sneak away for a few days? There have been times, like at your birthday party, when she looked like she could use a break."

"Everything is fine between us, Mitra, just fine."

Everything's fine? What a laugh. About a year ago, Kareena and I were spending an evening at Soirée when a hugely pregnant woman waddled past our table. I shifted my chair to let her pass. Kareena put her fork down and gazed at the woman.

In a teasing tone I asked, "Could that be you?"

"Adi doesn't want kids." She returned to her voluptuous plum-almond tart.

Now I hear a staccato rumbling in the background, a car cruising. Adi has nerve telling me everything was fine with Kareena. Kareena's everything and Adi's everything are obviously not the same.

"Did you check her closet?" I now ask.

"Looks like her clothes are all there."

Would he even recognize her alligator handbag, jeweled mules, flowing shawls she favored over the structured feel of a coat, or the new Camellia scarf? Would he be able to detect the nuance of her perfume? I believe he only remembers the superficial facts of her presence.

"Did you go to the safety deposit box to see if her passport is there?"

"No, yesterday I had to chair a three-hour offsite meeting. The market isn't as calm as it was last year. We need to get our cash-burn rate under control. It may be necessary to dehire some people."

I almost choke at the expression he uses for firing an employee. Then he begins to ramble on about market share, competitive disadvantage, and going public to raise new capital. In short order, his business-speak begins to grate on me.

I interrupt him by saying, "This is a life-and-death situation, Adi."

"It sure is," he replies. "This morning around 5 I got a call from the police. They asked me to go see a body at the morgue."

My vision blurs. "What?"

"A woman's body was found in Lake Washington. It wasn't her."

"Oh my God!" I shake my head. "Must have been difficult for you. I don't know what I'd do if . . ." I get a grip on myself. "Could we meet this morning? Put our heads together? The earlier the better. We need to mobilize our community. I'll be happy to drop by your office."

"Hold on now, Mitra. I *don't* want even my friends to get wind of this, never mind the whole community. You, of all people, should know how things get blown out of proportion when the rumor mill cranks up."

I sag on the couch. Losing face with his Indian peers is more important to him than seeking help in finding his wife. In a way, I get it. Our community is small. We have at most two degrees of separation between people, instead of the hypothetical six nationwide. Word spreads quickly and rumor insinuates itself in every chit-chat. Still, how silly, how counterproductive Adi's pride seems in this dark situation.

And that makes him more of a suspect.

There are times when I think Adi is still a misbehaving adolescent who needs his behind kicked. According to Kareena, he was an only son. Growing up, he had intelligence, if not good behavior, and bagged many academic honors. His mother spoiled him. Even on the day he punched a sickly classmate at school, she treated him to homemade *besan laddoos*.

Finally, Adi suggests meeting at Soirée at 7 p.m.

How empty the place will seem if I go back there without Kareena. But I don't want to risk a change with Adi. It'll give him an excuse to weasel out of our meeting.

I ponder why he's so difficult. Rumor has it that his family in New Delhi disowned him when he married Kareena against their wishes. Not only that, his uncle sabotaged his effort to obtain a coveted position with an electronics firm by taking the job himself. Adi endured that type of humiliation for a year before giving up. Eight years ago, he and his new bride left India and flew to the opposite side of the world, as far away from his family as he could possibly go.

He landed in Seattle, where he found a plethora of opportunities and no one to thwart his monstrous ambitions. Before long, he formed his own software outfit. There was a price to be paid: long hours, constant travel, and a scarred heart. In spite of this, he persisted and ultimately succeeded. These days he flies frequently to India on business, and rings his family from his hotel room, but his mother will not take his call.

What is Adi doing to locate the woman on whose behalf he sacrificed the love of his family?

Would he really show up at Soirée this evening?

I walk over to my home office and dial Kareena's office number. Once transferred to the private line of the agency director, I leave her a message to get back to me a.s.a.p.

Then I wander into the bedroom where I confront the unmade bed, sheets wavy like desire building to a crescendo. Herr Ulrich floats in my mind, a man who appears so strong and unyielding, but who turns out to be tender and pliant. Right now, his taut body is pushing, lifting, and stooping in the brown-gray jumble of a construction site, the angles of his face accentuated by the strain. Did he stop for a split second, stare out into the distance, and reexperience my lips, my skin, my being?

It's a little too soon to get moony about a man, friends would surely advise me.

Just picturing Ulrich, however, warms my body. Not just the electric tingling of sex, but a kind of communion.

Muted piano music floats from the Tudor across the street. As I reach for the phone with an eager hand, my gaze falls on the bedside table. The pad of Post-it notes is undisturbed. Ulrich hasn't jotted down his phone number or his last name. He promised he would, but he didn't.

My dreamy interlude is sharply broken. With a drab taste in my mouth, I realize that a promise is an illusion and so is "next time." It's similar to hoping that your parents will never die, your friends will forever be around you, and your tulips will always sprout back the next year. This morning I've learned how untrue my assumptions can be.

These days I feel like I'm living in a ghost town. I don't know where to go, who to see, what to do next, or even what to believe. The last five days have coalesced into an endless dreary road. I've reached an impasse in my search for Kareena. Adi cancelled our meeting at Soirée at the last minute. From my repeated phone calls to him, I've gathered that Kareena's passport is missing, an indication she's left deliberately. It strikes me as odd that Adi seems so blithe about her being gone for so long. He even had the nerve to joke about it.

"You know what? I think she's flown somewhere for an

impromptu vacation. She's punishing me for not taking her to Acapulco last February. Don't worry. She'll get a big scolding from me when she gets back."

Where might she have gone?

I've contacted the police and given them an account of the bruises I saw on Kareena's arm. Detective Yoshihama assured me he'd do what was necessary and gave me his cell phone number. This morning, I buzz him again, but he doesn't return my call. How high is this case on his priority list? To him, Kareena is no more than a computer profile of another lost soul, yet another *Have you seen me?* poster to be printed, whereas to me and our mutual friends she's a person of importance.

I'm not ready to give up. I call the Washington State Patrol's Missing Persons Unit, but am advised to wait thirty days.

I miss Ulrich too, even though he's practically a stranger. Everywhere I go, I see his broad face, neat haircut, wary green eyes. He appeared in my life about the time Kareena went missing. I haven't heard from him since he left my bed that fateful morning.

I have no choice but to get on with my life, except that the daily duties I took on happily before have become meaningless. I put off grocery shopping, misplace my car keys, and ignore e-mails from the library warning that three books are overdue.

Late this morning, I check the tulip patch. The buds are still closed and a trifle wan, despite the fact that the soil, sun, and temperature are just ideal for them to bloom, and there are still dewdrops hanging from them. Whatever the connection might be, I can't help but think about Kareena. Why didn't she confide in me?

What concerns me most is the nothingness, the no-answer bit, the feeling that the answer is beyond my reach.

I decide to make a trip to Toute La Soirée this evening. A voice inside has been nagging me to do just that, not to mention I have a taste for their kefir-berry cocktail. Kareena confided not long ago that she was saving the pricey Riesling for the next special occasion. Will her wish ever be fulfilled?

The café is located on busy 34th Street. To my surprise, I find a parking place only a block away. The air is humid as I walk up to the entrance. The stars are all out. I check my watch. Despite the popular spot's catchy name—meaning "all evening"—it closes at 9 p.m., less than an hour from now.

Inside, the café pulses with upbeat, after-work chumminess. It is nearly full. A middle-aged man fixes me with an appraising look over a foamy pint of ale. I ignore him and survey the interior. The décor has changed since my last visit. The smart black walls sport a collection of hand fans. Made of lace and bamboo, they're exquisitely pleated. The new ambience also includes a wooden rack glittering with slick magazines and jute bags of coffee beans propped against a wall. I don't find this makeover comforting.

As I thread my way through, a speck of tension building inside me, I overhear snatches of a debate on human cloning. Ordinarily, I would slow down for a little free education, but right now my attention is focused on finding an empty seat.

The table Kareena and I usually try for is taken; how could it be otherwise at this prime hour? I was half hoping for a minor miracle, but finding a parking spot must have filled my evening quota. "Our" table is occupied by a couple whose heads are bent over an outsize slice of strawberry shortcake.

Right now, I find even the thought of such sugary excess revolting. And the blood-red strawberry juice frightening.

Something about the couple nudges me and I give them a second look. Oh no, it's Adi and a blonde. He looks slightly upset. The overhead light shines over his copper complexion. He's dressed in a crewneck polo shirt in an unflattering rust shade—he doesn't have Kareena's color sense. The blonde wears crystal-accented chandelier earrings that graze her shoulders. I wouldn't bear the weight of such long earrings except on a special occasion. Or is this a special occasion for them?

Their presence so rattles me that I decide to leave. Besides, Adi might notice me and complain I'm spying on him.

On the way to the door, I knock over a chair, which I put back in its place. Then I almost collide head-on with an Indian man who has just entered the shop. Although he's young, dark, and devastatingly handsome, somehow I know he's not my type. Clad smartly in a silver woolen vest, this prince heads straight for the take-out counter. His impressive carriage and smoldering eyes have caused a stir among women seated nearby. A redhead tries to catch his glance. He touches the jute bag, an Indian-style *jhola*, dangling from his shoulder. Even Adi stares at him.

I slip out the door, too drained to absorb anything further, pause on the sidewalk, and take several deep breaths to cleanse my head. Please, Goddess Durga, no more intrigues this evening.

It's starting to drizzle, but the streets are mercifully clear. Within minutes, I pull into my garage and step out of my Honda. As I close the garage door, I flash on the enchanting prince from the café. Didn't Veen mention that Kareena was last sighted with a *jhola*-carrier at that very place?

A jolt of adrenaline skips through my body. Why couldn't I have been more alert? Stuck around longer to scrutinize another potential suspect and his belongings?

Should I drive back?

I check my watch: 9 p.m. Soirée has just closed.

Filled with nervous excitement, I enter my house. Neither a hot shower nor a mug of holy basil tea tempers the thought racing through my head: what really happened to Kareena?

In a need to restore my spirit, I retire early. As I lie in bed, I can't help but run through the day's events, foremost among them being Adi's public appearance with a blonde. Suspicions about him blow in my mind like a pile of dry leaves in the wind. Eventually, the atmosphere settles; my mind clears.

I'm worrying too much about Kareena. Worry is a sand castle. It has no foundation.

Could my assumptions about Adi be wrong as well?

Assumptions, like appearances, can deceive, I tell myself. Adi's cheerful façade and his lack of concern about his wife's unexplained absence just might be more sand-castle building on my part. I'm reading the worst in what might be a perfectly plausible and innocent situation.

You've been acting silly, Mitra, pure silly. You have no reason to fret. Pull your covers snug and get yourself a restful sleep. All will be well. The morning will come, the sun will be out, and Kareena will return, her bright smile intact, as surely as the swing of seasons.

I awake refreshed and invigorated. Last night's drizzle has evaporated, leaving behind a bright morning. The sun streams through a wide gap in the window draperies. A spider is building a nest outside the window, intricate but fragile.

I have the perfect task to usher in this new day. I shall

tend to Kareena's tulip patch. The plants will soon release their full yellow blossoms as emblems of beauty and renewal and she'll cradle a bunch lovingly in her arm.

I don my gardening clothes—faded jeans and a worn black cardigan—gather my tools, and hurry outside. The morning light shines brilliantly on my front flower patch. An errant branch of camellia needs to be pruned. Its shadow falls over the tulips. I step in closer to inspect, an ache in my belly. All the tulip buds are shriveled and brown, as though singed by blight, their dried stalks drooping over to return to brown earth.

Why are they dying on me so soon? I fall to my knees and caress the tulip plants, lifting them up and squeezing their brittle stalks and wilted leaves. I roll each wizened bud between my fingers, but don't find a single one with any hope.

Holding a broken stem in my grasp, I think of Kareena, so vibrant, so full of life, and brood about the promise of these tulips.

GOLDEN GARDENS

BY STEPHAN MAGCOSTA

Ballard

Dolores leaned forward against the back of the taxi driver's seat, eased her choke hold on the man's throat, and pressed the gun barrel harder into the side of his head. "If it helps," she said, "think of me as a messenger from God." In the rearview mirror, she watched a tear trickle from the driver's bruised and swollen right eye. "Tell me, Mister . . ." Dolores glanced at the Yellow Cab ID tag on the dash. "Farah, is it?"

"F-Farah."

"Farah. Almost sounds Spanish. How do you say your first name?"

"Ab-Abdelaziz."

"Well, that's a mouthful."

"It means—"

"What?"

"Servant of G-God." He bit the inside of his mouth to stop stuttering. "It means Servant of God."

"Really. Well, that's why you're here, Abdelaziz—serving God . . . God's messenger, anyway." Dolores appraised his raw head wound from the pistol-whipping she'd given him. "You're still bleeding. Keep both hands on the wheel." She let go of his throat for a moment and fished a tissue from her parka.

"I have to use restroom. My—"

"Shh." She dabbed at the blood coagulating on his scalp.

"It'll be light soon; just have to wait now, enjoy the view. Look, you can see the Olympics out there."

"Please—" Abdelaziz flinched, started to shake. "Take all money, I already say."

"Money?" Dolores shook her head. "You think I'd be wandering the streets during Easter vigil looking for money? I was looking for you, my friend, a man with a turban."

He turned, trying to look at her. "But—" She gave him a hard rap on the forehead with the butt of her pistol.

"I told you, *quiet*. Now you're bleeding again. And I'm out of tissues." She reapplied the choke hold on his throat. "You did a good job not getting stuck in the sand. I wasn't sure we'd make it this far." Dolores glanced over her shoulder. "Can't see us from the parking lot. That's good. You're a great driver for such a small man; I almost thought a boy was driving when you pulled over to pick me up." Her eyes drifted to the gun she held to his head—his blood trickling onto the barrel. "My son's a good driver too . . . that's what he did over there." She looked away, cheeks swelling as if she was going to vomit.

Abdelaziz started coughing and sputtering. "Too strong— you squeeze too much."

"You think I'm strong? That's funny. I'm dying. And I wasn't strong enough to protect . . ." She closed her eyes and ground the barrel deeper into the side of his head.

Abdelaziz whispered, "Please . . ."

Dolores cocked her head, listening; there—the approaching rumble of a southbound locomotive. "I forgot trains come through here," she said. "We took the bus here once, just for the ride. I told Roberto we'd go someplace special for his fifth birthday, a place with so much sand that they call it Golden Gardens. He thought I meant Mexico and he'd get to meet his *abuela*. But I couldn't afford that." Her eyes began filling with tears. "So we packed lunch; he had his little blue truck. We walked right through here, right along the beach. *Mamí, mamí, look at the train*, he was so excited." She gazed at a distant, moonlit embankment leading to the tracks.

"I have two child—"

She whipped the gun across his head. "I said QUIET! Now look, your turban's all ruined."

"Ku . . . faya."

"What?"

"Not t-turban." Abdelaziz thought his voice was broken—he hardly recognized it. "Kufaya. It is called kufaya."

"Well, it looks like a turban."

"But it is not—"

"It doesn't really matter anymore, does it?"

"Why?" he asked.

"That's what I want to know—*why*? He was so young! *Ay, mi'jo.* He was on foot, just walking across a street . . ."

Abdelaziz groaned and felt at the side of his head.

"Don't even think about moving!" She squeezed his throat harder, her grip lifting his eyes to the rearview mirror.

"Look at me," she said. "Does my face look strong?"

Abdelaziz stared into the mirror as Dolores pulled back the hood of her parka, gasping at the sight of her sunken, blood-shot eyes, faded teardrop tattoo, disheveled cinnamon hair curling across the ash smudged on her forehead. He blinked and envisioned a card from the special deck another driver had spread across the hood of his cab one night. The card showed a woman in white sitting up in bed, face buried in her hands, nine swords hanging on the wall. *A greater sadness the world has never known.* That's what Abdelaziz remembered the driver saying; that the cards predict the future and he'd better drive safe, he could die behind the wheel. *No, no,*

Abdelaziz had responded, *they're from Shaitan, the Great Deceiver.*

Abdelaziz squirmed. He had to urinate so badly. He wanted to reach down, pinch his member, ease the discomfort, the shame, in front of this woman who overpowered him and dared to call herself a messenger from God! Mocking the Prophet (peace and blessing be upon him). As if Allah would ever choose a *woman* as messenger!

A gull wheeled across the water, pale sliver against the gray marble Olympics. He thought of Mogadishu, endless golden sand, surf all the way from India, pounding the weary shoulder of East Africa. He thought of his mother and wept, tears falling on his captor's hand and wrist.

The woman was mad, caring not that he was no Arab or Iraqi, or even from that part of the world. If only he could explain . . .

"Is that a prayer you're mumbling?" asked Dolores. She had been lost in a waking dream, adrift above Baghdad on a magic carpet, searching for her son. But what she found was the glorious city of an age forgotten. The great Golden Gate Palace . . . an emerald dome . . . minaret voices across the Tigris, calling the faithful to morning prayer . . . a causeway with horsemen and their lances . . . dissolving into an American platoon on a potholed street two blocks from the Green Zone, Roberto's desert camouflage boot descending onto the trigger of a homemade bomb. A blinding flash, bloody and terrible, quartering his body like God's avenging sword.

"Are you praying, Abdelaziz?"

"I pray, yes."

"That's good," she whispered. "Even to a different God."

"But our God is the—*oow!*"

Dolores hit him again, then wiped the gun on his shoulder. "It's good to pray," she said softly. "That's all I've been doing. Got out in December, eight years locked up in Purdy. The doctor said the malignancy's too advanced, I have less than six months. I couldn't bear to tell Roberto, I'm all he had. I was going to wait till June, he had leave then . . ."

Was she was possessed by a *djinn*, Abdelaziz wondered, or could she even be one herself, a creature of smokeless fire, created by Allah? If she was a *djinn*, could she not, then, be bound to an object, as Süleyman once did, binding a great *djinn* to an oil lamp? But bind her how, and to what?

He could feel wind through the back window she'd cracked open. He should have known that no woman would be alone on this night, vigil of the resurrection of the last prophet before Mohammed (peace and blessing be upon him). But business had been slow, and he'd thought little of the hooded emptiness in her eyes when she'd asked to be taken to Golden Gardens. It wasn't far from where he'd picked her up, the restaurant whose name someone once told him meant *The Way* in the language of Mexico.

"You're mumbling again," Dolores said. "No matter, the sun's rising, it's time for you to choose. You understand?"

"N-no."

"What I mean, Mr. Farah, is that you choose when to pull the trigger. And, yes, *you* will pull it, not me. Now do you understand?"

"No."

"Give me your right hand . . . Ah-ah, slowly."

Abdelaziz felt her fingers tighten on his throat as she placed the gun in his right hand, wrapping her hand around his. Her iron grip made him wonder if the teardrop tattoo conferred power from Shaitan, the Great Adversary. She moved their hands till the pistol pressed against his right temple.

"Yes, like that," he heard her say. "Now, you choose when," she said. "Just calm your thoughts. Relax, and when you're ready, just slowly make a fist."

"Suicide is s-sin," he said. "Only Allah may t-take life. I will have to repeat this on Ju-Judgment Day. Please, no."

"Don't be afraid, this is God's will. I'll help you. We'll do it together."

"No." Abdelaziz watched a discarded holiday balloon bounce along the beach in the gathering light, the Easter bunny cartwheeling across tendrils of seaweed. The blasphemy of suicide! But no, she *forces* me . . . doesn't she? Did I not struggle? Was I not beaten senseless? And does not the Qur'an say that if we kill, unless it be for murder or a just . . . NO! She sees this as a *just* killing, for the death of her son!

"So-Somali," he said.

"Shh. No more talk."

"I-I am shamed, I have soiled . . ."

"It's all right. Anyone can have an accident . . ."

"Will it hurt?"

"You'll see light," she said.

"Light?" He was floating high above the cab; looking down, he could see right through himself. The cards were right, he was going to die behind the wheel.

Then across golden sand, streaking through the pale dawn, a rainbow rush of flashing lights. Abdelaziz felt ushered to the Garden gates.

"Do you know the Bible?" Dolores whispered.

"I know that which was written before Jesus."

"Then you understand an eye for an eye."

"Yes—"

"And a *vengeful* God."

"Please!"

Dolores saw red and blue lights strobe in the mirror. She heard a door opening, frantic shouts, footsteps stumbling in the sand as their hands closed, voices joining, blasted apart by the gunshot, "God forgive me."

THE CENTER OF THE UNIVERSE

BY ROBERT LOPRESTI

Fremont

Let me do the talking, says Petey.

Who's asking? says Fox.

Nobody yet. But they will. We gotta be ready.

No offense, dear boy, says Strabo. But you are the worst possible spokesperson. You're like Cassandra, of ancient legend. He warned and warned, but no one believed a word he said.

Was he crazy too? asks Fox.

Shut up, says Petey. Just shut up.

It's barely morning, the sun peeking from behind the clouds over Wallingford. Too early to be up, but the playground on Linden wasn't all that cozy, especially when the mist turned to drizzle.

Besides, fresh memories made sleep impossible.

I was up all freaking night, says Fox. Waiting for the Gestapo to show up and drag us away.

I'm too old to dodge *federales*, says Strabo.

But nobody found us, says Petey. Now it's an easy walk down the hill and out of enemy territory.

People were already leaving their houses and apartment buildings, getting into cars, or strolling toward the neighborhood center.

See all the worker ants, says Strabo. Starting their pleasant peasant days, serving their futile lords.

A bell jingles and Petey dodges as a bicyclist charges down the hill.

Bastard, says Fox. Don't pedestrians have the right of way on the freaking sidewalk anymore?

He's a wheeler-dealer, says Strabo. Hurrying to fuel himself on lattes and sushi before making his million-dollar deals. We, on the other hand, contribute nothing. We do not toil, neither do we sin. Society wouldn't care if we were wiped off the face of the earth by our bicycling betters.

Don't say that, says Petey, thinking of last night.

The biker parks his flashy white hybrid in front of a coffee shop.

See that? asks Fox.

Yeah, says Petey. Starbucks. Typical.

Get over that, will you? I meant Lance Armstrong there didn't lock up.

I didn't see that, says Petey.

You saw, lad, but you didn't observe, says Strabo. The lock dangles helpless from the rear rack. The ship is unanchored, gentlemen. Shall we be pirates?

I dunno, says Petey.

I do, says Fox. I know a shop near Pioneer Square where they'd pay cash for that bike, no questions asked.

That's the point, says Petey, shivering. We're out of our territory.

Out of this city is where we need to be, says Strabo. With the sugar from Sugarman and the ransom from the bicycle we could journey to Everett or Tacoma. Stay incognito until this blows over.

It's not gonna blow over, says Petey. That woman is *dead*. The cops won't stop looking till they pin a tail on somebody.

There's a cop by the Greek joint, says Fox. Let's hang a left.

Thirty-Fifth Street is quieter.

Condos everywhere, says Fox. When did this neighborhood fill up with freaking condos?

Why can't you swear like a normal person? asks Strabo.

Cause I was raised right.

Oh please, Foxy. You were raised by wolves, like Romulus and Rebus.

All these people going by, says Petey. They don't even see us.

If they did, they'd call the fuzz.

And why not? asks Strabo. What purpose does the constabulary serve if not to protect good citizens from homeless riffraff?

They didn't protect the girl last night, says Petey.

Something we have in common, dear boy.

We couldn't stop them, says Petey. By the time we knew what was going on, it was too late.

You said they were up to no good, lad. You could have done *something*.

You didn't either.

I'm not the hero, says Strabo. Just an old, old man.

You were scared, says Fox.

Damn right I was, says Petey. You saw Widmark's face.

Widmark?

The blond one. He looked like Richard Widmark used to. And the dark one with the big puppy eyes looked like Sal Mineo.

You and your cinema worship, says Strabo. What a waste of brain cells.

Sounds like you're queer for the shortie, says Fox.

I'm not . . . Damn! We gotta turn around. I'm not going under that bridge.

You're a real head case, says Fox. Scared of cops, scared of bridges, scared of Starbucks.

I'm not scared of *them*. I just hate them.

A red PT Cruiser squeezes into a parking space, and a family of tourists pops out, covering their cameras with raincoats and umbrellas, all talking at once.

The daddy comes up, smiling.

Excuse me, is this where they keep the troll?

No, says Strabo. It's where they keep the minotaur.

Shut up, mutters Petey. The troll's under the black bridge over there.

That's why he turned around, says Fox. Scared of the big bad troll.

The daddy frowns. I thought it was the *Fremont* troll. With a real Volkswagen in its hand?

That's the one, says Petey.

But that's the *Aurora* Bridge. Why isn't it under the Fremont Bridge over there?

What do we look like, asks Fox, the freaking road department?

Daddy jerks back, as if he just got a better look—or smell. Let's go, kids. The troll's over here.

I hate this place, says Petey. What kind of sick mind would put a giant troll statue under a bridge?

Someone who doesn't have much experience with monsters, says Strabo. There are enough real ones around without encouraging them with monuments.

Widmark and Mineo, says Petey. *They* were real ones.

Yeah, says Fox. You oughta tell the tourists what the movie stars did to their sister.

That girl was no tourist.

A deduction! How can you tell, maestro?

Fox picked up her address book, remember? All local names and numbers.

But she didn't put her own name in it, says Fox. That was dumb.

I guess she knew where she lived.

Har har, says Fox. Petey the comic.

We should have helped her, says Strabo.

We couldn't, says Petey.

In the long eye of the law, dear boy, silence breeds consent.

Now you're a freaking attorney, says Fox. Oh crap. Look what's around the corner.

Cops have gathered in force, surrounding the traffic island on 34th Street.

Speak of the devil and he shall appear, says Strabo. All the king's prowl cars and all the king's men.

They found her, says Petey.

She wasn't exactly hidden, says Fox. Just lying behind the gray zombies.

Don't be ignorant, says Strabo. That's another of Fremont's fine artworks. *Waiting for the Interurban.*

The six gray plaster figures are wearing T-shirts today. *FREMONT MOISTURE FESTIVAL,* reads one.

How did they get the shirts on with the cops around? asks Fox.

They couldn't, says Petey. The shirts must have been there last night. But we were behind the statues and didn't see them.

Another deduction, says Strabo.

Uniforms hustle around the statues and a small crowd has gathered on either side of 34th to stand in the drizzle and watch.

Are they looking at us? asks Petey.

It's okay to watch the cops, says Fox. Everybody's doing it.

A cat may look at a king, says Strabo. But curiosity kills them both. What killed Abby?

Nobody killed Abby, says Petey.

The young woman lying over there.

That's not Abby, says Petey. You're crazy.

I never met your dream girl, says Fox. But you said the chick last night looked like her. That's why you had us chasing her all over Queen Anne.

Marching after her like a parade, agrees Strabo. But no one was there to help when the beasts attacked.

What are *you* looking at? Fox asks a sidewalk gawker. The show's over there, jerk. Don't look at me.

Now you've done it, says Petey. Let's go.

Across the bridge of sighs?

Too visible, says Fox. Back up the avenue.

I want to get *out* of Fremont, mutters Petey. This is no place for us.

For Christ's sake, don't run, says Fox. In tourist land the three of us running is probable cause.

I used to live here, says Petey.

In the center of the universe, says Strabo. So says the sign, at any rate.

Hear the sirens? asks Fox. They're taking her away. Finally.

Whoever she is, says Strabo, she'll be a star now. Just like your cinematic friends.

Let's get something to eat, suggests Fox. How about this bakery?

Look what's in the window, says Petey.

Someone had put up photos from the Solstice Parade: giant puppets and naked bicyclists.

No wonder I went crazy. How could anybody stay sane in this place?

Abby did, says Strabo. That's why she left.

All the food here is too goddamn healthy, says Fox. Let's go to Starbucks.

Never, says Petey. I'm not giving those bastards one of my hard-earned dollars.

Hard-begged, says Strabo.

Same thing.

You're not being rational, dear boy.

Har har.

You can't blame a major corporation simply because your ex-wife married . . . What was he? A department head?

Coffee king, says Fox. Java general.

The bastard stole Abby from me, says Petey.

She married him—

Brew guru.

Hush. She married him after you went to bedlam, lad. Did you expect her to wait until you achieved *compus mentus*?

Stuff it.

So what do you want? asks Fox. Starbucks, this bakery, or starve to death? Your choice.

What else've you got? asks Petey.

Speaking of destinations, says Strabo, why were Bogart and De Niro—

Widmark and Mineo.

Why were they hanging around Queen Anne in the middle of the night?

To get to the other side, says Fox.

How would I know?

You were just playing detective, dear boy.

Petey sighs. Okay. They weren't bums like us. Somewhere

between yuppies and punks. Looking for drugs, maybe?

Bull, says Fox. They were looking for exactly what they found. A chick walking alone. Somebody to mess up. Two homeless broads got offed last year.

I didn't know that, says Petey.

Neither one looked like Abby, says Strabo. So you didn't notice.

They didn't exactly make the front page.

I wish last night never happened, says Petey.

It wouldn't have, if they hadn't been so far off their turf. Usually they stayed near Pioneer Square, where nobody complained much about grubbies and crazies.

But the previous morning they had run into Sugarman, a contractor Petey knew in better days, and he was looking for cheap labor.

Anybody with a green card. You a citizen? Even better. Hop on the truck and you can spend the day digging a trench for bamboo in Queen Anne.

The crew of half a dozen came in under budget and ahead of schedule. Sugarman got a bonus and was so pleased he bought pizza and beer and treated everybody to a picnic in the park.

When the party broke up, close to midnight, Fox had said he'd lead the three of them to a bus stop where they could get back to home base. But then Petey saw the brunette on Nickerson and fell in love.

I'm not in love, he had told them. I just said she looks like Abby.

Every white filly south of fifty looks like your lost angel, said Fox.

She was well under fifty. Maybe twenty-five. Brunette hair

pinned up in the back. Tight green dress. Wobbling a little on two-inch heels.

The angel is drunk, said Strabo.

Who isn't? asked Petey.

You a stalker now?

I just want to make sure she gets home all right.

This isn't home. She's cutting through a parking lot.

If she saw us following her, said Strabo, she'd scream for help.

Why don't you ask her to make you a double tall cappuccino? says Fox. That's how you met the bitch, isn't it?

Don't call her that.

Whoa. Catch those two on the other side of the street. They're watching her too. Six o'clock for your lady love.

What does that mean?

Behind her.

Two men, about the same age as the lady in green. The tall one had blond hair, was thin, almost gaunt, and vibrated with nervous energy. He wore a red jacket and blue jeans.

His friend was a head shorter and had dark hair. He walked with his shoulders hunched as if attacked by a wind only he could feel. Both of them were so busy watching the lady in green that they never noticed anyone behind them.

She's headed onto Fourth, said Fox. Up into Petey's no-go zone.

Petey stumbled to a stop.

Fine, said Strabo. Let's round up a bus and ride home. Discretion is the bitter part of valor.

I'm following them. They're up to no good.

What are you now, the freaking cavalry?

Our Petey is a man of chivalry, said Strabo. A white knight in vanished armor. That calls for a song!

Oh where are you going, said Milder to Moulder
Oh we may not tell you, said Festel to Fose
We're hunting the wren, said John the Red Nose
Hunting the wren, said everyone . . .

For the love of God, shut up, said Petey. I can't hear myself think.

The sounds of silence. Har har.

You Philistines! That's a medieval classic. Part of your heritage.

Yeah, but do you want those creeps across the street to hear you?

Why are they following her? asked Petey.

They like to watch Abby's ass, said Fox. Same as you.

She's not Abby. And don't talk like— Oh crap!

They were on the Fremont Bridge now and the drawbridge was going up.

Why the hell is a boat going by at this time of night? asked Petey.

Probably heading home, said Strabo. Like all sensible people.

They watched the city lights reflecting off the Ship Canal and the bright blue of the bridge.

Look over there, said Strabo.

Off to the right the Aurora Bridge stretched high above them.

Like a long black spider web, said Strabo.

Poetry sucks, said Fox.

Finally the drawbridge dropped into place. They made the long way across.

Where are they? asked Strabo.

Crap, said Fox. Take a look behind the zombies.

I don't see anyone, said Petey.

Not the movie stars. Your Abby clone.

Slow down, said Strabo. Impatient youngsters!

The woman in green lay on her back behind the zombies, staring up at the sky.

A goner, said Fox.

Where are Lerner and Lowe? asked Strabo.

Who?

The thrill-killers. I don't want them coming after me.

Gone, said Fox. We should be too.

The woman's purse lay open on the pavement, leaking its contents, just as her throat had done.

I'm taking the cell phone, said Fox.

No! They can trace us with that, said Strabo. Did the scoundrels liberate her wallet?

Black leather lay in the shadows of a statue. Fox picked it up.

Address book.

Why are we still standing here? asked Petey.

Hell, you're right. Let's get up to the woods.

You're the hero, dear boy, said Strabo. You should have saved her.

It's them.

Who? asks Fox.

Whom, says Strabo.

Widmark and Mineo, goddamnit. Across Fremont, in front of the music store.

The two stand in front of Dusty Strings. The tall blond bounces to a beat unrelated to the harp music playing through the speakers. His partner's hands are stuffed deep into his black raincoat.

You see them? asks Petey.

Yeah, yeah, says Fox. They're real.

But highly improbable, says Strabo. Returning to the scene of the crime?

You called it for once, old man, says Fox. They're thrill-killers and this is part of the freaking thrill. They were probably around the corner, watching the cops clean up their mess.

Screw it, says Petey, and starts across the street.

Get back here! Are you nuts?

Sure.

Petey strolls through traffic without even noticing it. Cars honk, but he ignores them.

He stops in front of the movie stars. Fox and Strabo are nowhere in sight. Big help, as usual.

You want something? asks Widmark.

Why'd you do it?

They stare at him. He looks back, poker-faced, though he feels like he's gonna puke.

Mineo backs up to the wall. Widmark just frowns. Do what?

Kill that girl.

Jesus, says Mineo, wide-eyed.

Widmark grabs Petey by the sleeve and pulls him closer, making a face at the smell. What the hell are you talking about?

You cut her throat. I saw you.

Sweet mother of God, says Mineo, and now *he* looks like he's gonna puke.

Listen, you freak, says Widmark. You can get in a lot of trouble making up stuff like that. People will think you're *nuts*.

Just tell me why you did it, Richard.

Richard? He blinks. Who do you think I am?

Richard Widmark, says Petey. You were great in *Kiss of Death*. I hated the remake.

Sal Mineo laughs, high-pitched squeals.

Petey curses himself. He *knows* the blond guy isn't the actor. But Fremont confuses him, tangles him in its fantasy world. He needs Fox and Strabo to tell him what's real, and the cowards have turned tail.

You're a whack job, says Mineo. No one will believe a word you say.

I've got her address book, says Petey.

That stops them for a moment.

So what? asks Widmark. That proves *you* killed her.

You thought it was her wallet, says Petey. You pulled it out of her purse and left it on the pavement. I'll bet it's got fingerprints.

The movie stars exchange a glance. I thought *you* had it, says Mineo.

Shut up, snaps Widmark. He looks around. The rain has given up and more people are on the street. He puts an arm lightly around Petey's shoulders.

What's your name?

Petey.

Okay, Petey. Let's take a little walk and I'll explain the whole thing.

He shrugs off the arm. I'm not going anywhere with you.

You've got us wrong, Petey. Whatever you think you saw—that woman had it coming. She was part of the problem.

Petey frowns. What do you mean?

Widmark chuckles. Think about it, Petey. Think of everything that's gone wrong in your life. All the backstabbers, all the pointless crap that's been dumped on you. You remember it?

I remember.

Well, she was the *reason* for it, Petey. Her and people like her. They're the cause of all our troubles.

Widmark shrugs. But if you don't want to know the truth . . .

Wait. Petey looks around but his friends are nowhere in sight. Damn it.

We can explain it all, but not in a crowd. Come with us, Petey.

Fox and Strabo would tell him to stay the hell away from these two, but they aren't here, are they? Screw them.

Petey walks between the movie stars, while Widmark talks casually, easily, as if this were any old day. Nobody, nobody *sane*, has chatted with him like this, like friends, in a long, long time.

They turn right on 34th, heading away from the gray plaster zombies, the scene of the crime, and toward the paved path that runs beside the Ship Canal. All the time Petey looks over his shoulder for Fox and Strabo, but they are nowhere to be seen.

Okay, Petey, says Widmark, here's the truth. That girl had to go because she was working for the bad guys.

What bad guys?

Widmark laughs. Come *on*, Petey. You're a smart man. You already *know* who the troublemakers are, don't you? Just say it.

Petey takes a deep breath. The movie stars are staring. He's all alone, and suddenly terrified of giving the wrong answer.

Starbucks?

Mineo laughs again. He hides his face in his hands, shoulders jerking.

Shut *up*, says Widmark. This is serious. That's exactly right, Petey. She was a spy for Starbucks.

Those bastards. They stole my wife.

Sounds just like them. But Petey, you have no idea what they're *really* doing. He leans close, eyes narrow. They put drugs in their drinks to control us.

Yeah?

If only Fox and Strabo were here. They were never gonna believe this.

Do you drink their coffee, Petey?

I used to.

That's what screwed your brain up, says Mineo. Java withdrawal.

Let me handle this, says Widmark. All the bad stuff that's happened to you is Starbucks' fault, Petey. All part of their *plot*.

He's stunned. It makes sense at a level logic never seemed to reach before.

That girl knew their plans, Petey. We asked her to help us but the bitch was gonna turn us in. It was self-defense, you see?

I guess so. Petey looks around again. They are deep in the dripping green heart of the trail now, and haven't seen anyone for almost a block.

Good man. The shame of it is, she wouldn't tell us what she knew. And she had the names and addresses of everyone in on the plot.

Widmark shakes his head sadly. Damn it, Petey. If we had those names we could catch them all. We could *stop* them!

I got their names! Petey reaches into his jacket and pulls out the black address book.

Bingo, says Mineo.

That's all we need, says Widmark, grinning. Give it to Jerry.

Who?

Me, says Mineo, and grabs it. Do it now. This is perfect.

Petey looks back at Widmark, who has pulled a knife out of his jacket.

It's time, Petey.

Wait a minute.

You can go quietly like a man, or squealing like a little girl. What do you choose?

What else've you got? asks Petey.

There's no one in sight. This piece of the trail is blocked off from the canal by bushes and trees, and blocked from the street by—

What the hell is that?

Mineo looks and laughs. That's a topiary dinosaur. A full-size brontosaurus made of plants. It's gonna eat you up, Petey!

You buffoon, says Strabo. It's an apatosaurus!

Where the hell have *you* been? asks Petey.

Who? asks Widmark, coming closer.

Run *now*! yells Fox.

Widmark swings and Petey raises his left arm. The knife cuts through his jacket, slices into his forearm. It hurts like hell.

Grab him! shouts Widmark, but Mineo sees the blood and hesitates.

Swing the fruit! yells Fox, and Petey grabs one of Mineo's skinny arms with both bloody hands and spins like a discus thrower. The movie stars collide and tumble to the pavement. The knife and address book go flying.

Run, boy!

Petey runs. He used to jog this trail, back when he lived in a funky apartment on Bowdoin, back before his mind betrayed him, when he had a job and a life.

You still got a life, says Fox, but not if they catch you. Step on it!

You need a bandage, lad. Use your coat.

Petey tears off his jacket and wraps it around his bleeding arm. That helps. He's still on the trail, which heads down and finally under the bridge.

We need crowds, says Fox. Go left!

Petey turns up Evanston Avenue. The movie stars had stopped for the knife and the book, but he can hear them on his track now.

On the hunt, says Strabo, and sings again.

Oh how will you cut him, said Milder to Moulder
Oh we may not tell you, said Festel to Fose
With knives and with forks, said John the Red Nose
With knives and with forks, said everyone . . .

The movie stars are gasping. They haven't run this hill route a thousand times like he has, before the world went to hell.

Petey's laughing, because this is really happening. There *was* a goddamned dinosaur made of plants. There really *is* a giant rocket on top of that building on the corner.

I'm not insane. I'm just in goddamned Fremont.

He dodges a bus on 36th Street and staggers to a halt.

Keep going! yells Fox. What's wrong with you?

A man stands in front of him, twenty feet tall. The familiar face scowls down from under his cap.

He's crazy, says Lenin. *That's what's wrong with him.*

Petey can't move, caught in the big man's glare.

It's just freaking Lenin! screams Fox. The statue they brought from Russia! You've seen it a thousand times!

Now hold on, says Strabo. It doesn't make sense, does it? Why would anyone put up a monument to a dead Communist in the middle of this merchant kingdom? No, I'd say the lad is delusional.

Out of his capitalist mind, says Lenin, and somebody hits Petey from behind. He slams into the base of the statue and bangs his head.

He rolls over on the plaza tiles and Widmark lands on top of him. Petey sees the knife going up but his left hand is tangled in his jacket. He can't stop the blade.

Freeze!

Widmark stops, looks up. He slides off and drops the knife.

Thank god you're here, officer! This man just confessed to murder.

Get away from him, says the cop, who looks a little like Matt Damon.

It's true, says Mineo. He told us he killed a woman near the bridge last night.

Damon's eyes widen. He's heard about the dead woman.

Is that true?

I didn't kill anybody, says Petey. *They* did it. You saw them attack me.

We took the knife away from him, says Widmark.

Ask him why she died, says Mineo.

The cop is frowning, not sure where to point the gun. Why'd she die, sir?

Be silent, boy, says Strabo, but Petey can't help himself.

She was a spy. For Starbucks.

See? says Mineo.

Petey shakes his head, trying to clear it. They attacked me by the dinosaurs. Then I came up here, past the rocket, and saw Lenin.

Damon nods. You were attacked by a dinosaur and came here by rocket. Was that after you killed the woman?

Dear, dear, says Strabo. The constable's not from around here.

Damon has his handcuffs in one hand, gun in the other. Put your hands on your . . . What happened to your arm?

He's afraid you'll get his cuffs bloody. Har har.

Your honor, says Strabo, my client pleads not guilty by season of inanity.

Petey falls back on the tiles. He's crying.

You're under arrest, says Lenin.

The detective is Bill Cosby, except his hair is gray and he has a thin mustache. He is scowling and Petey figures it is because he's only a TV star and the movie stars outrank him.

Mr. Gottesman, he says, you say you saw those two men following Ms. Mantello, but you didn't do anything about it.

I was scared. Did you see him in *Night and the City?*

Who?

Petey explains about Richard Widmark. Cosby frowns more. Mr. Gottesman, where do you think you are right now?

Petey looks around. I'm sitting at a patio table in a Mexican-style plaza in the middle of Seattle. Dozens of tourists are watching me. I'm handcuffed to an umbrella, staring at Lenin's giant butt, while a medic patches up my arm and a cop interrogates me. How much of that is real?

Cosby shrugs. All of it.

Petey repeats something Fox had said before disappearing

again. Just because you're paranoid doesn't mean there aren't two men chasing you with a knife.

The detective thinks that one over. He looks at the movie stars standing on the other side of the plaza by the taco shop, talking to Matt Damon.

You said Ms. Mantello was a spy for a coffee company.

They told me that.

Cosby sighs.

Okay. Here's what's gonna happen. You're still under arrest. We're gonna take you to the hospital to get that arm looked at. Then I think a judge will order an examination—

No hospitals, says Fox. They wipe your freaking memory there. You know that.

Think, Petey, says Strabo. Make him see the truth and the truth will set us free!

Listen, Bill, says Petey, I followed that woman because she looked like Abby, my ex-wife. I didn't go near those guys because they scared me. But I didn't kill her, and when it happened I couldn't get near them because of the drawbridge.

The drawbridge? She came from Queen Anne?

We all did. But the drawbridge went up—

You didn't mention that.

Nobody asked, says Petey.

I'm asking now. Tell me the whole route.

Petey does. Cosby nods and stands up.

He calls for Officer Bestock and Damon hurries over.

There's a bank on Nickerson Avenue and they've got a security camera out front. Tell 'em we need the tapes from last night. He looks at the movie stars and raises his voice. If that woman was over there, we'll know. And if someone was following her, we'll see who it was.

Mineo starts to cry. Widmark tells him to shut up, but it's too late.

Cosby turns to Petey. How'd you know my name is Bill?

It's in the credits.

Petey tells them he has no insurance, which usually saves him from medical care, but this time they insist he's going to the hospital.

Cause you're a hero, says Fox.

Indeed, says Strabo. A veritable Hercules or Adonis.

The paramedics strap him on a gurney and are ready to wheel him into the ambulance when another cop comes up, one who doesn't look like anybody.

Jesus, Petey, is that you?

You know him? asks Cosby.

Yeah. I do security shifts at the clinic downtown. He used to be a regular. Remember me, Petey? Officer Lazenby.

He shakes his head.

You went off your meds, didn't you, pal?

Had to. My friends didn't like them.

What friends?

Fox and Strabo.

They aren't your friends, pal. They're just voices in your head. You don't have any friends.

Thanks a lot.

I didn't mean it like that, says Lazenby. Oh, Jesus.

Should we notify anybody? asks the ambulance guy.

About what?

Tell 'em you'll be in the hospital.

No. There's nobody.

What about your ex-wife? asks Cosby.

Ex-wife, Lazenby repeats.

He said her name was Abby.

Jesus. Lazenby shakes his head. Abby wasn't his wife. She was just a nice barista who used to sneak free coffee to the homeless people. When she quit and moved away, Petey went on a one-man WTO against Starbucks. He got locked up for a while for throwing rocks through their windows. Didn't you, pal?

They took her away from me.

Lazenby pats his arm, the one that isn't cut. It's gonna be okay, pal. The drugs keep improving. You just listen to the docs and pretty soon you'll be back in the real world.

What else've you got? asks Petey.

PART II

WHAT COMES AROUND

BLUE SUNDAY

BY KATHLEEN ALCALÁ

Central District

 It was a blue night, a blue car, and Danny was full of shots of blue tequila.

"Slow down, man. Aren't you going too fast?"

"Can't catch me, I'm the gingerbread man."

"Shit, man, I thought I was the crazy one. Just get me back to my old lady in one piece."

"No problem, bro. How's she doing, anyway?"

"Good. She's happy to see me alive."

Chucho gunned it to make a light. That's when a cop car came out of the parking lot and the sirens started.

When Danny came to, he was lying on the ground.

"Get up . . . I said get up!"

A foot prodded him.

"Okay, okay," said Danny.

Danny was on his back. He slowly rolled over and got to his hands and knees. Chucho's car was nearby, the passenger door open next to Danny. He vaguely recalled Chucho's nervous laughter as they had careened past the fancy new condos on 23rd, past Garfield and the fire station to Jackson. The Seven Star Mini Mart was still open. Chucho made a bat turn left onto MLK in front of half a dozen cars and flew past the playground to Cherry.

"*Híjole*, man, that cop is mad!" he had said gleefully.

Danny wondered where his cell phone had gone. The last he remembered was Catfish Corner.

"Get up!" the policeman shouted again.

"Okay, I'm getting up now," said Danny as he began to rise. "I'm going to get up."

The policeman fired three shots into him.

"Shut the fuck up!" the cop shouted. "Shut the fuck up!"

Dying had seemed easy in Iraq—people did it every day. And when people were not dying in front of you, your buddies, the cooks, the officers, or the civilians who brought in supplies, they were telling you stories about people dying. About how they died, how long it took them, and what it looked like afterwards. Who killed them, or who might have killed them.

There was no death with dignity, only death. Danny spent most of his free time pretending he was someplace else. He plugged his iPod into his head, turned on some tunes, and tried to think about Aimee and the kid they were expecting early next year. Would it be a boy or a girl? It was too soon to tell, but when he went home on leave, they would visit the doctor, and maybe have an ultrasound done. Danny was ready to think about a little life—a little life after Iraq, if that was possible.

The next thing that woke Danny was sirens. A lot of them.

I ain't dead yet, he thought. A collar was clamped around his neck, and he was rolled onto a stretcher. "Hustle! Hustle! Hustle!" yelled a woman. "I need an IV here, as soon as he's in!"

Some more jostling, then a sharp pain in his arm.

"Go!" screamed another voice.

The ambulance, because he must be in an ambulance,

started up, the siren more muted from inside, and they flew. It reminded him of the cab to the airport in Iraq, but with fewer potholes. He wondered if Chucho was okay.

Danny wakes in a bright, noisy room. People keep leaning over him and yelling in his face.

"I'm not deaf, you know," he finally says.

"Oh good, he's conscious. We thought we were losing you there," a male voice barks at Danny. "Just keep talking to us."

Danny is in a curtained-off area, and he can hear people near him yelling. Triage.

"Uh, what do you want me to say?"

A bright light is shined in one eye, then the other. "No concussion. Let's give him some fluids . . . Are you in pain?" the man asks in that voice you use for the deaf, elderly, and foreign born. Danny recognizes it as the way he spoke to the Iraqis, as though it would somehow bridge the gap between his English and their understanding.

Danny has to think about this. "Actually, I'm kind of numb on one side."

"Not good," says the man.

Danny decides to pretend this man is a doctor.

"Can you feel this? . . . This?" The doctor pricks him with a pencil tip from his shoulder down his right side.

"It's my arm. I can't feel my arm," says Danny. Damn, he thinks. Back from Iraq just in time to die in Harborview. The room grows dark again.

Danny could say "stop" and "open" in Arabic. And, of course, *"Insha Allah"*—If God wills it. Sometimes, when he listened to the Iraqi men talking and smoking, he could hear them say to each other simply, *"Insha . . . insha . . ."* a sort of running refrain, an affirmation of hope, with a strong note of fatalism.

Danny had gotten used to stepping in front of speeding vehicles. Iraqi drivers seemed to have two speeds—stop and go flat out—so he, taking their fatalistic attitude, assumed the drivers of speeding trucks would stomp on their brakes before hitting him at the base checkpoint where he was usually stationed. If not, his fellow MPs would open fire. It was that simple.

This habit of driving as fast as possible was soon picked up by the Americans. It started when you got out of air transport and on the road. Since the highway between the airport and the capital was mined, and also without cover, you felt as vulnerable as an ant as soon as you hit the ground. The drivers stepped on it and went at a suicidal speed, swerving away from suspicious objects and people, even if it meant driving directly into the path of oncoming traffic. But the trucks and cars coming the other way were doing the same thing.

Danny becomes aware of a shooting pain down his left side. It jolts him from sleep, or wherever he has been. He remembers the doctor poking him along that side, and feeling nothing. The pain jolts him again. Is this good? Pain is probably better than nothing at all—it means he's still alive.

"Danny? Danny?" It's his sister Sirena's voice.

He feels a cool hand on his right arm, then against his cheek. He opens his eyes, then shuts them again quickly against the glare.

"Can you hear me?" she asks. Then a note of her old, mischievous self, his little sister: "Are you in there, Danny?"

He opens his eyes again, sees her silhouette against the window before shutting them again. It is raining outside.

Good. This means he's not in Iraq. Where is he, then? He remembers the car chase. The police.

"Chucho . . . happened to Chucho?"

"My cousin Chucho? He's fine. Don't worry about him. Only you were hurt." Sirena leans over him.

He can feel her breath on his face, and tries again to open his eyes, fluttering his lids briefly. "What?" he says.

"Do you remember what happened?"

"Yeah. Somebody shot me."

"A *cop* shot you. For nothing. Someone taped it, and it's been all over the news."

Danny grunts.

Sirena pats his hand. "Are you thirsty?" Without waiting for a reply, she reaches for a glass and places a straw to his lips.

Danny realizes he's in a neck brace. He opens his lips and sucks.

"Is my neck broken?"

"No. I don't know why you're in that thing. Maybe we can get them to take it off soon."

Danny can see a nurses' station, more bright lights.

Sirena looks up at the clock. "Aimee will be here pretty soon, as soon as she drops off the kids."

Soon. Soon. Soon. Her words echo in his head.

"Soon," he says, then closes his eyes.

At Sarge's urging, Danny tried driving the truck. After grinding the gears around the compound for a while, he got the hang of it. It was loud and hot inside. It was a hundred degrees outside. He had never learned how to drive a stick shift back home. His cousins in L.A., when he e-mailed them, teased him, told him he was finally a real man.

Danny met Aimee when he was stationed at Barksdale Air Force Base in Louisiana. Her friend was dating another reservist and the four of them went out one night. The other couple broke up after about two months, but Danny kept seeing Aimee, simply knowing that he felt better when he was around her. This must be love, he thought.

At twenty-five, Danny was one of the last in his family—of the cousins—to marry, except for his little sister. The relatives blamed it on their college educations.

"Gotta get 'em while you're young," said Freddy, a sleeping baby balanced on his thick forearm. "Gotta get 'em while you still have hair!"

At twenty-nine, working fifty hours a week in a detailing shop, Freddy already looked old to Danny. Danny had gotten his degree in industrial design and was starting to pay back his debt to Uncle Sam.

Aimee was a Cajun girl, not the sort anyone thought Danny would fall for, with wild red hair and a husky voice. She ordered up a plate of garlic shrimp and a mug of beer for each of them, and taught Danny the fine art of peeling shrimp. Then she taught him how to two-step to a zydeco band. It might have been the way she placed her boots on the sawdust and shrimp shell–covered floor of the nameless crab shack where they danced. It might have been the way she placed her hands on his chest during a slow number and took the wings of his collar between her fingertips before looking up into his eyes. But probably it was the way she double-clutched her pickup truck without ever glancing at the gear shift that won Danny's heart.

Winning over Aimee's family was another matter. Where Danny grew up, the place they lived would have been called "the tulees." In Louisiana, it was called the bayou. Aimee drove the two of them south from Shreveport to the end of a paved road, then onto a sandy track that ended in water. Swinging her vehicle off to one side, she parked next to a stake truck that could have been there five minutes or five years.

"Daddy's home," she said. Wading into the shallows, Aimee retrieved a flat-bottomed boat from the reeds and they climbed in. They set a bag of groceries and Rikenjaks beer at one end and tucked their coats around it to keep it upright. Then Aimee grabbed the oars and steered them out onto the dark waters. Danny felt like he was in a movie, or at Disneyland, and waited for the giant, audio-animatronic gator to rear up out of the water and snap its plastic jaws at them.

"Don't you think they ain't real gators out here," said Aimee, as though reading his mind. "Cause they is."

Danny kept his hands well within the boat as the sun slipped lower on the horizon.

Danny wakes to Aimee's kiss.

"Hey, stranger," she whispers.

"I feel like Sleeping Beauty," he says, "except woken by a princess."

"Were you dreaming?" she asks, pulling her fingers through his short hair.

"Yeah. About you."

"You seem better," she says, dragging her chair closer. Danny notices that he's in a regular hospital room with a door, not the ICU.

"What about Chucho? Is he hurt?"

"No."

"Oh, that's right."

"They arrested him, but he's out on bail. Your uncle put up the money."

"What's he charged with?"

"Drunk driving. Speeding. Resisting arrest. The works. You were too, you know."

"I was what?"

"Under arrest. You were chained to the bed. Don't you remember?"

"No. How long have I been here?"

"Five days."

"Am I still chained to the bed?"

"My God, no. Someone taped the whole thing. A police officer shot you without provocation. Now he's on leave and under investigation. Don't you remember anything?"

Danny tries.

"I can get flashes of things, like little snapshots. He told me to get up. I put my hands up, exactly like he said. But he shot me anyway." Danny feels himself heating up just thinking about it.

"Well, a couple of lawyers have called. They want us to sue the bastard. They say we have a good case."

"I'm supposed to rejoin my unit in a week."

Aimee throws back her head and laughs. "Soldier, you ain't going nowhere." Then she leans over and hugs him, and bursts into tears.

Danny itched even after he'd had the good fortune to shower, which happened maybe once a week; the constant dust and grit irritated his skin. It worked its way under his watchband, under his waistband, under the sweatband of his hat. When he took his boots and socks off, there was a fine mud between his toes that he tried to remove with baby wipes.

Danny wanted to wear a bandana over his face when he worked the checkpoint, but his sergeant said no, it would spook the Iraqi civilians if they couldn't see his face. When he coughed and spat, his phlem was brown.

A man Danny doesn't recognize reaches up and pops a videotape into the slot in the television bolted to the wall. Gray screen suddenly goes to black with white walls, an upswing motion as the camera seems to be thrust upward, then pointed down.

Danny recognizes Chucho's metallic blue Corvette, the front bumper crumpled, white streaks from side-swiping something.

"Get out. Get out!"

A figure on the right is holding a gun with both hands. The door opens and Danny puts his feet on the ground. He doesn't see Chucho, although he can hear him yelling.

"It's okay," says Danny. He has his hands up.

"Get out of the vehicle and down on the ground."

Danny hesitates.

"I said get down on the ground!" The voice is agitated, angry.

Danny kneels down slowly, then rolls onto the ground.

He remembers how he had been asleep, or so drunk as to be virtually asleep. That's why he had left his car and ridden with Chucho.

The camera is jostled as the operator tries to focus on the policeman, on Danny lying on the ground. He is a light-colored, prone figure on a black background. The quality is poor, bluish for lack of light. It reminds him of night vision goggles.

"Get up!" the voice barks. It cracks with tension, near hysteria.

"Okay, I'm getting up now," says Danny. "I'm going to get up."

He rises to his knees, starts to put his hands up again.

That's when the shots ring out, three of them. The camera wobbles wildly, but Danny does not see this part, because he's shut his eyes and turned away.

"It's okay, darlin'," says Aimee, clutching his right arm, the good one without all the tubes in it.

Danny can hear Chucho yelling again. He must still be in the car. Danny opens his eyes and sees himself slumped sideways, close to the open door of the car.

"I told you to lie down!" screams the policeman.

Another police car pulls up, and Chucho is pulled roughly from the driver's seat.

"He killed my friend!" Chucho screams. "He shot him in cold blood!"

"Shut up," says a voice.

Chucho is spread against the far side of the car, searched.

"We are not armed, officer!"

"Just shut up. I'm arresting you on suspicion of drunk driving and eluding an officer." He is led out of camera range as the officer tells him his rights.

There is the crackling sound of radios. An ambulance pulls up. The camera seems to sag with fatigue, again showing Danny prone on the ground.

The ambulance crew hustles out a stretcher, sets it on the ground next to Danny.

"What happened?"

"He has a gunshot wound. He tried to attack me."

Someone clamps a collar around Danny's neck, and two men turn him onto his back.

"Jesus!"

He is placed on the stretcher and taken away. There is a lot of shouting, doors slamming, and the sound of the ambulance siren starting up and fading away.

More radio noise, and a figure slams the door on the car. The video ends.

The man who played the video has been standing in the corner, watching it silently, observing Danny. "The officer's name is Troy Amboy," the man announces, "and we are going to sue him into the Stone Age."

"Who are you?" asks Danny.

"I'm your attorney, Jason Ritchie."

Danny glances at Aimee.

"He called," she explains. "He says we don't pay him. He only gets paid if we win the case."

"Why did he shoot me?" asks Danny.

"That's the million-dollar question," replies Ritchie. "He claims you lunged at him, that he thought you were armed, but it's pretty clear he was entirely unprovoked. Look here." He points a remote at the TV and rewinds the tape back to where Danny is about to exit the car. "Right there," Ritchie says, waving the remote and stopping the video where Danny has gotten up from the ground to a kneeling position. "He says you reached into your shirt, but you didn't even touch your chest."

Danny tries to look down at his body. In addition to the tubes, a complex web of bandages cover his chest, and he feels the pull of adhesive tape across the back of his left shoulder. "When can I get this damn neck brace off?" he asks.

There was the incident outside of Kirkuk. Two soldiers had died earlier that day, and everyone was jumpy. A rumor was spreading that a new shipment of weapons had just arrived from Afghanistan, including IEDs.

Danny had spent the previous day escorting a group of

Iraqi detainees from one prison to another, always a dangerous business. One man in particular haunted Danny. As he was led out of the foul-smelling holding area along with fifteen others, the man had fixed an eye on him and said in broken English, "I know you. You promised to get me out of here! Where we are going, they will kill me."

Danny did not recognize the man, had never been to that prison before. Did the man have him mixed up with someone else? Was it a ruse?

Danny didn't answer, had merely gestured with his rifle for the man to move along onto the truck that would take them to another foul-smelling prison. Danny knew there was torture. He knew there was death. On their way to reinforce the battalion that had lost two soldiers, they had stumbled across a trash heap with five more Iraqi bodies, hands fastened with plastic ties behind them, no IDs.

Danny did not want to be recognized by anyone in Iraq. He just wanted to do his job and get home.

The following day, he was back on the AFB checkpoint. Forbes, Yamada, Meyer, and he had been checking IDs and searching cars for five hours. Their shifts had ended an hour before, but their relief had not shown up. They couldn't leave their posts. All they knew was that there had been an "unexpected delay."

Later, it turned out that Vice President Cheney had made an unannounced visit to the Green Zone to meet with top officials. All members of Danny's squadron who had not been on duty at the time were called in to provide extra security.

"Dang!" said Sergeant Klein when they got back. "They've got hot water twenty-four hours a day in there. And a swimming pool! It's like paradise, while we're roasting out here like hot dogs on a stick!"

The incident started when a new black Humvee pulled into line for the checkpoint. The driver got out and walked up to Danny.

"We go around," he said, indicating that they wanted to skip the line.

"All Iraqi citizens must go through the line and show ID," replied Danny. Every day, a couple of people tried this stunt.

"He is late for meeting," said the driver, pointing back at the vehicle. Danny could not see in through the tinted windows.

"Sorry," Danny answered, "those are my orders. No exceptions."

The driver returned to the vehicle, and Danny went back to asking for IDs, demanding that car trunks be opened, peering into sweat-smelling interiors at frightened men.

About ten minutes later, the Humvee roared up to him and the rear window rolled down silently. Danny found himself staring at a man in sunglasses pointing a rifle at him. Danny cocked his own rifle, and swallowed hard.

"I mean you no harm," said Danny. He heard the hoarseness in his voice. He and the man stared at each other.

"I'll take it from here, soldier," announced a voice behind him. Major Samuelson and a translator approached the Humvee. The translator said something, and the man in sunglasses pulled the muzzle of the gun back into the car without taking his eyes off Danny.

Danny stood down, sweat pouring from his body. Samuelson and the translator got into the Humvee with the armed passenger and drove off.

Just then, Danny's relief showed up. "What the hell was that all about?"

"Oh, man," said Danny. "Not my problem. Not anymore."

* * *

"Okay, we're going to try sitting up today."

Danny opens his eyes to see Pilar, the day nurse, rearranging the tubes attached to his body. Almost everybody who works at Harborview seems to be Filipino. When they speak to each other, their soft, clipped language has a lot of Spanish in it, but even so, Danny can't understand it.

He thinks of an old punch line: "What do you mean 'we,' Kemo Sabe?"

"Very funny," says Pilar. "Okay, ready?"

"Yeah."

She puts one hand behind his back and pushes gently, while Danny uses his arms to press up. There is some pain and pulling. He catches his breath and grimaces.

"You okay?"

"Not too bad," he says. "Nothing I can't handle."

"Good. The sooner you start moving around, the sooner you can go home. Want to try standing?"

"Sure."

Pilar fits some slippers on his dangling feet. His legs look like somebody else's coming out from under the gown.

"You going to give me something to cover my butt?"

"As soon as you stand up, I can put a robe on you," she says.

Danny stands. Muscles pull. Bones creak as she holds him by the waist.

"How's that?" she asks.

"Good."

"Can you stand by yourself? Here, hold onto the railing." Pilar works a robe onto Danny's shoulders.

"Well, well! Look who's standing." It's Danny's father Sam in the doorway.

"Hey," says Danny, pleased in spite of himself.

"He's doing great!" says the nurse. "How about if I get a wheelchair and you can visit in the lounge?"

"What do you think, Danny boy?"

"Good deal." Danny is so pleased that he doesn't even object to the eternal nickname.

"Here. Stand right here," Pilar positions Danny's father next to him, "while I get a wheelchair."

"Have you seen Aimee today?" asks Sam.

"I think so." Time has been elastic for Danny in the hospital. "I think she and Sirena took the kids swimming. Is today Sunday?"

"Yes."

Pilar returns with the wheelchair and Danny's mother. "Look who I found."

"Aye, *mi'jo*," says Letty. She moves to hug Danny, already tearing up.

"Let him sit down first," cautions Pilar.

Even after two minutes, Danny is grateful for the rest. The nurse attaches his bags to a rolling stand and wheels him down the hall.

"Don't cry, Mom."

"I can't help it." She dabs at her eyes. "I'm just so happy to see you can stand, *gracias a Dios*. It means you're getting better."

Danny's father goes straight for the television. "Let's see if the game is on."

"Is that all you can think about?" says his mother. "You come to visit your son, and you want to watch the game?"

"Of course not! It's up to Danny. It's the Final Four."

"The game is fine, Dad."

Danny's father watches Florida vs. UCLA while his mother recounts what Aimee and the kids did that day. They are staying with his parents on South Plum in what had been meant as a short visit upon his return from Iraq. It isn't a big house, and Danny figures they must all be getting on each other's nerves by now.

"They got up and had cereal, then went out. So I've just been cleaning all day."

The sound of the game on the television suddenly rises, the announcers rabid with excitement.

"Turn that thing down!" snaps Danny's mother.

"I just want to hear the scores. I'll turn it back down in a sec," her husband replies.

When Danny spots Aimee and the kids coming down the hall, he breaks into a big grin. Sirena is with them.

"Daddy!" chirp the kids, running up and trying to climb in his lap.

"Careful, careful," says his mother.

Aimee holds them back, an arm around each waist. "You can't climb up on Daddy yet. Remember, he was hurt. Just give him a kiss."

Just then Danny's father turns up the volume on the TV again. "Here you are," he says.

The TV shows a clip from the grainy video taken the night Danny was shot. Danny sees the car window slowly roll down, the stone face of the policeman. The officer has his gun out. He yells at Danny, who stumbles out of the car, struggling to comply with the policeman's orders as he barks out commands and expletives, his voice rising higher and higher. Then he hears himself say it: "I mean you no harm."

The officer orders him down, then up, and Danny shuts his eyes, anticipating the sound of the gun.

"Not in front of the children," Letty hisses.

"Sorry." His father switches the channel to a commercial. Danny's parents continue to argue in low voices in Spanish, until his father switches off the TV and stomps out.

"Was that you, Daddy?" asks Jacob.

Danny turns his wheelchair at the sound of his son's voice. He continues to stare at the blank television, as though the ghostly blue-white images are still on the screen.

"No," he says, "that was somebody else who looks a lot like me, talks a lot like me, but gets shot by the police. That's not me."

"But you were shot. Who shot you?"

Aimee says nothing.

"Somebody," says Danny. "Somebody who thought I was a threat."

Eight months later, Danny is back in Iraq. For better or worse, the cop in Seattle had missed all his vital organs and he healed up as only a young guy can. Danny had gladly rejoined his company.

"Soldier," says his lieutenant, "you need to report to the CO's office."

Oh shit, thinks Danny. Now what?

The commanding officer has a desk, a couple of chairs, and an air conditioner. Danny removes his helmet and feels the sweat evaporate off his head and neck.

"Have a seat," the CO says. "We just got a call from Seattle."

Danny sits.

"There was a shooting incident there last night."

Danny swallows.

"Same place, same block where you were shot. The police think the officer in question was deliberately targeted."

"What do you mean?"

"It was the cop who attacked you."

A pain shoots up Danny's side from his leg to his shoulder. Amboy had been cleared of all wrongdoing and put back on the street. Danny tries to keep his face impassive. "Nothing to do with me."

"We know that. And that's what we told them."

"Thank you, sir."

"I just wanted you to know."

"Thank you. May I go now, sir?"

"Yes. Dismissed."

Danny stands to leave.

"Oh, by the way . . ."

Danny turns.

"Just like cops, MPs take care of their own."

The CO holds his eye for a moment, then waves him out.

THE TASKMASTERS

BY SIMON WOOD

Downtown

The bar fight was over. Matt staggered to his feet. The loudmouth was down and he wasn't getting back up without assistance. None of the barflies volunteered to help him, though they closed in to examine Matt's handiwork. Matt ran the back of his hand across his mouth, leaving it streaked with blood.

Police sirens wailed in the distance. Matt's heart rate quickened just as it had finally started to slow down. He couldn't afford to be busted again. The spectators swarmed for the exit. This wasn't one of those trendy downtown bars where management called 911 at the sound of a raised voice. Everyone was a little cop-shy at The Dive. The Dive lived up to its name—literally and figuratively. It was a basement place, part of Seattle's subterranean past. An underground bar for underground people.

Matt went to follow the crush out the door, but someone held him back. He shook off the hand gripping his shoulder and whirled around with a readied fist to face his new challenger. The middle-aged guy held up his hands in surrender. He had six inches and fifty pounds of muscle on Matt.

"Easy, pal," the guy said. "I'm not trying to stop you. Backdoor, before the cops get here. You kinda stick out in your current condition."

Matt glanced at himself in the mirror behind the bar. Ripped clothes. The red blooms of burgeoning bruises.

The sirens intensified. Matt didn't argue and followed the man out the fire exit. It opened up into an unlit stairwell. The guy burst through the door, casting streetlight onto Matt's escape. He clambered up the stairs and into the service alley.

"C'mon, this way," the man urged.

The alley ran from Cherry to Columbia. He jogged down the alley away from The Dive's entrance on Cherry, sidestepping busted trash bags and puddles containing more than just water. Matt followed the man uphill on Columbia a couple of blocks, then into another alley lit by a thumbnail moon.

"We'll hang here until things are cool."

Matt didn't reply. His guardian angel didn't sit well in his stomach. He didn't trust him. He didn't trust anyone.

Late for the party, two cop cars roared down 2nd toward The Dive, spraying red and blue light. Matt's stomach clenched. They'd start combing the surrounding streets for someone matching his description soon. He needed to get moving.

"Get into a lot of fights, don't you?"

The sudden question jolted Matt from his thoughts. "What makes you say that?"

"The way you handled yourself in there. You didn't learn those moves in a boxing ring or a dojo. You've had a street education. Besides, I recognize a bottle scar when I see one."

Instinctively, Matt touched the thin mark beneath his left eye with his thumb. Although it was faint after so many years, he remembered the fight like it was yesterday. He'd been eighteen and it had been over a girl. Frank Tremaine hadn't liked the idea of losing his Susie. Matt thought it would be easily settled, but he hadn't expected Frank to go for him with a bottle of Bud. He nearly lost his eye that night. There'd been a lot of Frank Tremaines over the years and a lot of fights over lesser reasons than Susie. Tonight was no exception.

"Have you done time?" the man asked.

"Once."

"Carry on like you're doing and it's easily going to be twice."

"Who the hell are you?"

"Harry Sharpe." He thrust out a hand.

Matt looked at the hand warily. This attempt at an introduction could be a stunt to take him down. He ignored the handshake and said, "Matt Crozier."

Harry let his hand drop without showing any signs of being insulted. "Good to meet you, Matt."

"What do you want? Why are you helping me?" Matt backed up a step. He'd rather take a chance with the cops than this guy if something went down. At least he knew what to expect with the cops.

"I represent a group that helps young and wayward men like yourself. We try to turn their skills toward more positive outlets and keep them out of trouble."

Matt was already shaking his head. He knew where this was going. A dark alley, a sensitive older man, and a misguided youth; a cry for attention and a sympathetic ear, leading to a tender moment. It was pathetic really.

"Sorry, dude, you've dialed the wrong number. I don't answer those sorts of calls."

"I'm not trying to pick you up," Harry snapped. "I'm trying to keep you out of trouble."

Matt backed up toward the street. "Okay, whatever you say, reverend."

Harry lunged and snared Matt's arm. Matt took a swing.

Harry blocked it and slammed him up against a dumpster.

"I'm not a priest. I'm trying to teach you something. If you want to end up dead or serving a life sentence, then carry on doing what you're doing, because believe me, you will overstep the boundary of a bar brawl to manslaughter one of these days. But if you want to change that, learn something, make yourself a better man, call me."

Harry released Matt and jammed a business card in his palm. Matt watched him leave and turn the corner. Once he felt Harry wasn't coming back and the police weren't waiting for him, he stepped out into the street. He examined Harry's card under the streetlight. It had no information other than TASKMASTERS, followed by a local telephone number.

Matt spent the following day mulling over what Harry Sharpe had said. He didn't need some do-gooder telling him where his life was heading. He knew already. He couldn't keep from getting into fights. He wasn't a kid anymore. He was fast approaching thirty with nothing to show for it except calluses and scar tissue. He'd eventually cross the line and it would end his life one way or another. Harry had handed him a much-needed reality check. This was certainly the time to wise up.

He hadn't heard of the Taskmasters and neither had anybody else he asked at the oil changers where he worked. The consensus was they were something like the Toastmasters or the Rotary Club. He took some shit from the guys about not being Rotarian material. More concerned about who exactly the Taskmasters were, the jibes bounced off him. He wasn't sure what he was expecting, but a public speaking group wasn't it. Harry didn't seem the type to sit around over a pleasant meal, challenging others to speak on a subject suggested by one of the other Taskmasters. How this would make him a better person he couldn't imagine, but he'd heard they were connected with the business community and helped members find jobs. He could do with a boost in that direction. He'd go—just this once.

He dialed the number. Harry picked up on the first ring.

"Yes."

"It's Matt, from the bar last night."

"I remember you. I wasn't sure you'd call, but I'm glad you did. You want to join, then?"

"I thought I'd check it out."

"Good. We'll pick you up at 9. What's your address?"

Matt waited outside his apartment block so that Harry couldn't see the hole he called a home. Not that standing outside helped. It wouldn't be hard for him to work it out from the address. The five-story converted residential hotel on the wrong side of I-5 looked almost as bad from the outside as it did on the inside.

A horn tooted and a blue-black SUV pulled up in front of him. Harry was driving, but he wasn't alone; three other men sat in the vehicle with him. Matt wandered over and the guy in the back flung open a passenger door. Matt got in.

"Guys, this is Matt," Harry said. "Okay, quick introductions. Riding shotgun with me is Brett Chalmers. Sitting next to you is Frank Tripplehorn. And taking up too much room in back there is John Stein."

The Taskmasters smiled and nodded. Matt tried to do the same, but they were nothing like he'd imagined. Matt had taken the trouble to dress up, nothing too fancy, but then again he didn't have anything too fancy. Surprisingly, however, he was the overdressed one. Everyone else was in jeans, polo shirts, and windbreakers. They all had Harry's muscular build, except John Stein, who was another X-size up. His head scraped the underside of the SUV's roof.

Introductions over, Harry turned the car around and took Madison over the freeway and into downtown. The Taskmasters bantered with one another, talking about nothing much. Matt interrupted them.

"Where are we going?" He hadn't intended the level of fear in his voice. It didn't go unnoticed by the others.

"We have a clubhouse where we meet," Tripplehorn said.

"Is there anything else you'd like to know?" Chalmers asked. The jagged edge the man placed on his question didn't invite further questioning. Matt shook his head and the Taskmasters returned to their conversation.

The clubhouse was an exaggeration of mammoth proportions. Before Matt had called Harry's number, rich Corinthian leather and dark mahogany had sprung to mind. All that went out the window when Harry drew up in front of a largely ignored stretch of Yesler Way. By day, this area was home to the court and city workers. By night, it was nothing. Matt was checking out the restaurants dotted along the streets when Harry pointed across the road at a decayed building. Graffiti-strewn boards covered old busted-out windows.

"Home sweet home," Stein said, sliding out of the SUV.

Harry popped open on a giant padlock on a security shutter protecting the entrance from bums and thieves and slid it back. He unlocked and opened the dark wood doors with amber-colored, leaded glass insets.

Stepping inside, Matt remembered this place. It was going to be some fancy five-star restaurant headed by some TV chef and financed by a dotcom millionaire. When the dotcom bubble burst, it took the millionaire and his restaurant dreams with it. The place had been festering ever since. It was a shame. The turn-of-the-century brick structure gave the place class, but only when it was in tiptop condition. In its current shape, the heavy brick construction turned the place into a dungeon. The place was rainproof, but the brick held the damp and didn't let go. Someone had gotten into the building at some point. Graffiti covered the walls and either the contractor or opportunists had made off with anything that had salvage value. Someone at sometime had urinated in the building. A startled rat scuttled across the floor to hide in a darkened corner.

Harry closed the doors and locked them. The dead bolt sounded like a gunshot and echoed off the walls.

If the Taskmasters owned this place, they had a lot of work to do. But Matt knew these guys probably didn't own it. Something was very wrong and Matt started planning how he was going to get out of this. He knew when he was out of his league. Harry and Co. weren't the kind of guys he could punch his way past. He wondered if the Taskmasters were connected to someone he'd hurt, but couldn't think of anyone with that kind of muscle on tap. Harry dropped a heavy hand on Matt's shoulder and guided him toward a circle of raggedy looking La-Z-Boys.

"Don't be put off by the surroundings. Take a load off and have a beer."

Tripplehorn carried over the cooler he'd retrieved from the SUV's trunk and deposited it at the center of the circle. He flipped it open and tossed Matt an MGD. "You're in good company."

Matt did as he was told and sat down.

Harry took a beer from Tripplehorn and flopped into a chair next to Matt. "I declare this meeting of the Taskmasters is now in session." He raised his bottle and so did the other Taskmasters. Matt shifted in his seat. "Only two items of new business tonight," Harry continued. "The first being our new member, Matt."

"Good to have you, Matt," Stein said, and raised his bottle to him.

"I think Matt can be an asset," Harry said. "I believe he has a good heart, but he's a little misdirected. I hope becoming a Taskmaster will straighten him out and put him on the right track."

Harry's character assessment embarrassed Matt. It made him feel like a kid at parent-teacher night forced to listen to a report being given about him. He hid his embarrassment behind his beer, drinking it too fast.

"I don't know if Harry has explained what we do here at the Taskmasters," Tripplehorn said.

"Not really," Matt replied.

"Well, once a month we challenge each other."

"One person from the group is given a specific task chosen by the others," Chalmers chimed in.

"Which must be completed by the next month," Stein added.

"Which brings us nicely to our second piece of new business," Harry said. "This month's challenge."

Tripplehorn fished out a pack of playing cards from his pocket, but Harry stopped him.

"No low-card winner this time." He looked at Matt. "Taskmaster rules state that the new Taskmaster member is automatically assigned the challenge."

Stein and Chalmers grinned at each other. An invisible noose tightened around Matt's throat and he shrank into the damp-smelling La-Z-Boy.

"Harry, you're right. I forgot the rules." Tripplehorn did nothing to hide his smirk. "Matt, you're this month's automatic low-card winner."

"Don't let these goofballs scare you, Matt," Harry said. "There's nothing to worry about. As fellow Taskmasters, we'll make sure that everything goes smoothly."

"What do I do?" Matt's fear began bubbling to the surface.

"Didn't I tell you Matt is a born Taskmaster?" Harry said.

"You guys give speeches, right?" Matt asked. "Like Toastmasters do, right?"

He knew his assumption was wrong. This was no conventional organization. They were something else and their burst of raucous laughter confirmed the fact.

"I think you need another beer," Chalmers said, and tossed another bottle at Matt.

"No," Harry said. "We do things a little differently. Stein, why don't you tell Matt here what you did for the Taskmasters last month."

"Surely." Stein wiggled in his seat, making himself comfy. "I killed a no-good pimp. Put a bullet," Stein put a finger to his own forehead and made a popping sound, "right between his eyes."

Stein handed around half a dozen Polaroids of a stick-thin Latino man lying dead in a gutter with a small hole in his face. He went on to describe how he'd stalked the pimp, some guy named Hernandez, and finally lured him to his death with the promise of a big score. The Taskmasters laughed and joked with each other as Stein walked them through the story. Matt didn't laugh. He was too busy trying to hold it together. His worst fears struck him with freight-train intensity. He'd guessed the Taskmasters weren't on the up and up when they'd picked him up in the SUV. Philanthropic tendencies were the last thing he felt from them now. He remembered Harry's words in the alley. When he'd said that he could help Matt turn his life around, Matt had thought he would help him straighten up his act, not teach him how to hone his violent tendencies.

Chalmers fished out a letter-sized manila envelope from inside his jacket and tossed it over to Matt. Matt opened it, failing to hide his trembling hands. The Taskmasters glanced at each other, exchanging naughty schoolboy smiles. Matt scanned the details on the plain typed sheet and the handful of photographs.

"That's Terrance Robinson," Chalmers said, confirming the details Matt held in his hands. "He's a hit-and-run driver. Killed a little girl six months ago."

Matt examined a surveillance picture of Robinson crossing 1st with Pike Place Market behind him. He was twenty or thirty pounds overweight. According to the CliffsNotes, he was the same age as Matt, but his extra bulk aged him a good ten years.

"Why haven't the police arrested him?" He hated how his fear brought the formal out in him.

Stein snorted. "A friend is giving him a bogus alibi."

"So what do you want me to do? Get him to confess?"

Harry laughed at Matt's suggestion. "We don't give anyone a shot at redemption."

"We don't solve problems," Chalmers said. "We eradicate them."

"You're going to kill this guy," Tripplehorn explained.

It wasn't a shock. When this went south, he knew it was going all the way to China, but it still left him cold. He was glad the poor lighting hid his expression.

"Don't worry about the cops. We've got them covered," Harry said.

Stein handed Matt a small semiautomatic. "It's untraceable. Just use it and lose it."

Harry went into fine detail about how Matt should stalk and kill his prey. Matt nodded, taking in the words, but he was too numb to comprehend the ABCs of killing a complete stranger. When Harry finished his speech, the Taskmasters drank and joked amongst themselves for a while. Matt drank but didn't join in the hilarity. He waited for them to have their fun and take him home.

They dropped Matt off first. Harry followed him to his apartment block's entrance, under the watchful gaze of the other Taskmasters. He stuck out a hand for Matt to shake.

"Now, you're cool with this, right?" Harry asked.

"Yeah, of course."

"You went a little quiet on us."

"Well, you know."

"Yeah," Harry said, nodding. "It's a big step up from bar brawls every other night, but this will be good for you. This will put some meaning in your life. Look, don't worry, son. It'll go great. You'll see."

Matt attempted a confirming laugh. "Yeah."

"Remember, this guy isn't innocent. He's guilty as hell. You're just doing what the law can't. You just have to keep telling yourself that."

"That helps. Thanks."

"So the Taskmasters can trust you? There's no going back after tonight."

"You can trust me."

"Good man."

Matt sat at his kitchen table with a mug of coffee in his hands, watching the dawn creep up on the city. Daylight spilled over the skyline, casting fingers of light between the gaps between the buildings. Sleep hadn't come easy, not while a loaded gun and a picture of the person he was meant to kill sat out on the kitchen table. This was way beyond bar brawls. He had to kill a man. If he failed to follow through, his imagination didn't have to wander too far to know what the Taskmasters would do to him.

He'd made such a hash of his life. The really embarrassing thing about it was he didn't know how he'd achieved the feat. There were no excuses for his predicament. He wasn't a total idiot. He was reasonably smart. His parents had been good people who'd only wanted the best for him. So how come he couldn't hold down a job or go for a drink without bruising his knuckles on someone's face? *Questions without answers,* he thought—or not ones he could answer, at least. He picked up the gun and examined it.

Time to answer some of those questions.

Terrance Robinson left his bank job twenty minutes after 5, having had a pretty easy day of trying to arrange loans at a branch of Bank of America. Matt knew this because he'd spent the day in Westlake Plaza watching Robinson through the glass-fronted building. He'd even gone into the bank to ask about opening an account, just so that he could get a close-up look at the man he was supposed to kill. Matt didn't get the impression that Robinson's child-killing escapade weighed heavily upon him. He was easygoing around his colleagues and the people at the sandwich place where he went for lunch, and he negotiated rush hour traffic with infinite patience.

Robinson pulled up in front of his home on Queen Anne Hill, a respectable slice of suburbia where nasty crimes could be hidden from the world. He parked on the street to let his two sons, around seven and nine, continue playing a little one-on-one in the driveway. Pulling his tie off, he jumped into the fray, snatching the ball away to attempt over-ambitious layups, which his offspring managed with equal accomplishment.

Matt slid past the Robinson home and parked a couple of blocks away. His aged Ford Escort stuck out in the neighborhood, but he wouldn't be staying long.

He wandered back up the street for a closer look. Excited giggles and shrieks carried on the air. Robinson exhibited no signs of remorse about his deadly action and the lives he'd wrecked. A man like that deserved to die, didn't he?

"Hate is the key," Chalmers had said during their meeting. He tapped Robinson's file. "To kill him you have to hate him. Read what this man has done and hate it. Stare at his picture and hate him. Do that and this will be easy."

Matt watched the man at play with his children. Did he hate Robinson? He'd let that girl die instead of doing the right thing. He despised Robinson for that, but did he hate him in the way Chalmers and the Taskmasters wanted him to hate him?

Matt found himself staring at the kids and not their father. Killing Robinson meant destroying those boys' lives too. Devastating another family didn't make up for what had already happened. Matt couldn't kill Robinson. He returned to his car and drove to the one place that would end this game.

Matt stopped his car in front of the Seattle Police Department's West Precinct and stared at the industrial-looking building. In there was salvation. Harry told him he could make him a better man and he had. He was going to do the right thing. He didn't know what he was going to say, but he was planning to spill it all—the Taskmasters, their clubhouse, the unregistered gun, Terrance Robinson, the lot. He guessed he'd be dropping himself in the crapper along with everyone else, just by association with these madmen, but he couldn't help that. The Taskmasters had to be stopped and he had to take some responsibility for once in his life. He left the car parked on the street and went in.

The clean and modern but drab reception area was awash with people. Victims wandered around waiting to be helped, while those in custody needed a different kind of assistance. Cops floated between both sides of the law, in front of and behind the bulletproof barriers. Matt stopped a passing policewoman reading a report.

"Hi, I wonder if you could help me?" Matt said. "I need to talk to a police officer about a crime."

"You'll have to check in first," she replied, and pointed at the occupied people behind bulletproof shields. The policewoman went to leave, but Matt sidestepped her to counter her escape. Her features tightened.

"I'm not here to report a stolen VCR or anything. This is important," he said, scanning the room for eavesdroppers.

The policewoman read his face to determine whether he was genuine or a whack job. She made her decision after a long moment. "Wait here."

She retreated into the depths of the building after punching a code into a door marked *Authorized Personnel Only*. A couple of minutes later, the policewoman opened the security door with a uniformed sergeant in tow and pointed at Matt. The sergeant approached him.

"Officer Hansen says you want to speak to someone?"

Matt didn't answer.

"Sir?"

Matt still didn't answer.

"I don't have all day." An edge of irritation crept into the cop's voice.

Matt wasn't answering because he recognized two familiar faces in the crowd—Harry and Tripplehorn—and both of them were wearing police uniforms. His urge to do the right thing for once turned to lead in his throat and he struggled to swallow it down.

"I've made a mistake," Matt said, backing away.

The sergeant placed his hands on his hips. "What?"

"I'm sorry."

"Is this a joke?"

Seeing the Taskmasters there, it did seem like a joke—a bad one. Matt continued to back away, tuning out the angry cop. The Taskmasters, engrossed in their conversation, hadn't spotted him and he wanted it to stay that way.

Matt's back struck the double doors and he thrust them open and bolted. He left his car. He'd come back for it later. He didn't want them knowing what he drove. He tore down Virginia until he hit 8th. He glanced back and saw the sergeant was surveying his escape from the doorway, but the Taskmasters were nowhere to be seen. Matt kept on running.

The apartment building manager was gone for the night. Tuesday was singles' night at the VA social. Matt hoped the old coot got lucky tonight, and even if he didn't, it wouldn't take long for Matt to skip out. He crammed all his belongings into an army surplus duffel and a box for an RCA TV. It was depressing to see that his worldly possessions accounted for so little, but he'd change that. The Taskmasters had given him a new perspective on life. He hooked the duffel over his neck and carried the box down to his Escort.

With no lot at the apartment building, he'd been forced to find street parking. He'd left his car four blocks from his place. He half-walked, half-jogged to his parking spot.

Reaching the spot, he slowed to a crawl and cursed. Another car rested in the space that had been filled by his car only hours earlier. He could be on the wrong street, but he knew better. His car was gone. He couldn't believe someone had stolen the heap of junk on the one night he needed it.

Well, there was no way Matt was going to report the theft, and it wasn't going to stop him from leaving town. The loss of the car meant he would be traveling even lighter. He carried the box of possessions over to a nearby dumpster. He'd hefted it to head height when someone kidney-punched him. Matt crumpled and the box crashed down on his head.

"Leaving town, son?" Harry brushed the box aside and hoisted Matt to his feet. "I thought you had a job to do."

Resignation washed over Matt. There was no point lying or being scared. They'd tagged him at the police department. They'd probably been watching him all day.

"Where's my car?"

"On the way to impound. Would you believe it was parked illegally in front of a fire hydrant? But I wouldn't worry about that. You have other things to worry about."

Harry signaled and the familiar SUV pulled a U-turn in the street and stopped in front of them. Stein was behind the wheel; Chalmers and Tripplehorn weren't around. Harry jammed Matt into the rear of the vehicle and Stein reversed back into traffic. Stein kept to downtown, driving for a bit with no particular destination in mind.

"You betrayed us, Matt," Harry said eventually.

Stein shook his head and said nothing.

"You wanted me to kill a man."

"He killed a child."

"But I can't kill him. That would make me no different."

Harry snorted. "If you don't kill him, you're no different than him. He's a coward and so are you."

This logic made Matt's head swim. He wasn't an executioner and the Taskmasters had no right thinking they could be either.

"Hang a left here," Harry instructed.

Stein turned down an alley and stopped the SUV in front of a tow-away zone. Harry flipped Matt over and zip-tied his hands together. Both men dragged him from the vehicle and shoved him through a doorway. Matt didn't know where he was. Panic blinded him.

The cops dragged him up flight after flight of stairs. Matt knew he should be pleading for his life, but he didn't have the words. What argument was there worth making for saving his life?

Stein kicked open a door and the three of them ended up on a rooftop amongst vents and air-conditioning units. The sun had long escaped over the horizon. The streets below were alive with activity—everyone looking forward, but not up.

Harry shoved Matt down onto his knees and put a revolver against his forehead. Matt closed his eyes and waited for the trigger to be pulled.

"Open your eyes," Harry growled.

Before Matt had a chance to respond, Stein kicked him in the back, sending him sprawling onto his face. With his hands tied behind him, he couldn't lift himself up. Harry lifted him back to his knees, then bent forward and put his face in Matt's.

"Play time is over, son. You've got to make your mind up. Are you going to kill this guy? Because if you aren't," Harry cocked the revolver, "you know we can't have you knowing what you know." Harry straightened and pointed the gun at Matt's forehead again. "What's it to be, son?"

Matt stared at the muzzle. Kill or be killed. What a choice. He would have liked to tell Harry to go to hell, but the man was probably right about him. He was a coward.

"I'll kill him," Matt said.

"Are you sure about that? I don't want you repeating this disappearing act tomorrow night."

"Don't worry, you'll get your head for your trophy room," Matt snarled.

Harry smiled and lowered the gun. "Good." He nodded to Stein, who cut Matt's wrists free.

"I think you can find your own way back," Stein said.

The Taskmasters headed for the stairs.

Reaching the doorway, Harry said, "And I wouldn't think about running. Your picture is in the hand of every cop down at the bus station and train station. You could always thumb a ride or even steal one out of town, but know this: We're watching you. You're on a very tight leash from now on. Oh, and Matt . . ."

Matt looked up.

"You've got two nights. If Terrance Robinson isn't wearing a toe tag by then, you will be."

Terrance Robinson smiled and shook hands with the young couple. Their loan application must have been successful judging from their broad smiles. When the couple walked away, Robinson beckoned to Matt. Robinson walked him through the loan application procedure. He was very thorough and Matt nodded at all the right times. Robinson printed out an application, then excused himself while Matt completed the form.

Matt scanned the paperwork, then wrote across the top of the form: *You're a hit-and-run killer.*

Robinson returned to his desk and Matt handed him the application. The color drained from the loan manager's face as the sheet of paper slipped from between his fingers. A response failed to make it past his lips.

"I know you killed that little girl and I've been sent to kill you."

"I . . . I . . . didn't."

Matt held up a hand to silence Robinson's gibbering. "Doesn't matter. It's been decided that you have to die."

Robinson's eyes flitted from person to person in the bank.

"They can't help you." Matt let him see the gun tucked into the front of his pants. "It's closing time in a few minutes. Just excuse yourself early. You're having a business meeting with me. Make a fuss and you'll still have to explain the girl you killed. It's a no-win for you. Are we cool?"

Robinson nodded.

"Good. Let's go."

Matt followed Robinson to the tellers. He told them he was leaving, then Matt guided him out the doors and onto the street. This was the tricky part. Robinson kept his car parked in a garage two blocks away. It wasn't an inconsiderable distance in itself, but it was when there were hundreds of people filling the street and you had a frightened hostage in tow. But holding the barrel of the gun where Robinson could feel it kept him docile.

Matt made Robinson drive. When he pulled onto the street, Matt scanned for the Taskmasters. He didn't spot them but he sensed them shadowing his every move. He couldn't imagine them not being there at the kill. They'd still be worrying about him. Oh yeah, they would be close.

"Don't shoot me," Robinson squeezed out between sobs.

"You brought this on yourself. You shouldn't have killed that girl."

"I didn't."

"The least you could do is man up here."

Robinson shook his head. "They sent you, didn't they?"

Matt went cold. Robinson knew the Taskmasters. That couldn't be right. "Who's *they?*"

"Jesus, I told them I wouldn't say anything. I even paid them. Ten grand. All the money I have. I should've known they'd send someone to get me. Lying bastards."

Robinson's ramble came out too fast for Matt to take in. "Whoa. Slow down. What are you talking about?"

"The cops. I saw them kill that guy. Shot him in the face. I'd never seen anyone die before. It was horrible. I can't get it out of my head. It's so stupid. I shouldn't have been there. Wouldn't have been there if I hadn't needed to take a short cut through the alley to Spring Street. I didn't want to pay for parking and I have a space I use sometimes. Christ, I tried to save a buck and it's cost me everything."

The revelations slammed into Matt one after another. But instead of leaving him punch drunk, they gave him clarity. Pieces fell into place of a much larger picture.

Robinson had broken down into nonsensical sobs. If he didn't get his shit together, he was going to crash the car.

"Hey, snap out of it. I need you straight. This guy you saw killed, what'd he look like?"

"I don't know. Skinny. Hispanic. All I saw was the hole in his forehead and four pissed-off cops." Robinson stared at Matt. He'd picked up on Matt's change of heart.

Some things had changed. Some things hadn't.

"Keep driving."

"Do I get a last request?" Robinson asked.

"What?"

"All condemned men are granted a last request."

"What is it?"

With a shaking hand, Robinson reached inside his jacket. Matt's grip tightened on his gun and he fixed his aim on Robinson's stomach just in case the bank worker carried a weapon. Instead, Robinson brought out a phone.

"Can I call my family?" Tears ran down his face. "Just this last time?"

Matt was softhearted but not soft in the head. He snatched the phone away. "No way. Do I look retarded? I'm not giving you the green light to call 911."

Robinson broke down. Matt examined the phone. He wasn't too up on these things but it looked to be the latest in cell phone technology.

"Does this thing have video capability on it?"

Robinson palmed away his tears. "Yes."

Matt punched in a number and waited for an answer. "It's me. I'm going through with it. I'll be at the clubhouse as arranged." He hung up.

Robinson looked at him with questioning fear. "There'll be others?"

"Don't look so worried. This'll all be over soon."

Matt directed Robinson to the derelict restaurant on Yesler that served as the Taskmasters' clubhouse. He pulled Robinson out of the car and shoved him toward the rear of the building, ignoring the slowing sedan across the street.

The backdoor wasn't as fortified as the front. Matt kicked it in without too much trouble. The dead bolt remained intact, but the rotted frame gave way. He pushed Robinson inside the building and into a large dining area. He wished he had the keys to the main doors; he only had one means of escape. He stopped Robinson by a table with a missing leg.

"Show me how to record a message."

Robinson helped Matt record two video messages of him, one for his family and the other about the hit he witnessed.

"I'll send these when it's all over."

"Thank you."

Up until this point, there'd been a pleading element to Robinson. Everything from his posture to his expression had revealed a thin hope that Matt wouldn't go through with the execution—but not anymore. He knew these were his last moments on earth.

"Facedown, please." Matt pointed to a nook which must have served as some sort of station for the waitstaff. Robinson did as he was told and lay in the dirt and rubble without complaint. "I'm sorry to put you through this, but it should be all over soon."

Matt waited for a response, but Robinson said nothing.

Matt took a breath, aimed, and fired the gun twice.

With the reports still bouncing off the walls, the Taskmasters, in uniform, poured in through the rear entrance with guns drawn and spread out until they each had Matt in their sights.

"Drop the gun!" Harry shouted.

Matt dropped the gun and raised his hands. "I figured this would come next. There's no Taskmasters. No vigilante hit squad. Just a group of dirty cops who got seen killing a pimp. Who was Hernandez?"

"A scumbag who didn't want to pay a toll for working our streets," Stein answered.

"You should have taken him up to the roof to do your business," Matt said. "Fewer witnesses up there."

Stein ground his jaw in quiet fury. Chalmers and Tripple-horn didn't like having their noses rubbed in their own mess. Harry was the only one unaffected by Matt's jibes.

"So I'm the patsy you need to take the fall for Robinson. What happens now? You shoot me, pin it all on me, and you guys walk off into the sunset?"

"I'm afraid so, son," Harry said. "You're just a punk kid, a loser who's going to pay for our mistakes. I hate to do it to you, but it's for the greater good."

"You left it a little too late to get smart," Tripplehorn added.

"Maybe not." Matt nodded at the cell phone. "That's one of those phones with the video camera built in. It's recording right now."

Chalmers cursed and shot the phone off the table.

"There's still the problem of the murder you just commit-ted," Harry said. "You're still a killer."

"No, I'm an innocent man with a witness."

Robinson rose awkwardly to his feet, looking dazed and confused. He stared at the two bullet holes in the ground to the right of his head.

"We'll just have to do it the old-fashioned way," Stein snarled, and made for Matt's gun on the ground.

"Hold it right there!" a voice barked.

The Taskmasters froze as the men wearing King County Sheriffs' windbreakers from the courthouse just a street away stormed the room through the upper level and kitchen area. The Taskmasters quickly surrendered and the sheriffs relieved them of their weapons. The Taskmasters cursed Matt—except for Harry, who just smiled.

Matt walked up to Harry. "You kept a tail on me to keep me from leaving, but you couldn't stop me from using the phone. I've been talking to some friends."

"I underestimated you," Harry said, as a deputy cuffed him.

Matt grinned. He'd underestimated himself. "You said you'd make me a better man."

"Enjoy this moment." Harry leaned forward and whispered in Matt's ear: "Smile while you can. Do you honestly think we're the only Taskmasters inside the SPD?" He winked at Matt as the deputy hauled him away. "You've still got a lot of work ahead of you, son."

WHAT PRICE RETRIBUTION?

by Patricia Harrington

Capitol Hill

G us Maloney struggled awake, fighting the pain that shot electrical currents through his head. "Who the hell's out there?" His words rasped, hurting his raw throat. The sound of his own voice thudded in his ears. His mouth tasted foul, like he'd been guzzling Lake Union's polluted waters.

How long have I been out?

He pulled off his tangled blankets, belched, and tasted bile. He rubbed his gut.

When was the last time I ate?

The tin door to his shack rattled again.

I'll kill Sweet Sue for making that racket!

"Mister Mayor, ya gotta get up."

Gus swung his feet to the dirt floor and sat on his cot, elbows on thighs, and cradled his head in his hands. Then he ran a hand over the stubble of whiskers on his face. Slowly, it sunk through the fog in his brain. The voice yelling wasn't Sweet Sue's.

Gus staggered to the door and moved the heavy metal trunk he'd placed there. It was his insurance that no one could push the door open without him knowing. Dead drunk or not, his old cop instincts kicked in when trouble was about to kick *him* in his face.

When he pulled the makeshift door open, Muffler Man stepped back on his good leg. His face puckered up and his faded blue eyes stared over Gus's right shoulder at nothing. He had his signature plaid wool scarf around his neck.

At the sight of Gus's murderous scowl, Muffler Man hitched back a step. "We got bad news," he said. He half turned around and nodded at the small woman standing behind him. "Me and Bets here, we been hollerin' a long time."

Gus looked around Muffler Man at Bets, who seemed scared as a kid about to be whipped. She didn't return his look but bent her head and hunkered down inside the worn pea coat dwarfing her skinny body.

Gus had slept in his clothes and couldn't remember the last time he'd changed them. His stink hung close. He felt like hell and looked worse. "Where's Sweet Sue? Why the hell are you bothering me?"

Even with his alcohol-hazed brain, Gus knew something had gone very wrong in the camp. Like it or not, he'd been elected the "go to" man by its inhabitants. That's because he was an ex-cop. Once the word had gotten out in the homeless camp set up below St. Mark's Cathedral, Sweet Sue had started calling him "Mr. Mayor." The label stuck. So did the responsibilities. He'd questioned himself. *Why stay?* But then he'd shrug. *Why not!*

Maybe it was Sweet Sue, the thin old relic who'd attached himself to Gus. The man had been drifting since he was a boy. He'd been called a tramp and a vagrant then, and not the niced-up label of *homeless.* Sweet Sue liked to say that he was Mr. Mayor's "aide-de-homeless-camp." Then he'd laugh his high-pitched cackle.

Just about everybody in the camp went by a street name. Sweet Sue's came about because he liked to suck on hard candy and told over and over about hearing Johnny Cash sing "A Boy Named Sue" in San Quentin.

Mudflat Manor was a loose collection of pitched tents, tarps, and a few lean-tos set on the wooded hillside below the Episcopal cathedral. When the rains came, the place was a muddy, slippery slope. But Gus kept the camp clean, so to speak, so that the Seattle PD and the do-gooders, including the big church's minister, left them alone. Gus didn't allow dope dealers or druggies—he could be persuasive. And he made damn sure there weren't any syringes or used condoms littering 10th Street in front of the cathedral. That way, the police and uptight citizens in the Capitol Hill neighborhood could pretend the homeless squatters didn't exist. If they did, then they'd have to do something about them.

Gus let alkies like himself stay—if they didn't make trouble. A core group of drifters and homeless came and went with the seasons. Before he'd gotten the news about his daughter and went on his bender, some had already left and headed south. It was closing in on November. The rains had started and the temperature dropped the last few nights.

Muffler Man's fingers twitched at his pants legs. He looked away from Gus and mumbled, "I gotta say this: Sweet Sue's hurt bad."

Gus grabbed Muffler Man's arm. "What happened? Where is he?"

Muffler Man stammered. "Huh-huh-Harborview. A dope dealer beat him up. He was a b-b-big black man. Wore his hair in them funny kind of braids. Sweet Sue tried to stop him peddling his dope. Had all kinds on him—kinda like a one-stop drugstore."

"Why the hell didn't you get me?"

Muffler Man stumbled back into Bets. "We tried. Honest. But you was worse'n dead—out cold."

"Did the cops come? How'd Sue get to the hospital?"

Bets wrung her hands behind Muffler Man, her face crumpling like a child's about to cry.

Muffler Man shook his head. "He dragged off old Sue, said he'd teach him a lesson. Billy found him in the alley up by the brick apartments. He had kicked in Sue's face. We called 911 from a pay phone and said we'd seen this body and where and hung up, quick."

Bets raised her hand to catch Gus's attention. "Mr. Mayor, I went to the emergency room at the hospital and asked if someone found on Capitol Hill had been brought in. They said yes, he was being operated on. I got scared and didn't stay. I was afraid they'd ask questions or call the cops on me."

Gus groaned and rubbed his shaved head. "When did this happen?"

"Last night. Late-like." Muffler Man wrung his hands together.

Gus glanced at his watch, forcing his eyes to focus. It was almost noon. He shivered. It was getting colder.

He nodded at Bets. "You did good." She dimpled and smiled. Then Gus added, "Can you give me any other description of the man?"

"He had a long kind of a blouse on." Bets peered down at her clothes and then shyly back to Gus. "It had a picture of that singer on it . . ." She paused, her face distressed. Then she started humming and her face brightened. "Bob Marley. That's who it was. No, not the bad man who hurt Sweet Sue. I mean the face on the shirt. Bob Marley." Then Bets backed up, as if she'd done something wrong.

Gus smiled to reassure her. His teeth hurt; everything on him ached. "Way to go, Bets. Now, heat me up some water. I need to clean up and take care of business."

* * *

Gus made it to the hospital an hour later, his face raw from shaving because he used an old blade. He'd put on decent clothes, a pair of clean Levi's and a T-shirt under a Mariners jacket. He kept them stashed in a plastic garment bag for emergencies. He didn't want a nurse calling security when she saw him, hollering to get the bum out of the hospital. Gus knew he could pass, at first glance, as a middle-aged, common Joe; someone with a house, a wife, and a kid he was putting through college. He'd had them once—he could play the part. The hospital security wouldn't shuffle him off.

Gus also had a stash of cash in a bus station locker and a drop mailbox in his name at a place on Capitol Hill. That's where he received his disability check. It was a kiss-off from the San Jacinto Police Department: leave the force, get out of the state, and don't come back. Gus had been working a child molester case where a six-year-old kid died after being repeatedly raped. Following a four-month trial, the monster got off on a technicality. Gus couldn't let him do it to another kid. The boy's bruised body, his face like an angel's in one of the cathedral windows, haunted him. He saw him in his sleep and would wake up crying. Hitting the bottle didn't make the images go away. So Gus tracked the guy down, tailing him day and night and stoking himself on good old Jose Cuervo. When the guy took off on Highway 101 to get out of town, Gus followed him. On a lonely stretch, Gus did some fancy tailgating that he had learned in police academy training, fished the asshole in his Toyota off the road and over an embankment. The car rolled and then caught fire when it hit bottom. The perp toasted inside. Better than going to hell, the way Gus figured it.

Of course, the San Jacinto PD had their suspicions but didn't work the case hard. Gus's captain didn't do much talking, but some suggesting. So Gus left the department after eighteen years, with a couple of commendations, a hearty handshake, and the warning, "Don't come back." Same held true for his marriage. "You've changed and I can't live with you anymore," his wife had said. She kept the kids and booted him out of the house.

He didn't look back.

Gus had called from a pay phone to find out what room Sweet Sue was in—found he was in a ward, the kind with beds in rooms that ringed a nurses' station. Gus fingered the hard peppermint candies in his pocket, Sweet Sue's favorites. The ends of the cellophane wrappers crackled when he touched them.

The nurses and hospital aides at the station were deep in conversation when Gus walked by and entered Sweet Sue's room. His roommate was sleeping, and so was Sweet Sue. The tread mark from a sneaker was outlined in ugly red and purple bruising on the old man's left cheek. A bandage covered part of his skull and one eye. His arm was in a cast, and he had more bandages around his chest. A fury that Gus hadn't felt in a long time boiled up in him, so thick and red that he couldn't see for a moment. Then it subsided, chilling, turning into a sharp edge of calculating revenge that cut through the fuzz in Gus's brain.

He stared at Sweet Sue. The man didn't have a mean bone in his body and was as simple as they come. His shallow breathing hardly moved the covers on him. Gus thought he'd slammed the door on caring for anyone. But now Gus groaned and bent over the bed. He didn't want to hurt, to feel. He couldn't open up the logjam inside that kept everything behind it sealed out of sight and touch. Neither his daughter Jenny nor this old, broken-down hobo deserved what happened to them.

Gus leaned over and put his mouth close to Sweet Sue's good ear. "I'm here, buddy. Gawd. I'm sorry." He lightly clasped Sue's scrawny good shoulder. "I'll get the bastards. I promise." Then he put the hard candy on the nightstand and left.

Gus took a bus and transferred and then got off on the east side of Lake Union. He had a favorite spot, a bench, where he could watch the boats and the seagulls. It was too cold, and there were no boats out sailing. The waves were an ugly gray, looking as mean as Gus felt. The seagulls did their thing, squealing and wheeling about, and he took the lid off his triple-mocha shot that he'd bought at Starbucks. He shivered in his thin shirt and windbreaker—but welcomed the cold. It crystallized his thinking. He didn't have a lot of time. It was strange that a Rasta had kicked in Sweet Sue's face—not any Rastafarians around, except the wannabes he'd seen from time to time. And the guy sure as hell wouldn't be hanging around in the cold and rain of Seattle if he didn't have to. He'd be on the first plane out of SeaTac, headed for Jamaica or wherever he came from, as soon as he'd peddled his weed and made some bucks.

The cold seemed to freeze the fuzz in Gus's head, but made clear channels, letting ideas flow. It was like the synapses in his brain were snapping together, ones he hadn't used in a long while.

He'd learned the hard way in investigations: look first for the obvious. Why was this guy hanging around a homeless camp, peddling dope to someone who probably only had chump change? He'd have easier chances making a sale with the potheads who hung out on Capitol Hill. A black man with dreadlocks, wearing a T-shirt with Bob Marley's picture on it, would be accepted, fit in.

Gus reached into the bag of cookies he'd bought with the coffee. He broke off a piece from one and threw it by a dirty gray seagull, which inspected and then rejected it. Gus reflected again on the Rasta and thought about the stores and cafés that lined Capitol Hill's main drag. They catered to a cultural mix of apartment/condo dwellers, community college kids, fringies, and refugees. Gus blew out his breath and it turned white in the cold air. Damn. He should have remembered before. A Caribbean jerk chicken place had opened up recently on Broadway. What if the creep was related or connected? It would make sense. Could be a reason for him setting up shop on the hill, making it his territory. Not much to go on—it was a stretch. But better than nothing. Gus drank the last of his cold coffee and then threw the remaining cookies on the grass. It'd be sunset soon. The leaden sky promised a dark night.

He shivered and stood up. What he needed was a plan . . . and a warmer jacket.

On the way to his locker at the bus station, Gus stopped at a liquor store and bought a couple bottles of Jose Cuervo. Then he continued on to the station to collect his winter jacket and stow away the one he had on. He took out his emergency envelope of cash and a gym bag that carried his essentials for late-night work. Then he stopped in the washroom. Now he had the beginning of a plan. But first he had to find this creep.

On the bus ride up Pill Hill, he kept his mind on Sweet Sue, picturing his pale, stomped-on face. He wanted to keep his focus. But then at his stop, a young woman stepped in front of him as the bus door opened. She flashed an apologetic smile, and Gus's heart froze for a moment. She looked so much like Jenny—at least his memory of her. How long had it been since he'd seen his daughter? Six years? No, seven. She was fourteen then. Now a mother . . . No, not a mother. That's what the letter from his ex-wife was about. The one that sent him on a long-term bender. The baby had been stillborn.

Gus,

    I'm only writing because Jenny wanted you to know. She was going to name the baby after you. Why, I'll never know. I don't even know if this letter will reach you. You're probably dead too. But I did what our daughter asked me to do and it's done.

His ex hadn't even bothered to sign her name.

Gus didn't blame her.

Old emotions, the guilt and anger, and a sorrow he couldn't handle, collided inside him. They churned in his stomach and his hands trembled. He clutched the sack with the two bottles of tequila in it like they were his only lifelines. He needed a drink bad. He needed a whole damn bottle worse.

Gus forced himself to walk in the direction where he thought the Caribbean restaurant was located—he remembered it as a kind of hole-in-the-wall place. Along the way, he wandered around the area sizing up the traffic and turning down drug offers. Doorways and alleys drew dealers and buyers like old lovers who could sense a soft touch and a score a block away.

After a couple of hours, Gus stopped and asked a couple of punks with dyed hair if they knew of it. They shrugged, pointed down the street, and kept walking, their laughter trailing behind them.

Once Gus found the place, he went in, sat at the counter, and put the gym bag by his stool. There was a couple seated at a booth, but otherwise the place was empty of customers. A large woman who probably topped two hundred pounds took his order for jerk chicken and coffee and then waddled into the kitchen. Gus struck up a conversation when the woman came back to wipe down the counter. He found out that she was the Caribbean Breeze owner and came from Kingston, Jamaica. But she didn't hum the song. Her eyes said she'd seen and heard it all, and Gus didn't try to play her for a fool. She looked at the bulky brown paper sack that he'd laid on the counter; the tops of the bottles showed. She shrugged and walked away.

Gus ate slowly when his food came, small bites because his stomach couldn't handle much. He bided his time, waiting until he was sure that the owner was watching him. Then he took out his wallet, bulging with bills, and opened it so she could see the twenties and fifties. She brought over his check and he studied it. "Seems fair. That was a nice meal," he said. He glanced down, pulled out a couple of twenties, and murmured, "Any ganja around here?" He riffled through the money in his wallet again, but didn't look up.

The owner didn't answer. She took Gus's two twenties and his bill to the cash register. She turned and glanced at the couple in the booth. When she brought back Gus's change, he left the extra money on the counter. "You keep it."

She scooped up the money. Then in a low voice she said, "Go behind, in the alley. Mon there, he help you."

Night had fallen, streetlights had come on and shadows crept into the alley. Walking down it, looking for the dealer, made Gus feel as if he had a big S, for *stupid*, on his back. There was a naked lightbulb over the backdoor of the restaurant and a big metal dumpster to its right. Gus looked up and down the deserted alley. A few doorways further along had lights over them. When Gus drew closer to the restaurant's backdoor, a shadow shifted and a figure stepped out from it.

Bingo! It was the Rasta. Bets had given a good description. Except she left out the evil grin, the stringy body, and his lean, muscled arms. His dreadlocks hung to his shoulders. He'd be a standout in a line-up.

"You wan' somet'ing, mon?"

"Could be."

Gus knew better than to be too eager.

The dealer nodded at the gym bag in Gus's hand. "Wah you got."

"The woman inside, the restaurant owner, says you have something I need. And I have something you want." Gus picked up his bag slowly. He gestured as if opening it. "Okay?" he asked. The Rasta nodded.

Gus slowly unzipped the bag. He'd tucked the sack with the tequila in it when he left the restaurant. Now he pushed the sack to one side. Under it was a clean shirt, his jeans, and underwear. They covered a loaded Glock, duct tape, and a pair of handcuffs. On top of the clothes, though, was an envelope with his stash of cash. Some of the bills fanned out from it. They were easy to see. Impressive too.

Gus pointed at the bag. "I'd like to do some international trading. Your dope, my money."

Even in the alley's poor lighting, Gus could see greed overcoming caution on the Rasta's face.

Then Gus prodded: "Is there some place where we can talk business?" He reached down slowly and pulled out one of the bottles of tequila. "This makes negotiations more fun."

They ended up in a back room in the restaurant at a small table. The woman closed early and left some big pots soaking in the kitchen. She didn't look at the men or say goodbye. Gus figured she wanted no part of what was going on. He was glad. It made things easier for him.

He set the bottles of tequila on the table, one for the Rasta and one for himself. Jose Cuervo grinned back at each of them.

They haggled over price as they took straight shots from their bottles. The Rasta brought out his dope; Gus whistled when he checked it out. The creep was doing some serious business. The Rasta had everything from weed to meth and even some OxyContin. Gus didn't pay close attention to the Rasta, who was pretty much out of it. The whites of his eyes were a spiderweb of red veins fringing his dark, dilated pupils. Gus poked at the dope, stalling, thinking ahead, while the man talked about the Seattle women and how they couldn't get enough of him. He made an obscene gesture and pointed to the words *No Woman, No Cry* under the headshot of Bob Marley on his T-shirt.

With a drunken leer, the Rasta said, "Me mek woman happy."

Gus let the silence build. Then he asked, "You score big with your weed around here? I hear some of the guys out in the homeless camp by the big church carry cash on them. Heard they made some big scores and don't like banks."

The Rasta sneered and took a deep drag on his tequila. "No way, mon. Me been there." He shrugged. "Old mon try to stop me. T'ink he boss? Me fix him." The Rasta punched the air and twisted his two hands, like wringing a chicken's neck. He grinned with drunken satisfaction.

Gus leaned back in his chair and looked away. He didn't want the guy to read the deadly anger in his eyes. Gus had his answer. The time had come.

The tequila had gotten to the Rasta, but not to Gus. Earlier, in the bus station washroom, he'd dumped one of the bottles in the sink and refilled it with water. The Rasta was the only one drinking the real stuff.

Gus was as sober as a judge and about to pronounce sentence.

He took the money from his bag and put it on the table. The Rasta leaned forward to count it—and then Gus pulled out the gun from his bag and pointed it between the Rasta's scared eyes.

"Hand over the weed."

The Rasta tried to focus, pull himself together, but he was too drunk. He fumbled for the package with the weed and put it on the table. Gus dumped it into his bag. Then he picked up the money lying on the table and jammed it beside the weed in the bag.

Gus motioned with the gun. "Stand up, scumbag, and take off your clothes."

The guy looked at Gus, blinking, weaving on his feet.

"You heard me. Strip, take off your shirt and pants."

The Rasta looked around, fear growing in his eyes. Slowly, he removed his shirt and then his pants.

"Underpants too, stud."

The Rasta stood naked as the day he was born, except for his bare feet in large loafers. "Put your hands behind your head and keep them there," Gus commanded. He could see the man was trying to sober up. But he'd had way too much to drink. The dealer couldn't get his brain into gear; he could only let his eyes flick about, trying to find a way to escape.

For a moment, the image of Sweet Sue's battered face and body replayed in Gus's head. He felt like shooting the bastard weaving in front of him. But Gus had a better plan. He motioned the Rasta over to the backdoor and made him stand beside it. Then Gus opened the door, stuck out his head, and checked the alley. It was clear, and it was cold—freezing cold. The Rasta hung back.

Gus made him turn around so that he stood in the doorway, facing the alley. Then Gus cold-cocked the Rasta behind his left ear with the gun's butt. The Rasta crumpled and sagged to the floor. Gus flipped him over and removed the handcuffs and duct tape from his bag. No ex-cop should leave home without them, he thought. He cuffed the dealer's hands behind him. And then Gus stuffed a wad of the money in the dealer's mouth and wrapped duct tape around it and the Rasta's head. The man wouldn't be running his mouth off any time soon.

Gus slipped out the backdoor and opened the dumpster's cover, swinging it back against the building. Then he dragged the Rasta to it and, grunting, heaved the man over the side and into the dumpster. Gus looked over. It was about a quarter full. He figured the city wouldn't be doing a pickup for at least a few days. No matter. He wasn't through with the Rasta yet.

Gus took a deep breath in the cold air. It hurt his lungs—he wasn't used to breathing that deep. Next, he hoisted himself up and into the dumpster, gingerly stepping into the smelly mess. He pushed aside the gunk until he'd made a place for the dealer's body. Gus turned him over so that he lay facedown, his dick on the freezing metal bottom of the dumpster. Then he covered him with the stinky mash of rinds and peelings and other discarded food.

It was a fitting end and a lesson the dope dealer would live with painfully for a long time.

Gus climbed out, closed the lid, and went inside again. He tidied up after himself, cleaning his pants and shoes and socks. He found white vinegar in the restaurant kitchen and wiped down all the surfaces he had touched, then moved outside and wiped down the dumpster too.

He went back inside and checked around one more time before he turned out the lights, flipped the lock, and closed the door.

Gus collected the drug money that hadn't gone into the Rasta's mouth, and he took all the dope and stuck it in his gym bag. The money would make a nice anonymous contribution to the Gospel Men's Mission. The dope he'd unload into the nearest sewer drain. He hoped the salmon would get a good buzz when it reached the Sound.

Gus heard the heavy motor of a truck pulling into the far end of the alley and the squeal of brakes. He ducked around the corner and looked back. It was a city garbage truck, the big kind that compacted the garbage. Gus stayed to watch. He saw the truck's long skid arms slip under the dumpster, lifting and then emptying it into the truck. The dumpster's lid clanged as it was lowered. Then the mechanical sound of the compactor's motor revved as it efficiently ground up the contents.

Gus leaned back against the rough brick side of a building, hidden from view of the garbage crew in the alley. Then he bowed his head, but it wasn't in prayer. He was staring at the realization, as clear as if printed on a poster in front of him. He could've stopped the truck—and the compactor. Maybe shouted or waved his arms before the terrible sound of the grinding wheels.

But he hadn't. Now he'd have to live with that memory too. Gus shrugged.

It was a bad end to a bad creep.

Gus stuffed his free hand in his pocket and started walking. Before he caught the bus for downtown, he fed the dope and pills into a sewer grate and tossed the bag into a garbage can.

Gus got off on First Avenue and walked to Pioneer Square. He found a dank tavern and had some quick shots—he knew from practice exactly how many dulled the sharp edges of memory but still left him able to figure out next steps.

The odds were that the trash collectors would find or see something funny. Maybe the dealer's skinny bones would jam the mechanism. Or the garbage collectors would notice a lot of blood and do some checking. Once something like that was reported, it would be carried on the local news. Probably say, *What's Seattle coming to?* Do-gooders would be up in arms at such a heinous crime. Gus laughed at the image. Peaceniks armed with pitchforks, not rifles.

Gus welcomed the mellow numbness beginning to spread in his body. He wanted it to reach his chest, to surround his heart. Still its beating. Gus shook himself. Now was when he had to be really careful. He needed to think, and he pushed his shot glass away with a shaking hand.

Seattle PD had good cops. They might not care if a dope dealer ended up as beef stew in the city dump. But they'd follow through with their investigation. The headlines and the City Council would demand that.

A good investigator would interview all of the shopkeepers and restaurant folks around the alley. Ask the drifters and bums if they'd seen anything. The cops would sure as hell assume there was some connection between a Rastafarian and a Caribbean restaurant. And the owner could ID him. So could some of the punk kids he'd approached about buying drugs.

If they did a sketch from the café owner's description and ran it over the wire, his picture might turn up. Sure as hell, his name and the fact that he'd been a cop in San Jacinto would come out. And why he'd left the police force.

The word would spread. *Rogue cop.*

Gus threw a couple bills down beside his glass and left the bar. He started walking, not caring where. He had a headache that was the granddaddy of all headaches, knocking the sides of his skull and traveling down to his shoulders. Suddenly, Gus felt too weary to move, his feet, dead weights. He couldn't lift them. He shuffled into a doorway and leaned against the shop window.

Gus thought of Sweet Sue . . . and Jenny, and he wanted to cry. But couldn't do that. The well had dried up a long time ago. He muttered, "Gus Maloney, you've screwed up your life. Big time."

He nodded in agreement with himself. Then, after a long while, he slowly pulled himself together and swiped his eyes with his hand.

There's no going back.

But Gus did change direction.

He headed for the hospital and Sweet Sue. Gus knew what he had to do. After he checked on Sweet Sue, he'd pack up and get out of town, head south, maybe just to Tacoma. Lay low. But be close enough that he could check on Sweet Sue. Soon as the old geezer was well, he'd let him know that he wanted his aide-de-homeless-camp with him again.

PART III

LOVE IS A FOUR-LETTER WORD

TILL DEATH DO US . . .

BY CURT COLBERT

Belltown

I hate domestic cases. As long as I've been a private eye, they've been as unpredictable as counting on a sunny day here in Seattle. Harry Truman upsetting Dewey in last year's election was no big surprise at all compared to domestic cases. They can ruin your day faster than losing a bundle on the wrong nag or saying "I do" to the wrong dame.

So why did I do it? Take the Dorothy Demar/Harold Sikes case, I mean. I've been asking my bottle of Cutty Sark that question ever since it was full and I still don't have a good answer. It *has* been getting a little easier to ask the question, though. Decent Scotch doesn't do a thing to solve the eternal mystery of sin and sordidness, but it does make it slightly easier to swallow.

Dorothy Demar entered my office without knocking while my girl Friday, Miss Jenkins, was out having her usual at the Woolworth's lunch counter. At least Miss Jenkins could afford to go out to lunch. Me, I was dining on yesterday's liverwurst slapped between two hunks of last week's bread. I had some slight money troubles. It was payday and I'd sucked my bank account dry forking over my girl Friday's salary. Worse, I'd blown the last C-note I had in reserve for the down payment on the fancy-schmancy two-way radios that I'd had my sights set on for the better part of a year. Cops had them, why not me? Yeah, well, now I had my two-way radios, but my name was going to be mud at Queen City Electronics without the dough for the balance of the account, which, coincidentally, just happened to be due today. Nothing I hated worse than a welcher—and that was going to be me, I was thinking, when Dorothy Demar sashayed in.

"Jake Rossiter?"

Husky voice for a female. More like a command than a question.

"Who's asking?"

I glanced up from my desk, startled that the owner of the whiskey voice turned out to be such a hot number.

"Dorothy."

The way she peeled off her long white gloves reminded me of a woman slowly taking off her nylon stockings. This dame just dripped with sultry allure. Got me excited—got me nervous—didn't know which emotion to act on.

So, there I sat—and there she stood—tall, slim, busty, early thirties at most, with a blond Veronica Lake hairdo over high cheekbones, perfect skin, and a button nose, her powder-blue, two-piece silk ensemble so snug that I had to catch my breath.

"Dorothy Demar," she said, adding a last name, her eyes a deeper blue than the last swimming pool I dove into.

I noticed she wasn't wearing a wedding ring. I drew on all my years as a professional to compose myself.

"Glad to meet you. Have a seat. What can I do for you?"

"I want to hire you." Curvier than ten miles of bad road, she slid into the green wingback chair across from me.

"I figured you weren't collecting for the Milk Fund." I pushed the liverwurst out of my way and replaced it with my stenographic notepad. "I might be able to squeeze in a new client. Shoot," I told her, uncapping my fountain pen. "What's the scoop?"

"I need you to keep an eye on me."

"From what I've seen so far, that won't be difficult."

She smiled for the first time, her pearly whites glistening between her full red lips.

"Just for the record, though," I continued, "why do you need me to keep an eye on you?"

"I think I'm in danger, Mr. Rossiter," she said, a little quaver in her otherwise strong voice.

"Why's that?"

"Does it matter?" she snapped. "I want to hire you! Isn't that enough?"

I studied her for a moment, a bit put off by her sudden fire. "Not quite."

"I think I'm in danger," she repeated.

"Look, let's try this again," I told her, taking out a Philip Morris and lighting up. "Maybe you're new to this sort of thing, but I'm not really big on mysteries. I like my cases nice and straightforward. And my answers plain."

Dorothy jumped to her feet. "Maybe I've come to the wrong man."

I stayed seated. "Maybe you have," I said, thinking about how fast lust can go wrong.

She reached into the small ivory clutch that she carried, and laid four fat C-notes face up on my desk. Ben Franklin never looked more handsome. "Is that enough to make you the right man?"

"Well, now . . ." I pulled the bills toward me. "I could maybe handle a certain amount of suspense for this kind of dough."

"Thought so." Looking smug, she sat back down and took a gold-filigreed cigarette case out of her clutch. Tamping one of her smokes against it, she said, "Now maybe you'll start doing like you're told."

"Could be." I offered her a light. "But you haven't *told* me anything yet. No, strike that, you've spilled loads just by the way you've been acting. Let's see . . . you're rich; undoubtedly spoiled rotten as a child; used to getting your own way and you tend to throw tantrums when you don't. How am I doing so far?"

"Good as a gypsy." She took a deep drag off her cigarette and gave me a wry look. "I can tell a few things about you too. Let's see . . . you're *not* rich, otherwise you wouldn't have this crummy office in the Regrade; you probably had to do for yourself as a child; you're used to making your own way in this world and you tend to be cynical and sarcastic when things don't go like you think they should. How am I doing so far?"

"Good as a gypsy."

"There's one other thing."

"What's that, pray tell?"

"You seem to be one of those people who act just the way they look, Mr. Rossiter. Smart but tough. Exactly the type of man I need to help me."

This dame was smart herself. And definitely drop-dead gorgeous. Volatile, potentially explosive mix. Whether it was the edgy thrill she gave me, or the fact that her moola would more than cover my two-way car radio debt, I don't know. All I can say for sure is that I could feel my better judgment flying away as fast as a pheasant that you'd missed with both barrels.

"Okay. You're rich, I'm not. That about covers all the bases except one: I still need to know why you feel threatened and want me to watch over you." I pushed the money back toward her. "No answer, I'm afraid I'll have to decline your case, even though I might kick myself later."

"You have integrity. I don't need integrity. But it will have to do, I suppose." She slid the C-notes back at me. "I strongly suspect that my husband is planning to kill me."

"That so? I didn't know you were married."

"We live apart," she said, a definite sense of finality in her tone. "I have my own place; Harold has his."

"Harold, huh?" I wrote his name down. "Tell me about Harold, Mrs. Demar. What makes you think he's got it in for you?"

"It's Mrs. Sikes, actually," she corrected. "Demar is my maiden name."

"Sounds better than Sikes; I don't blame you." I fixed Harold's name in my notes. "So, once again, why would Harold have homicide on his mind?"

"He thinks I'm two-timing him."

"Are you?"

"Yes."

Her candor brought me up short. For want of anything better to say, I replied, "That's refreshing."

"Harold thinks he owns me. He doesn't. That's why I need you."

I leaned back in my chair and blew a smoke ring. "What exactly do you want me to do?"

"Keep an eye on me, like I said."

"That could get expensive."

"I have my own money. I was rich before I married Harold, and I'm still rich."

"Have you tried marriage counseling? It's bound to be cheaper."

She laughed. Only the second time I'd seen her crack a smile. It vanished as soon as she began talking. "You have a sense of humor too. Keep it. Do you want the job? Yes or no?"

"When would you want me to start?"

"Now."

"How close do you want to be followed? I can tail you from a distance or so close we might have to get engaged."

Another smile—very small, very brief. "While the latter method might prove interesting, Mr. Rossiter, just keeping an eye on me from a distance will be more than adequate for the time being."

"In that case," I said, picking up the phone, "I'll have my right-hand man on the job before you leave the office."

She stubbed out her butt in the ashtray. "You won't be watching me personally?"

"I'm saving myself for you." I grinned. "I want to be fresh as a daisy if you ever need the close tail work."

"I see," she told me, the hint of a flirt forming in her eyes. It disappeared the instant I got Heine on the horn.

"Heine. Got a gig for you." I could hear the click and clack of pool balls caroming in the background. As usual, he was downtown, just a few minutes away, at Ben Paris's pool hall. He haunted the joint trying to shark a few simoleons whenever I didn't have him working a case.

"That so?" Heine asked. "Good. Where do ya want me and when?"

"Over here at the office. Now."

"What's up?"

"Dame I need you to keep tabs on. She's with me as we speak. Make it a discreet tail, but don't let her out of your sight. Her life may be in danger. Name's Dorothy Demar. Just honk when you show up. She's got better gams than Betty Grable. You'll like the work."

"Say no more, brother," Heine answered quickly. "I already left." The line went dead.

"Thank you," Dorothy told me as I hung up the receiver.

"For what? The compliment or for taking the job?"

"Both. I'm very grateful."

"Maybe you should save your gratitude until I'm sure I can keep you safe."

"You will. I have no doubt."

"You're pretty certain about me, huh?"

"Everybody says you're the best."

"Can't argue with that. Even so, I'd advise you to lay low for a while if you think your life's in danger."

"No, I won't do that." She stood up like she was preparing to leave. "I'm going to lead my life as usual. Neither your well-intentioned advice nor Harold's ill-intentioned behavior are going to stop me." She glanced at her diamond-studded wristwatch. "I hope your man hurries. I have a final fitting for my winter trousseau at Frederick's, after which I have a date for dinner and a night out on the town."

"Not with Harold, I presume."

"Heavens no."

"Your date's a lucky man."

"Yes, he is."

Her eyes flirted with me again. This time, I let mine flirt back. Our orbs danced that way awhile, getting closer and closer. They say you can look right into another person's soul through their eyes—I don't know what she saw in mine, but what I was seeing was pretty much what I thought the moth saw instead of the flame.

Heine tooting his horn outside saved me from getting singed. He had a trick air horn on his hot rod '47 Ford that sounded just like a wolf whistle.

"That'll be Heine." I walked over to the window, pulled it open, stuck my head out, and threw him the okay sign.

Dorothy came up behind me and put a light touch on my shoulder. "Am I going to be safe with him?"

I turned around—we were so close that her ample bosom brushed against my chest. "Maybe safer than with me," I told her, taking a step back. "What kind of car are you driving?"

"The new Packard. Black. It's out front."

I yelled down at Heine a couple stories below. "Her ride's the black Packard!" He couldn't miss her expensive white side-walled sedan considering he'd parked right behind it. "She'll be down in a minute, compadre. Stay loaded for bear and keep in touch. It's worth a C-note."

"I'll stick to her like a fly on you know what!" he hollered at me.

Closing the window, I smiled as I noted the new radio antenna sported on Heine's Ford. Twice as long as a normal aerial, it made his coupe look almost like an unmarked police cruiser. At least I'd be able to pay for it now.

Dorothy slipped on her long white gloves, took her clutch from the top of my desk, and headed for the door.

"Maybe we'll see each other again," she said over her shoulder.

"Up to you," I told her, liking the way her curves curved when she walked.

She paused at the door. "Yes, it is." Then she went out.

I watched out the window as she got into her ritzy Packard and drove off, south toward downtown, Heine's Ford rumbling close behind. Then I pulled out my bottle of Cutty Sark and had a belt. I hate domestic cases—could've kicked myself for taking this one—except for the big moola and Dorothy Demar's deep blue eyes. There was something about her that I didn't trust. That's why I had Heine tailing her instead of me. I figured I'd do some digging on her and see if there were any concrete reasons for my qualms. Besides, you never knew when another fat cat could walk through the door and offer a bundle for a simple job. Crazier things had happened.

A few minutes later, a man walked in just as I was about to start snooping on Dorothy. He doffed his gray Hamburg and said, "My name's Harold Sikes. I want to hire you."

I could've choked on my Scotch. Instead, I kept a poker face and studied him for a moment. Dressed to the nines in a double-breasted gray suit, with a pink boutonniere and a diamond stick-pinned tie, he looked to be in his mid-fifties, paunchy, balding, and thick-browed, with a heavy, jowly face bordering on ugly. For the life of me, I couldn't tell what Dorothy Demar had ever seen in this joe.

"What's your interest in hiring me, Mr. Sikes?"

"I need protection." He strode over and took a seat across from me like he owned the place.

"Protection from what?"

"My wife. I think she's planning to kill me."

I almost choked on my whiskey again, so I set the glass down. "Really? How did you happen to pick my little detective agency?"

"Everybody says you're the best."

"Can't argue with that."

He took his billfold from his breast pocket, pulled out four C-notes, and pushed them across the desk at me. "Will that cover it, Mr. Rossiter?"

Ben Franklin looked just as handsome as before, but the déjà vu added a real fishy smell to him. I decided to play along anyway.

"What makes you think your wife wants to do you in?" I asked, leaving the bills where they lay.

"She's jealous."

"That so?"

"Hysterically so."

"There a reason for that?"

"I'm a man of wealth. It draws beautiful women like a magnet. I have healthy appetites."

"That's laying it on the line."

"Come, come, my good man. You must like attractive women."

"Can't deny it."

"There you have it." He gave me a curt nod, took out a leather cigar case, and withdrew a Corona that probably cost more than a whole carton of my fags. Snipping the end off the cigar, he carefully lit it with a gold Ronson lighter. "As this seems to be settled," he continued, the pungent smoke curling up from his lips, "I shall consider you in my employ."

"That depends." I lit up a smoke for myself. "How do you feel about your wife, Mr. Sikes? Bear her any ill will?"

"Dorothy?" He looked flabbergasted. "Heavens no. Well, I suppose I should, her wanting to do me harm. But I love her very much. We've just never been able to make a go of it."

"She after your money, maybe?"

"Hardly. She has plenty of her own." Harold frowned. "See here, Mr. Rossiter, I'm a busy man. You're welcome to a few questions, certainly. But you've had them. Will you help me—yes or no?"

I thought long and hard.

Harold put an extra C-note on my desk.

This was all some kind of setup, no question.

Another C-note landed in front of me.

Somebody was trying to pull the wool over my eyes.

Yet another Ben Franklin hit the pile.

Old Ben was simply irresistible. "Sure, Mr. Sikes," I said,

raking in the seven large bills. "You've just hired your own personal shamus."

"Good." He ground out his barely smoked cigar in my ashtray, which raised quite a stink. "But you must be discreet."

"I suppose that means I should do my surveillance from a distance."

"Quite. I deal with a number of very important people. It wouldn't do to be seen in the company of a . . ."

"Low-life private dick?"

"Well . . ." He cleared his throat.

"That's all right." I gave him my best smile. "I've been called worse."

He threw me a return smile, albeit very tight-lipped. "Then we understand each other."

"Quite."

His eyes narrowed. "Are you mocking me, Mr. Rossiter?"

"No, I talk that way all the time. When do you want me to get started?"

"Immediately." He looked at his wristwatch—big and gold, studded with diamonds. "I have an appointment with my tailor, then I have a date for—"

"Dinner and dancing," I said. "And not with your wife."

"Uh, yes . . ." He gave me a queer look. "How did you—"

"Just a wild guess," I said. "Well, shall we get to it? Wouldn't want to keep the lucky girl waiting."

I grabbed my fedora while he put on his Hamburg. He carefully adjusted the hat to a jaunty angle, though it did nothing to improve his bushy-browed, beefy mug. As we went out, I left a quick note for Miss Jenkins to run down any info she could find on Harold Sikes and Dorothy Demar. Then I accompanied Harold to the elevator and down to the lobby.

His car was a new, black '49 Packard just like his wife's.

While he got it started, I hopped into my Roadmaster, parked only a few cars back, turned it over, and dropped it into gear. After we pulled out into traffic, I settled into a medium-distance tail, never letting more than one car get between us. Then I called Heine on the two-way radio.

His gravely voice came loud through the static. "Hey, Jake, what's shakin'?"

"Where are you?"

"Just pulling into the Frederick & Nelson parking garage. Dame came straight here except for a quick stop for smokes at Pete's Grocery by the office. Man, you were right about her gams. They're swell! So's the rest of her. Real treat following this broad. You got many more jobs like this, I might even take a cut in pay."

"Don't get too excited," I said. "We just got thrown a major curveball."

"What d'ya mean?"

I gave him the scoop about Harold Sikes hiring me for the same reason his wife did.

"Don't monkey around, ain't funny."

"It's the straight skinny."

"No shit?"

"No shit. I'm on Harold's tail right now."

"Ain't that the shits?" There was a long pause. "Somebody's playin' us for suckers!"

"I agree. Nothing we can do presently, though, except keep our eyes and ears open."

"Hey, she's pulling into a parking spot. Dame's about to get out of her car."

"Stay on her," I said. "And stay in touch."

"You got it. Over and out."

I put my radio microphone back into its holder and continued following Harold Sikes through the moderate mid-afternoon traffic. So far, Dorothy Demar had done exactly what she'd told me: gone to Frederick & Nelson. We'd have to see about the rest. Likewise for Harold—I was real interested to see if he, too, would stick to the itinerary that he'd laid out for me.

He did. Made a beeline to his tailor, J. Berrymann & Sons, at 4th and Union. Swank joint. Had lots of polished brass and green marble fronting the plate-glass windows by the place's entrance. I didn't see any price tags on the display suits in the windows, so I figured it was one of those places where if you had to ask the price you couldn't afford it. At least I had a decent view of Harold from where I was parked. I could see him pretty clearly past the window display as his tailor went to work on getting him fitted. So I stayed put, had a cigarette, and bided my time. Kept my eye out for danger, of course, but the only real danger turned out to be me smoking too much.

I was halfway through my fourth Philip Morris when Harold came out, got into his car, and promptly headed for the Rolf of Switzerland Beauty Parlor near 1st and Pike. I wondered what business he had at a beauty parlor, but my question was soon answered when he tooted his horn and two glitzy bimbos came out and met him at the curb. One had flaming red hair, was about half his age, and looked cheaper than the prize in a box of Cracker Jacks. The other chicken, also a redhead, wore a pop-your-eyes-out, bright blue evening dress that revealed the deepest cleavage this side of the Grand Canyon.

A perfect gentleman, Harold got out of the car and held the passenger door open for them. They scampered into the front seat, but not before each got a playful smack on the rump from the old boy. Then Harold slid behind the wheel and hit the road again, where he hooked up with Highway 99 and headed north.

Half an hour later, we ended up at our destination: an updated Prohibition-era roadhouse a few miles past the city limits called the Jungle Temple Inn.

I found parking fairly close to Harold's car in the Jungle Temple's big gravel parking lot. Instead of getting out and going inside, though, Harold and his chippies stayed put in the Packard for a while, the three of them busy kissing and horsing around as they nipped from a bottle of liquor that somebody had brought along.

While they had their playtime, I put in a radio call to Heine. I could hear the loud jazz music blowing out from the Temple as I waited for his reply. Place was a swinging hot spot. I knew it well, having done a little bootlegging for the original proprietor back when I was in my late teens. Now the booze was legal and the joint was even bigger and more popular than it had been during its speakeasy days. They featured jazz and swing that really got your feet moving. Had a huge dance floor, Class A hooch, good eats, and some of the best bands around. Even late on a Friday afternoon, the joint's parking lot was filling up fast.

"Hey, Jake," came Heine's voice over the radio. "Where you at?"

"Jungle Temple."

"The Temple, huh? Got some sweet memories of that place."

"Anything out of order on your end?"

"Nah," he said. "No kind of threats or anything, unless you count this Romeo that Dorothy's with: he's been all over her like hot fudge on a sundae."

"Yeah? Where are you exactly? And tell me more about this Romeo."

"He's some swarthy joe she hooked up with at Vic's Grill on Third Avenue. They had a couple drinks there, hardly touched their steaks, though—looked to me like they were hungrier for each other than the meal. Anyway, right now I'm tailing them past Chinatown up South Jackson Street. Nothin' out this way except those Negro jazz clubs. Bet that's where they're planning to let their hair down. What about you, Jake? Anything exciting?"

"Not really. Except that Harold's got *two* dames with him. They've been playing plenty of Post Office, but I haven't seen a hint of anything sinister . . . Wait. Hold on a minute." Harold and his redheads were getting out of the car. "Gotta go, Heine. My people are fixing to go into the club."

"Likewise for mine, I think," he told me. "Yup. They just parked outside the Rocking Horse. You know the place." I could hear him opening his car door. "Talk to you later. Over and out."

I signed off the radio and watched Harold, a girl on each arm, make his way across the parking lot. Then I piled out of the Roadmaster and followed them inside the Temple, both dames giggling and kicking up their heels the whole while.

The sound of their laughter was soon drowned out by the crazy combo that had the joint hopping. It was jammed to the rafters already, the parquet dance floor and most of the sixty or so tables ringing it almost full. Harold had no problem getting seated, though: slipped the floor manager a couple of bills and was promptly led to the one empty table front and center to the dance floor. Me, I was lucky to find a spot clear in back by the long saloon-style bar. But that was okay; it suited my purpose just fine. I was far enough away to be the epitome of discreetness, but still close enough to have an eye on business if somebody tried anything with Harold.

As if reading my mind, Harold turned my direction, looked straight at me, and smiled, like he approved of how I was keeping watch. Then he went back to nuzzling his chippies, both seated so close to him that they were almost in his lap.

I needed a drink if I was going to keep this up for long. No waiter in sight, I stepped to the bar to place my own order. That's when the phone on the bar's back counter began to ring. It kept ringing while the husky crew-cut bartender set up a round of drinks at the far end of the bar, then finally made his way down to me.

"Be with you in a second, bud. Gotta get this damned phone." He jerked the receiver from its cradle. "Yeah? Who? Jake Rossiter? Look, I'm too busy to—"

"Hey, that's for me; I'm Rossiter." He handed me the phone. "This is Jake," I said.

"Jake! Bad news." It was Heine, all agitated. "Dorothy Demar's been killed."

"What?"

"Happened a couple minutes ago." I could hear sirens in the background as he spoke. "Her and her Romeo both."

"Damnation. Where and how?"

"Outside the Rocking Horse. They were about to go inside when all of a sudden this big DeSoto speeds right up over the sidewalk and squashes them against the wall. Hit so hard it almost cut them in half. Couldn't do a thing about it. Car sped away by the time I got over to check on them."

"I'll be a sonofabitch."

"Sure wasn't any accident," said Heine. "Dorothy Demar was telling the truth about her hubby. Had to be him behind this."

"Yeah. And he made me his chump," I said, now seeing the true reason why Harold hired me. "I'm his damned alibi, Heine. Get it? Harold will claim that I was watching him the whole time and he wasn't anywhere near the Rocking Horse when his wife bought the farm."

"That dirty bastard." He was as angry as I was. "But what can ya do?"

"I'll tell you what I can do." I looked over at Harold with blood in my eye. "I'm going to take him out back and beat the truth out of him!"

"Don't get yourself arrested."

"If I land in jail for finally doing something right on this case, so be it."

"Jake—"

I hung up on him. I was too pissed to listen to reason. All I could see at the moment was being too tough on Dorothy Demar when she had truly needed me. So I came out from behind the bar intent of rearranging Harold Sikes's face.

A waiter was fixing to serve Harold and his party girls as I neared their table. But instead of setting up their drinks, he tossed the serving tray aside and exposed a silver pistol his right hand. It barked rapid-fire, putting three slugs into Harold's chest before I could clear leather with my Colt.

Instant pandemonium. Harold was flat on his back, everybody screaming and ducking for cover around him. I got a bead on the shooter as he beat feet across the dance floor trying to escape. I yelled for him to stop. He turned and aimed at me. My .45 dropped him in his tracks.

I ran over to him, gun at the ready, to make sure he was no longer a threat. He wasn't: I'd hit him square in the heart.

What the hell was going on?

I went to Harold next. Found him barely alive, his redheads cowering partway under the table, squealing and sobbing as Harold gasped and moaned. The blood spurting from his white shirt told me he wasn't long for this world.

I knelt at his side. His glassy eyes stared into mine. "What . . . happened?" he asked.

"You tell me, pal. Your wife got murdered just minutes ago. If you know the score, you better cough it up before you meet your maker."

He spat up a mouthful of blood. "I got her, then . . ." He managed a weak and bloody grin. "But this . . ." He grimaced in pain. "This . . . shouldn't be happening to me . . . You're supposed to be . . . my alibi . . ."

"Dorothy's too, by the looks of it. Your wife was playing the same game you were, by God," I said, finally getting the big picture. "She also hired me for protection today—had somebody ready to punch your ticket just like you did hers."

"No . . ."

"Yeah. She set me up to be her alibi the same as you."

"I don't . . . believe it . . ."

"Believe it."

"That devious . . . little bitch . . ." Then he shuddered and breathed his last.

I got to my feet. The two redheads were whimpering and blubbering even louder now that Harold was dead.

"Aww, shuttup!" I told them.

Then I waited for the cops. There being nothing else to do in the meantime, I went to the now empty bar and helped myself to a shot of Chivas Regal, the most expensive Scotch in the house. But like everything else, it tasted off.

I hate domestic cases. I hate feeling sorry for myself. I hate having no good reason to feel sorry for myself. I hate drinking half a bottle of Scotch and having it do absolutely nothing to make me feel any better.

It was all crap and bound to get crappier, especially when the newspapers inevitably picked up the story. I could see the headline now—*Local Private Eye's Clients Murdered Right*

Under His Nose. It would do my reputation a whole world of good.

The only thing that hadn't gone south on this case was the big moola I'd gotten for taking it in the first place. I had the eleven C-notes fanned out on my desk like so many playing cards. But the longer I stared at them, the worse they looked. I'd never had so much dough look so bad. Like everything else, even the damned money was tainted. Yeah, I'd earned it, but I didn't want any part of it. Yet there wasn't any choice—I had to keep at least some of it, I was flat broke. I needed a couple hundred for the radios and a hundred for Heine. The rest, well, I'd just as soon eat beans for a month than hold onto it: all it would do is serve as a constant reminder of what a rank and amateur sucker I'd been.

I swilled a little more booze and wondered what I was going to do. I was giving serious consideration to donating the remaining eight-hundred bucks to charity when the realization struck me. A wonderful, happy realization that gave me such good cheer it put bells on my toes. It was so obvious.

I scooped up the dough and gladly put it into my wallet. Of course I'd keep it. This had been no ordinary domestic case. Far from it. In fact, it was a model of what a domestic case could and *should* be. It even had a happy ending.

After all, it was the first case I'd seen where each of the spouses trying to get out of a bad marriage got exactly what they wanted *and* deserved.

THE BEST VIEW IN TOWN

BY PAUL S. PIPER

Leschi

There was not a more beautiful sight in Seattle. For the present at least, I owned it: Keri seated legs crossed on the metal heater as she stared out my window. A cigarette smoldered in her hand, its smoke drifting lazily to the ceiling. Her crystal-blond hair snatched the moon and starlight and magnified it. I had some Miles Davis—*Bitches Brew,* to be exact—on the Goodwill stereo, a little scratchy, but to my liquor-besotted ears it sounded good enough. It sounded fine. And this woman . . . Damn! She wasn't the kind of woman who gave me a second look, but here she was sitting in *my* room.

Beyond her the night stretched back and away, dropping from the 30th Street ridge onto the glittering surface of Lake Washington. Diamonds, diamonds everywhere. And beyond that blinked the golden lights of Bellevue; and much further to the east were the Cascades, towering snow-capped peaks. Above them the sky was radiant with stars.

It made me dizzy staring at it all. I looked back at Keri and felt even more dizzy. Then the room began swaying, and that was a different kind of dizzy altogether. I grabbed the Cutty bottle off the table for balance.

"Wanna nother drink?" I slurred, giving her my sexiest smile.

She turned and gazed at me with the same distant look she gave to the stars. "You've had enough."

"But this isn't about me," I said, feigning indignation.

She turned back to the window.

"Ish beautiful isn't it?"

"Yeah," she muttered, taking another drag off her cigarette. I didn't normally let people smoke in my apartment, a second-floor duplex on 30th atop the ridge just off Yesler, but I wasn't going to damage my odds with her. This woman could spray the whole place with skunk juice for all I cared.

"What the hell is he doing?" Her voice had a sexy rasp to it. Like Dietrich, I thought, though I couldn't remember if I'd actually ever heard Dietrich talk.

"Who?" I was sitting on a beat-up swivel chair in front of the doorless closet I used for an office. A couple of Paul Klee prints stared at my back, and my cat, Lady Chatterley, was curled on a pillow. Her tail twitched as she chased after dream mice.

I spun the chair around, coming to rest a bit off-kilter, but Keri was still in view. I swung the chair around again. This was fun.

Divorced thirteen months yesterday, I'd been on a downward spiral with life and love ever since. Thirty-eight and working as a dishwasher at the Lakeside Broiler. I used to say I was a writer. Now I didn't even bother. I couldn't even say I was much of a reader. I was rapidly becoming what I did nine to twelve hours a day: a dishwasher. And believe me, that's not how I had pictured it when I stepped onto the graduation stage in Palo Alto to receive my Bachelor of Arts in history from Stanford.

I'd met Keri earlier that evening at a bar in Fremont. I'd traveled by bus to see my favorite all-women bluegrass band, The Coal Miner's Daughters. The friend I was supposed to meet never showed, so I began a slow beer crawl toward the end of the night. I was already toasted, which loosened me up enough to dance alone, when Keri stepped in from out of the blue and took my hand, swinging me into a haphazard rendition of the lindy hop. We ended up back at my table where I immediately ordered more drinks and launched into a nonstop narration of my life, with a few detours into Charlemagne, Pépin the Short, Redburga, and the flaws in Einhard's biography. It was the sort of rant that usually left me talking to an empty chair, but this time, when I came up for air, a gorgeous woman was listening attentively with the hint of a smile on her lips. I ordered more drinks but she declined. I waited for her rendition of her life but that never came either. My leading questions, "Where did you grow up?" "What do you do?" "Was your mother a model?" were met with curt, polite responses. So we listened to music, and danced sloppy jitterbugs.

The band finally shut it down around 1:45, and although I could still dance, after four or five additional drinks I could barely walk. When she offered to drive me home in her rusted gray Taurus, I figured we must have something in common.

"Hey, I own a shit car too," I said. "A Honda Shivic."

"It's a loaner," she said. "My Beamer's in the shop." She looked at me and smiled. "That's a joke."

As we drove, she searched the night radio realm for tunes, homing in on those lonely calls for love. This woman was playing my song.

"My parents grew up in this neighborhood somewhere," she said as we climbed the hill toward 30th. The streetlights dropped circles of yellow light onto the street, and an occasional hooker walked her walk in them. Bobby Vinton, of all people, was singing "Mr. Lonely" when we pulled up in front of the eighty-seven steps that led to my flat.

* * *

"Who?" I said again, still spinning the chair. "Who, who?" I sounded like an owl.

"That old man." She paused to take a drag on the cigarette. "He's carrying buckets of dirt out of the house and pouring them into a wheelbarrow."

I laughed. "The corner building?"

"That's the one."

"Ricard. He and Wanda the towering Swede own that place. Turned it into a coffee house."

"So what's with the dirt?"

"The place is tiny. He's trying to expand it. He's digging up the cellar. Going to put another room in. Maybe a pool table; home movie theater; bowling alley, I don't know . . ." I started laughing, but it sounded more like soprano hiccups.

"At 1:38 in the morning?"

"Hey, they drink a lot of coffee. How should I know? Maybe he's an insomniac. Maybe he pays himself more for working the night shift."

She turned and stared at me. It was a hard stare, and in a momentary flash of sobriety I felt like a weak joke. Women, particularly gorgeous woman, had that effect on me.

"Come here."

I got up obediently and caught the door jamb as I tipped too far. I righted myself and drew a bead on her. It wasn't easy but I walked over.

"Look at him."

Below, the streetlights illuminated the intersection in front of the shop. It was so bright that I could read the sign. *OPEN HEART COFFEE & PASTRIES*. They'd just put it up last week and the paint still gleamed. Ricard was pushing the wheelbarrow up the sidewalk to an abandoned concrete foundation, and when he got there, he turned the wheelbarrow into the weeds, pushed it to the edge, and dumped the contents. Then he wheeled it back to the front of the shop and went inside.

"Weird, huh?"

There were no cars, few lit windows. No one was around. The night belonged to itself, and we were all strangers. I had to admit it was an odd sight.

"What movie would this be out of?" Keri asked, sucking her cigarette and tipping her head back, exhaling hard toward the ceiling.

"It depends if we are in it or not. Hitchcock's *Rear Window*. I'm Stewart in the wheelchair. You're Grashe Kelly."

"You're Stewart? Not."

"Whaddya mean *not?*" My near-perfect Stewart imitation.

"I mean we're not in that movie."

"Then I take the fithh. I refuthe to appear without you at my side." I raised the near-empty bottle of Cutty to my lips.

She drummed her fingers on the heater. "He's up to something."

"You're crazy. Are we going to bed?" I reached over and slopped my hand onto her shoulder but she shrugged it off with a casual flick.

"I'm going down there to find out." She ground her cigarette into an ashtray I'd dug out of a forgotten cupboard full of my ex-girlfriend's flotsam and jetsam. And they say history is dead.

I raised the bottle again and took a slug but there was nothing left in it. Just like my life.

A few minutes later I saw Keri striding purposefully across the intersection and walking into the yawning front door of the Open Heart coffee shop, following Ricard's trail. This beautiful creature was beginning to piss me off, and I felt I better control her before she pissed off my neighbors. She could leave, but I was stuck here. I felt strongly enough about it that I got up and leveled one of my lamps on the way to the door.

I weaved my way across the street and paused by Ricard's overturned wheelbarrow. I brushed it with my fingers, the kind of caress men give tools. Something solid about metal. It was a sturdy wheelbarrow, its red body worn to the metal in places by hard work. I felt like it would be a good companion, so I sat next to it on the curb. I could hear the crickets singing in the blackberries and a siren winding its way through Chinatown over on Jackson. I began talking to it but don't ask me to remember what I said.

I have no idea how long it was before Keri shook me awake. It was a rough shake, and I stared at her glassily. Who was this goddess sent to save my soul?

I tried to ask her something but it came out something like, "Splefff."

"Come here." She jerked me to my feet, hooked her arm under mine, and then led me across the street and to my front steps. We made it up twenty-three, I was counting, and she bade me sit, although *bade* may be the wrong word.

"Sit!"

Sit I did. I could be a good dog if there was a bone waiting.

"That bastard," she hissed, plopping herself next to me.

"Ricard?" I was beginning to remember things. Unfortunately, with the return of memory came a splitting headache.

"I found out what's going on, and I don't mind saying I'm really, really pissed."

"Whaaa?" I wiped some stray drool off my chin. My goddess was beginning to sound downright scary.

Keri started talking, ranting actually.

"Remember I told you my parents grew up around here?

Well, it started coming back to me. My grandparents owned that place."

"What place?"

"The corner place. The place where that guy is digging. They had a business, kind of a pawn shop. I've seen pictures of it. I think it was called Thirtieth Avenue Resale. My dad told me once when we drove by it, and then he showed me pictures."

"Wow. This is karmic. Or cosmic. We're like past-life neighbors or something."

She ignored me.

"They took in tons of jewelry from the Chinese and Japanese immigrants who came on hard times. Family heirlooms, a lot of it. My dad said much of it was jade. High-quality jade. Well, the interesting thing is," she stabbed the air in front of her, "the interesting thing is that my grandparents stockpiled it all. Never sold it. And most of the immigrants couldn't afford to buy it back. So they ended up with a shitload of really expensive jewelry."

She turned and peered directly at me, an insane fervor in her eyes. "A shitload of jewelry is still in there somewhere. I know it!"

"Really?" I moved back a few inches. Her vibes were too intense.

"Yes, really," she told me. "When my grandparents died the jewelry was supposed to go to my dad, but it never did. My parents couldn't find it. They searched all my grandparents' possessions, bank accounts, safety deposit boxes. They searched the store a number of times. I remember my dad saying that he thought they'd hidden it in the basement, but it never turned up. In the end they had to sell the store to pay some debts, and that was that.

"I'll bet that old bastard Ricard found out about it," she continued. "He's looking for it. He knows! Maybe he even found it. That's *my* jewelry!" She stood up quickly and shook her fist in the direction of the Open Heart. "That's my jewelry, you bastard!"

"Shhhh! You'll wake the landlord."

"Screw the landlord."

"Well," I said, standing unsteadily, "I'd rather you saved that for me."

"No chance, loser. I'm out of here."

When I woke up—I think it was still morning—I went over to the Open Heart, Lady Chatterley sashaying behind me across the street, our shadows playing tag. Wanda and Ricard were cat friendly, but their cat Tufts was not, so Chatterley sat outside on a sunny bench, as if it were exactly what she wanted to do. Wanda was behind the counter smiling her Swedish mother's smile. She'd adopted every hungry boy and girl in the neighborhood, and half of them sat crammed into little tables, their knees bumping the tops, pastries piling into their mouths.

"Morning, Wanda." My voice sounded worse than it felt, but not by much.

"Albert. You look so pale."

"Sun's bad for you, Wanda. Gives you cancer. Could I have a pear Danish and a cup of coffee to go?"

"Sure." She bent over and carefully extracted the pastry with wax paper. "Three dollars," she said cheerfully, passing it to me.

I handed her three crumpled bills.

"Get some sun, Albert, and forget about cancer. Take some risks. You'll have a better life. You worry too much."

"I know." I bit into my Danish. "Thanks." I went outside and sat next to Chatterley and watched the neighborhood happen. As I ate, I wondered which was worse, pastries or worry. I guess you had to choose your poison.

* * *

Three weeks later the digging stopped. Since that night with Keri, I'd become more attuned to it. The wheelbarrow remained tipped against the white stucco wall next to the buckets on the sidewalk.

When I asked, Ricard had invited me down to see the progress. It wasn't much: thirty square feet of dank, dark space propped with timbers and stinking of mold and wet clay. When he lit the second lantern I saw an opening covered in ocher muslin. The corner of a rusted flour container stuck out. Ricard stepped in front of it and fiddled with the lantern, which fizzled out. He cursed.

"A cellar restaurant, perhaps. Some day. Like the old country." Avoiding my eyes. "That's it. Let's go."

I continued to do my thing, which was washing dishes and catching some local music. There was no more action in the girl department, and I was curiously waiting for construction on the basement to begin. Ricard had tapped local talent in Josh Bullford, who lived across the street and ran a small construction company. He'd built most of his own house, and worked fast and cheap. But it never happened.

Some salesman found Ricard laying at the bottom of the foundation with his head split open. The death was ruled accidental. Wanda collapsed into a nervous breakdown. A friend of Wanda's tried to keep the place open, but the Open Heart closed down a few weeks later. Life went on, as it always does, even after the direst tragedies. As my uncle used to say, the bigger the rock, the more ripples, but the surface always smooths out eventually.

It was no surprise that when I ran into Keri again, at a pub in Pioneer Square, she was wearing better clothes, Issey Miyake to be precise. She was sexily wedged between two young dudes dripping with wealth. A leach. I wanted her to squirm, so I walked up, torn jeans and dirty Sonics T-shirt, and sat down.

"Ricard's dead," I said, stopping the conversation and the superficial laughter.

"Who?"

"You know who." I pulled out a chair, flipped it, and sat down.

Keri picked up a fancy-looking purple drink and stirred it with a tiny red straw. I had to admit she looked terrific, but then so did cobras.

"How much do you remember from that night anyway?" she asked. I noticed the two men pulling back into their drinks.

"I remember enough."

"I had nothing to do with that old man's death, if that's what you're thinking."

I leaned forward. "You mean you just went home and forgot all about those piles and piles of jewels you were telling me about?"

"I didn't forget about them. But what could I do? I checked into it with a lawyer and they legally belong to whoever owns the property. Besides, I read about his death in the paper. It was ruled an accident. What can you expect from an old man who's dumping dirt all night?"

"What indeed? Sounds like you've got all the ends neatly tied up then."

She sipped her purple drink.

"You are cold."

"There's a breeze in here."

I'd given her what I wanted and she hadn't flinched.

Three beers later, I watched her get into a black BMW

with one of the two jerks, and with a puff of blue smoke from the exhaust pipe, Keri drove out of my life.

A few nights later, feet up on the heater, I gazed out in near awe at that gorgeous view. A full moon was cresting the Cascades and its light flooded the lake surface. I missed Chatterley already, but Cindy who lived next door was a sweetheart who would give her love and food. My landlord, John, had already advertised the apartment, and he'd taken my advice. *Best view in town,* the ad read. I took a sip of beer.

Ricard had been keeping the jewelry in containers of flour—over eighty pieces, dating back to the Ming and Han dynasties. Jade, gold chains, ornamental necklaces. I'd sold the lot north of the border in Richmond, BC for over $400,000, and I knew I'd gotten ripped off, but I didn't have time to shop them around. It would have been a shame to sell it all, though, so I kept a few necklaces. Maybe I'd meet a woman in Rio.

The taxi honked outside. I headed out the door, descended the eighty-seven winding stairs through the cotoneaster, streetlights illuminating the intersection in front of the Open Heart. The *Closed* sign on the door gave the evening a sense of finality.

I handed the bag to the cabbie, who tossed it into the trunk. I started to get into the backseat and noticed her ice-blond hair, unlit cigarette, and cool smile. She was tucked against the far door like a shadow.

I was struck catatonic.

"I can't imagine why you chose Rio," Keri said, "Nice is much more charming. But there's plenty of time to change *our* plans." She patted the seat next to her. "Come, sit."

THE WRONG END OF A GUN

BY R. BARRI FLOWERS

South Lake Union

S outh Lake Union was the Seattle neighborhood I called home. Located just below its namesake, Lake Union, it was bounded by Interstate 5 on the east and Aurora Avenue on the west, and was in the midst of an economic redevelopment. So what else was new? There were still places in the neighborhood that allowed you to escape the gentrification.

I spent every night at such a place on Aloha Street called Rusty's Bar and Grill. Dark and dreary, it was one of those retro dive bars that refused to apologize for turning its back on the present (and offered cheap cocktails).

The décor was fashionably outdated, with garage-sale tables and stools and framed photographs of city landmarks. A jukebox in the corner was playing B.B. King's "The Thrill Is Gone." There was a worn-out pool table where on the night in question two men were playing to impress a chick who couldn't decide which one she wanted to take home.

I sat by my lonesome, caught up in what might have been. Fresh off a bitter divorce and not looking for any company, I was content to finish off my mug of beer and call it a night.

That was before she walked in.

A cross between Halle Berry and Beyoncé, her complexion was like maple syrup over buttered waffles. Shiny raven Senegalese twists framed a heart-shaped face that featured full ruby lips. With plenty of curves in a tight red dress and three-inch heels, she really caught my attention.

She wore dark shades, but seemed to be scanning the place as though searching for a reason to stay.

When she sat at the table next to mine, I wondered if this was my lucky day.

I didn't wait to find out.

"Buy the lady a drink?" I asked.

"Sure, why not?"

I smiled and slid over to her table. "What's your pleasure?"

"Gin and tonic."

I flagged down a barmaid and ordered two cocktails. "You're new here," I said to the gorgeous girl beside me.

"I've been around," she said coyly.

"I think I'd remember if you had."

"That's sweet."

I've never been known for my sweetness but wasn't about to argue. "By the way, I'm Conrad."

"Hi, Conrad." She stuck out a small hand with long, polished nails. "Gabriella."

I shook her hand and didn't want to stop there.

"Anyone ever tell you that you look like Will Smith?" she asked.

"Not in this lifetime." I saw myself as more like Denzel Washington. But who was I to bicker with this Halle/Beyoncé red-hot chick?

Gabriella smiled but left it at that.

The drinks came quickly. I stayed focused on the object of my interest.

"Why don't you tell me something about yourself?" I suggested.

She removed her sunglasses. Her irises were the color of

rich chocolate. "What do you want to know?" she asked.

Everything came to mind, but something told me that might take more time than she had. So I cut to the chase.

"How about how you ended up here with me?"

She laughed. "Don't sell yourself short."

"I never do."

"Good." She took a sip of her drink, her lips lingering on the rim of the glass for a moment. "I'm married."

"Where's your husband?"

"Does it matter?"

I wasn't necessarily looking to step into another man's shoes, but I'd done it before. "Not in my book."

She looked relieved. Maybe a little nervous too. I couldn't be certain.

"He's home right now, probably wondering where I am," she said.

"That's too bad for him."

"He's not very nice when he's angry."

"So why make him angry?"

"Why not?" She batted her big brown eyes. "Sometimes a girl just wants to have fun."

I flashed my best smile at her. "So does a guy."

Gabriella licked the gin off her lips. "You probably have a wife and kids at home."

"Not quite," I said. "She's an ex and has full custody of the kids. So I'm on my own."

She gave me a dazzling smile. "Doesn't have to be that way."

"Oh . . . ?"

"Maybe we can have fun together?"

"Maybe we can."

The smile left her pretty face. "This isn't really a good place to talk."

Our conversation seemed to be working fine up to that point, as far as I was concerned. "You have a better place in mind?"

"Meet me tomorrow night."

I wondered if I could wait that long. "When and where?"

"Denny Park at 7 o'clock—near the play area."

"I'll be there."

Her smile returned. "See you then."

Gabriella put on her shades, then got up and left.

I wanted to follow her, but decided to honor her wishes. So I went home by myself to the apartment I rented on North Yale Street. It was a studio—a big step down from the house my ex walked away with in the divorce settlement.

At least I had a roof over my head and a bed to climb into. I would've preferred to do so with Gabriella, but that would have to wait for another day. I hadn't been looking for anybody, but now that I'd found her, I put my head on the pillow and counted down the minutes before I could see her again.

Denny Park was Seattle's oldest park and a cornerstone of South Lake Union. Once a cemetery, it had undergone extensive renovations over the years and given people a place to hang out (and hope muggers looked the other way).

But I was less interested in its past than my near future with Gabriella.

I found her occupying a bench by the children's play area. What I had in mind was strictly for adults.

Gabriella was dressed to kill in a low-cut fuchsia dress.

I sat next to her. Her flowery fragrance smelled like a slice of heaven.

"I wasn't sure you'd come," she said.

"I was too intrigued not to."

"I'm not that interesting."

"I beg to differ." I moved over, close enough that we touched. "What's your husband think you're doing right now?"

She smiled. "He thinks I'm visiting my sister."

I grinned. "I'm okay with that."

"I'm just looking to have a good time."

"Isn't that why we're here?"

She looked away. "My husband is a very jealous man."

"Why are you telling me this?"

Our eyes met. "I want you to know what you're getting into."

"Thanks for the warning, but I can take care of myself. And you too, if that's what you want."

"Eric's much older than me and he's been married twice before. I think he just sees me as a beautiful woman, somebody he can control and show off at parties."

"Like a trophy wife?"

"Something like that."

"What did you see in him? Is he rich?"

"He's someone who makes my life easier."

"At what price?"

She looked away. "I can't answer that."

"Can't or won't?"

She chewed her lower lip. "He cheats on me. Still sees his last wife and probably other women."

"Why do you stay with him?"

Her eyes narrowed. "Why do you think?"

"You tell me."

"Isn't that what all men do? Cheat?"

I thought of my ex who started fooling around with her boss before the divorce.

"Some women cheat too," I said.

Gabriella put a hand on my knee. "Why shouldn't we get our fair share?"

I put a hand on hers. "You're right, why shouldn't you?"

"Eric will be going out of town on business tomorrow."

I liked where this was headed. "I'm listening."

"If you come over around 8 tomorrow night, we'll have the whole houseboat all to ourselves."

"A houseboat, huh?" I'd never been inside one before. "Eight o'clock it is."

She gave me the address. "I like you."

"Works both ways."

She kissed me hard on the mouth. "Till tomorrow . . ."

Gabriella got up and sashayed away. I went in the opposite direction.

Things were beginning to look up again in my life. I had this lady with the shimmering Senegalese twists to thank for that.

The next day I made my way to the Yale Street Landing marina, eager to hook up with Gabriella and see how many ways we could please each other.

Only a smattering of houseboats were moored there, but enough to tell me I had moved up quite a few notches in wealth. I was beginning to understand why Gabriella was in no hurry to pack her bags.

I'd barely stepped onto the floating walkway leading to the moorages when a dark-haired, well-dressed Latino man bumped into me from behind.

"Excuse me," I said.

He gave no response, just hurried past me toward the houseboats.

I continued on my merry way, sure that I was headed for a night to remember.

Her houseboat was hard to miss. It had an end moorage and was the biggest and classiest of them all.

The wraparound lower deck afforded a full view of the city skyline. The surrounding water caught reflections that danced across the lake. This place must be worth a mint, I thought. Even so, the main attraction for me was obviously inside.

Gabriella opened the door before I could ring the bell. I gave her the once-over and liked what I saw. She was wearing a carnation-colored kimono that revealed a lot of cleavage. I wondered if she wore anything under it.

"You're right on time," she said.

"Did you think I wouldn't be?"

"Not really." Her cheeks flushed. "Come in."

I walked into a wide, open living and dining area. It had cane furnishings, rich, paneled walls, multiple picture windows, and more than a touch of class.

Gabriella looked perfect in this setting. She was everything I ever dreamt about. With luck, this could turn into a regular gig.

"Would you like a drink?" she asked.

"Sure, why not."

"I've got wine, whiskey, brandy, beer . . ."

"Wine." I liked beer, but wine sounded more romantic.

She handed me a long-stemmed glass and filled it with a Cabernet Sauvignon.

"Does your husband go away on business often?"

"Often enough."

I grinned. "Works for me."

"I'm glad it does."

I sat my glass down and pulled her close. I kissed her deep and long.

After a while, she pulled away. "Why don't we go in the bedroom where it's more comfortable?"

"Lead the way."

She took my hand and we ended up in a spacious master suite on the main floor. It had a king-size four-poster bed and crisp red satin sheets ready to be wrinkled.

"I'm yours," Gabriella cooed.

I didn't want to give her a moment to change her mind, so I untied the belt on her kimono. Indeed, she wore nothing beneath it. Her voluptuous naked body just begged to be caressed.

She kissed me, ran her tongue through my lips, then laid down on the bed, her long, shapely legs making me forget any woman-trouble I'd had in the past. She curled a finger and beckoned me to join her.

I got undressed in a hurry, eager to get between those satin sheets.

But I didn't hurry through our lovemaking. It had been a long time since I'd been with a woman, especially a woman like this—I spent what seemed like forever lost in her touch and her firm breasts, her smooth, velvet-soft bronze skin, her legs wrapped around me, her hands cupping my buttocks.

A loud noise in the hallway interrupted our passion.

"What the hell was that?"

Gabriella's eyes went wide. "I think my husband's back."

My heart skipped a beat. "You said he was out of town."

"He must have taken an early flight," she said, jumping out of bed and grabbing her robe. "You have to get out of here!"

Hell . . . I doubted I could get dressed and past her husband without him seeing me.

I'd just put on my pants and loafers when a sixty-something white man burst into the bedroom. He was heavyset, paunchy, and wore a designer suit. His eyes narrowed to slits as he glared at Gabriella.

"You bitch!"

She cowered behind me like she expected me to go from lover to protector.

"Hey, why don't we talk about this?" I told the guy.

He sucker-punched me on the chin, stunning me. My legs gave out, but I got up quickly. He was bigger than me, but I was half his age. He swung again. I ducked and hit him twice in his big belly.

He doubled over, gasping for air.

I thought it was over, but he suddenly charged me like a battering ram and got me in a headlock. We both tumbled to the floor.

He ended up on top in our struggle, then got his huge hands around my neck and started to choke me.

I couldn't break his grip. Desperate, I balled my hands and slammed them against his temples as hard as I could.

He groaned and released his grip on my neck. I scrambled out from under him and got to my feet. But so did he . . .

Man, this dude was as strong as an ox and ready to go at it again.

Then a shot rang out.

The big man clutched his chest and fell flat on his face.

I turned and saw Gabriella holding a Glock in her hand.

"Damn, you killed him," I said, attempting to catch my breath.

"Yeah." She looked at me with eyes that had gone cold.

I tried to collect my thoughts as I moved toward her. "Look, you could say that you shot your husband in self-defense."

A man appeared behind her in the bedroom doorway. "That won't be necessary," he told me.

It was the Latino man I had run into on the dock. Gabriella handed him the gun and he aimed it at me.

"What are you doing?" I asked, staring into the wrong end of the gun with nowhere to run. "Who are you?" I looked to Gabriella. "What the hell is this?"

"Shall I tell him or do you want to?" the man said to Gabriella.

As he put a protective arm around her shoulder, she smiled at me. "You followed me home, Conrad, and beat and raped me." She said this in a stone-cold, matter-of-fact tone. I couldn't believe what I was hearing.

"What a bad man you are," she continued. "But when my dear husband came home early, he tried to save me, and the two of you got into a fight. Then you shot him to death. That's when Enrique, my husband's lawyer, came over for a meeting. Thankfully, he got hold of the gun and shot you. You might have killed me too." She looked at Enrique. "Hit me in the face," she told him. "We've got to make it look good. Leave some marks; just don't spoil my looks."

Enrique made his free hand into a fist. "Don't worry, baby, nothing can spoil *your* looks." Then he punched her. Twice. Pretty hard—left a big welt on her cheek and bloodied her nose.

"Damn, Enrique," said Gabriella, wiping at the blood with the palm of one hand.

"Why me?" I asked Gabriella.

"You were available." She glanced at Enrique. "Shoot him, *now*," she ordered. "Get it over with."

"My pleasure." He cracked a cocky grin. "So long, sucker. Hope she was worth it."

"Just do it!" Gabriella yelled, giving Enrique an impatient shove. The unexpected jolt caused the gun to go off. Lucky for me, the bullet missed but I actually felt it whiz by my head.

I did the only thing I could in that moment of confusion: I barreled straight into Enrique, buried my right shoulder in his mid-section, and grabbed hold of his gun hand.

Gabriella screamed. As we struggled for the gun she stepped in to help her man. She hit me a good one, then scratched my face, but I held on.

That's when the Glock went off again. A couple times. *Bam bam!*

Gabriella collapsed to the floor, blood gushing out of her like a fountain.

"Baby!" Enrique yelled. "Baby!"

He forgot all about me for a second. I wrenched the gun away from him.

The man fell to his knees beside her and cradled her head in his arms. "No, no, no," he repeated when he realized she was probably dead. "No, no . . ."

"Get up, you bastard," I said, my head swimming, my knees weak. The Glock was shaky in my hand, but still aimed square at his head.

I took a deep breath. It was over. I had him.

Then he surprised me.

He charged me just like I'd done to him.

Except it didn't work for Enrique—I squeezed a shot off at the last moment. His head exploded like a melon hit with a sledgehammer.

Blood and brains all over me, I sat down on the bed and tried to gather my wits. I felt sick. Felt even sicker as I stared at the three lifeless bodies sprawled around me in the bedroom.

How long I sat there like that, I don't know . . . All I know for sure is that I finally picked up the phone and called 911.

August 24, 2009

Editor
Noir & Intrigue Mystery Magazine
PO Box 473
New York, NY 10051

Dear Editor:

So, that's my short story, "The Wrong End of a Gun." I sure hope you'll publish this. I worked very hard on it. It's all true. And I also hope you won't be put off by me being an inmate here at the Twin Rivers Correctional Facility.

I know it sounds clichéd, but I got the kind of justice that African Americans get all the time: lock us up and toss the key, never mind the evidence. I am innocent, I swear. I couldn't afford a decent attorney. I'm doing fifteen-to-life. That's the best my public defender could get.

I've tried the newspapers, TV, and radio—I even tried 48 Hours and 60 Minutes—but nobody would listen to me. That's why I have written this like it's a mystery story. I figured maybe it would be good enough to publish in your magazine. I sure do hope so. My appeal was turned down. You're my last chance. I think a lot of people will understand this story and like it and buy your magazine. It could do you and me both a lot of good.

I have enclosed a SASE like it said to do in the Writer's Market.

Thank you for your consideration. I look forward to hearing from you.

Sincerely yours,

Conrad Sinclair
Inmate #SN/IR-4569
Build. C
c/o Twin Rivers Correctional Facility
Monroe, WA 98057

PART IV

To the Limits

PAPER SON

BY BRIAN THORNTON

Chinatown

The grizzled morgue attendant manhandled the make-shift plank table to the center of the hot, small, noisome viewing chamber. James Robbins Jewell took an involuntary step back as he watched. Not since attending the funeral of an uncle who had stepped off a curb on New York City's Canal Street and directly into the path of a beer wagon had Jewell seen someone who had met a violent end. He had been twelve that summer.

Now twenty-four, he put a handkerchief to his nose and mouth, then willed his stomach not to betray him and add to the charnel house smell of Seattle's Cherry Street morgue. *Hardly a predicament in which I expected to find myself*, he thought. Jewell had been an Immigrant Inspector with the Treasury Department for all of four months.

As if reading his mind, the attendant, a squat, copper-haired fellow with the map of Ulster stamped all over his brogue, said, "First time with a corpse, hey?"

Jewell shook his head. "No, but it's been years." He didn't mention the fact that this was his first opportunity to do anything besides sit behind a desk and copy forms in the regional office since he'd been posted to Seattle three months earlier.

"And why, pray tell," the attendant continued, "comes a Treasury man to claim this Chink?"

"Ask your cousins among the bulls about that one," Jewell

replied drily. It was 1889, and Washington Territory stood on the cusp of statehood. The Irish, among the first non-Anglo-Saxon immigrants to the region, had set about doing in Seattle what they had done in such large Eastern cities as Chicago, New York, Philadelphia, and Boston: filling the ranks of the local constabulary. Seattle's tiny police force numbered right around twenty men; split almost evenly between Sons of Erin and Norwegian immigrants.

The attendant reached beneath his filthy apron and retrieved a pipe and tobacco pouch. "Wouldn't touch a Chink, hey?"

Jewell shrugged. "Where did they find him, again?"

The little Irishman struck a match, touched it to his pipe, and puffed a couple of times while pulling back the sheet where it covered the corpse's lower half. Squinting at the tag attached to one big toe, he read haltingly, "*South shore . . . Mercer Island . . . half-mile west of Clark Beach.*" Straightening up, the man said, "No wonder our city fellas wanted nothin' to do wi' this one. Mercer Island's unincorporated county, not city turf."

"The King County Sheriff disagrees. Says the currents running through south Lake Washington pass right by the city proper, and that's most likely the place where the corpse originated. Says he's too busy and hasn't enough deputies to put on the case of—"

"A dead Chink," the Irishman finished for him. "McGraw's no Chink hater. Gave a fair account of himself a couple of years back, during the Queen business." He said it as if he expected the younger man would be familiar with the reference. He wasn't.

But Jewell nodded as if he was, thinking it must have something to do with the Chinese troubles with the local

Knights of Labor back in '86. "So, since this fellow is obviously a foreigner, the city and the county decided that this becomes a federal matter, and they contacted my office. My superior in turn fetched me and sent me down here to take possession of the poor unfortunate." Steeling himself not to vomit, he motioned for the attendant to pull back the sailcloth tarpaulin covering the body.

The dead man had obviously spent a lot of time in the water. His eyes were gone, and his features so bloated that it was difficult to tell whether he was Chinese, Indian, even white. Jewell stepped closer to get a good look at the cold, quiet lump of mortality laid out on the plank slab like a feast on a trencher.

The Chinamen Jewell had seen before, both back home in New York and during the three months he had spent in Seattle, had all worn their hair in the same manner. They completely shaved the front, sides, and back of the skull, leaving only a circular topknot along the crown of the head: grown long and braided down the back.

The naked corpse before him sported a similarly shaven head. There was, however, no topknot to speak of. This man's hair was far shorter, and lay in a loose halo about his head, as if to draw attention to the deep, jagged cut that ran from ear to ear along his throat. The only other injury that Jewell could find on the body was a missing right pinky finger. Bloating caused by the corpse's watery sojourn made it impossible to discern how long its owner had gone without the finger. Old wound or new, Jewell had no idea.

Lake Washington had done equal damage to the corpse's remaining fingers, expanding them to the size of sausages. These appendages sported long fingernails, blackened by what Jewell had come to recognize as prolonged opium use.

"Poor devil," he muttered. "How do we even know he was Chinese? See?" he pointed at the corpse's head. "No pigtail."

"Likely cut off," the Irishman said. "Big insult to the Chinks, cuttin' their hair. Did ye mark how the rest of his hair is cut like a slant's, though? And," he said, pulling a canvas bag from one of the shelves that lined the walls of the gruesome little room, "he was wearin' these when they found him."

Jewell inspected the contents: heavily wrinkled black trousers and an equally bedraggled red tunic, both of Oriental design and obviously made of silk.

"No shoes, no hat, no other possessions?"

"He'd washed around in the lake for a while, captain."

"These clothes are not much to advance upon. Aside from arranging for a burial up on Capitol Hill, I'm uncertain as to what other service I or my office can be of in this matter."

"Lovely fabric, silk," the little man said.

"I hardly think—" Jewell began.

"Strong," the morgue attendant went on as if he hadn't heard. "Holds a design or a dye better than most other fibers. Oh, I'll allow that it shrivels right up and looks an ungodly mess if it's gotten too wet, just as this Chink's togs have. But look." He held up the red silk of the dead man's shirt for Jewell's inspection. "It's even got the poor soul's laundry mark right here inside the collar."

"A pauper's grave over in Lake View is the only place this is headed." H.M. Porter looked at his new gold watch, wound it, then returned it to the pocket of a vest so expansive, ten dead Chinamen might easily have hidden within it.

H.M. (short for "Hamilton Menander") Porter, a Treasury Department agent of countless years' service, and for exactly two more days head of the territory's Immigrant Inspection

Division, stretched his considerable bulk backward in the chair he'd had shipped west by Sears, Roebuck, and Co. the previous year.

"Dead Chinaman; in the water since the great fish swallowed Jonah. No one's reported a Chinaman missing; ergo, no one cares."

Jewell stood staring out the window of the single-room clapboard building that had housed the territory's sole Immigration Inspection office since it had ended its previous incarnation as a dry goods store the previous winter. Like nearly every other Seattle street, Seventh Avenue was unpaved, rutted, and prone to turn into a morass when it rained.

But that spring of 1889 had been unseasonably warm, especially for Seattle. Many an old-timer had remarked upon the unlikely pleasant weather they'd been having. Now the first week of June, Seattle's infamous late-spring rains showed no signs of reasserting themselves in their wonted seasonal patterns.

When Jewell had arrived in the city only a short three months before, the street on which their window faced had been home to the usual assortment of rivulets, puddles, and wagons stuck here and there in mud up to the axle. And "puddle" was too tame a word, a poor choice of descriptor for the standing rainwater that by turns eroded and covered the byways of Seattle's primitive urban grid. Horses had been lost in them. Pigs had gone squealing in them. Drunks had been fished from them. Children had been known to drown in the intermittent quagmires that dominated Seattle's streets.

Looking out upon the sunlit street from the musty confines of what was rapidly beginning to feel like a prison to him, Jewell balked at the thought of even three more days spent shuffling papers. He might as well just be locked up in the iron cell that occupied one corner of the building, the place where illegals were held while awaiting deportation. After Porter's retirement things might be different, but at the moment, two days felt like an eternity.

"It's a laundry mark, sir," Jewell said. "How long might it possibly take to pursue it in the Chinese community?" He looked from the street over to where Porter sat waiting out the remaining hours until his retirement. "Besides, they're Chinese. Just where would they have been able to go to report one of their number missing?"

Porter reached for his new watch again, looked longingly at it, as if willing the minutes to go by more quickly. "Immigrant Inspectors are not to involve themselves in local civil matters."

"Perhaps you ought to have thought of that before you sent me down to collect the body, sir."

Porter gave a sigh so violent that for a split second Jewell thought he might be having a seizure. Looking at his watch a third time, the older man said, "If only Clute were here. He'd know what to do."

Clute. The man Jewell had been sent to replace. The fellow whose abrupt resignation had reportedly been greeted within the hallowed halls of the Treasury building back east in Washington City by a satisfied and protracted silence.

Clute, who had an answer for everything. Clute, whose efficiency and commitment to his profession had allowed Porter to commence his life as a pensioner a couple of years early in everything but name. Clute, who understood and respected the Celestials who Immigration Inspectors were supposed to be encouraging to return to their homes in China. Clute, who had left his letter of resignation on Porter's desk and promptly vanished.

"But Mr. Clute isn't here, Mr. Porter. I am. In scarce two days' time you're to be pensioned off. In the three months I've been here you've had me hard at it, mastering the intricacies of our particular bureaucracy. This is an opportunity for me to gain some experience working outside of our office, while I still have you as a source of advice. Your sagacity and good counsel will be sorely missed once you've returned home." That last part was sheer flattery. Porter had done little over the past three months save arrive late, take long lunches, and leave early. "Why not make the most of this opportunity while I still have you here?"

At first Jewell thought he might have overplayed his hand. Porter sat there staring at his watch for a number of heartbeats. At length he asked, "Where's the body, anyway?"

Jewell blinked once while Porter's question registered. "They need a day to release it. Paperwork, I was told."

"You're hell-bent on following this up, aren't you, lad?"

"In this man's shoes I would want my mother to know what became of me." When Porter said nothing, he continued, "It's the Christian thing to do, sir."

Porter gave a loud rumble that might have been a chuckle or it might have been a grunt. "The Chinese," he said slowly, "seem to know very little of either Christianity or sentimentality. In China, life is a cheap commodity. This fellow's family likely wrote him off the day he set out for *Gum Shan*"—he used the Cantonese name for America; it translated as "Gold Mountain" in English. After pursing his lips and squinting at Jewell for thirty seconds, Porter finally said, "If I forbid you to pursue this, you'll just wait out my remaining days and then set about it on your own anyway, won't you?" Rather than wait for a reply, Porter sighed and looked at his watch again. "You have one day, young man; all of today and till 12 noon on the morrow. I expect you here not one jot later. After all, there's still the matter of the collection of that body."

When Jewell began to thank him, the older man cut him short.

"I can spare you the rest of today and tomorrow morning, but nothing further. Do I make myself clear?"

Jewell savored the feel of the sun on his face as he headed downhill in the general direction of Chinatown. No clouds today; the sky bright blue. Off away to the west across the Sound the jagged snow-capped peaks of the Olympics showed themselves. Gulls reeled and swooped overhead, looking for their next meal.

Taking the Skid Road, Jewell wove his way in and out of the foot and wagon traffic to be expected on so glorious a June afternoon. Known alternately as "the Mill Road" and "Yesler's Drive," the Skid Road was the first (and, to that point, only) paved street in town.

Built at public expense at the direction of former mayor Henry Yesler in order to more easily get freshly cut logs downhill to his huge sawmill on Front Street, the Skid Road ran straight down Seattle's steep western slope all the way from the timberline where it crested First Hill to the fill-dirt of the waterfront. Surprisingly, Yesler's primitive plank pavement did its work, serving as the "skid" that gave the avenue its name, and keeping logs being sent down the hill from sticking fast in the ever-present Seattle mud.

Such a reliable thoroughfare quickly sprouted residences and businesses running along both its sides. The Skid Road already boasted saloons, general stores, two millinery shops, a carpenter, a tinker, a hostelry, a cobbler on the corner of Fifth, and, at the foot of the hill, the elaborate cornice work and hand-carved façade of the three-sided, three-story Occidental Hotel stood on the corner where James Street dead-ended into it right in front of Yesler's massive mill.

This growth had made the Skid Road the anchor of Seattle's burgeoning downtown, and had spilled over onto neighboring streets, such as the spot a block to the north where the significantly pious whitewashed bulk of Trinity Church rose. As far as Jewell knew, Chinese were not welcome within. Furthermore, not a single business lining Seattle's busiest street was Chinese-owned.

The first Chinese to come to the area during the labor shortage of the late 1850s had been welcomed by Seattle's white settlers. When businesses began to fail in response to the panic of 1873 and available jobs dried up, Chinese laborers, always willing to work hard for lower pay than white men, became less welcome. Anti-Chinese riots periodically broke out across the Northwest, culminating in the Knights of Labor successfully running nearly two hundred Chinese out of Seattle aboard a steamer bound for Victoria only three years earlier.

In the time since then, most of the Chinese still residing in Seattle had been pushed out to the south end, clinging to a few blocks between the businesses downtown and the Duwamish mud flats that ran east from Elliott Bay right up to the foot of the craggy, flat-topped escarpment that the locals called Beacon Hill. Washington Street bordered Chinatown on the north, and since the mud flats were just spitting distance south from it, Seattle's Chinese population of between three and four hundred found itself crowded into the narrow space between.

While many of the neighborhood's structures were single-story frame affairs like most of those occupying the slopes of other areas such as Capitol Hill, First Hill, Belltown, and Magnolia, Chinatown's buildings doubled as both businesses and tenements, with living quarters in the back for both owneroperator and staff. The Chinese had been known to sleep ten men and more to a room. According to the records with which Porter had kept him so busy, no less than twenty-seven Chinese houses occupied the block of Washington Street that ran between Second and Third alone.

Because the Scott Act of 1882 had made it almost impossible for more Chinese to get to Gold Mountain, Seattle's Chinese denizens tended to be American residents of long standing. Since the Scott Act further effectively barred all women of Chinese extraction from entering the country, the overwhelming majority of the neighborhood's residents were male. Rare indeed was the sight of a woman of any race in Chinatown.

Jewell had once wondered aloud why these men, barred by state and local laws from working mining claims or owning mineral rights, bothered to stay in a country so different from their own, and so far from their homes.

"The Chinese can make more money in one month doing white men's laundry and laying railroad ties in Gold Mountain than they can clear in a year at home," Porter had told him. "That's why they stay. They put in their time here and go back home to much fanfare from the family they've supported for the past ten or twenty years."

These thoughts occupied Jewell during the fifteen-minute walk down the hill to where Yesler's big frame house dominated the northwest corner of the intersection of the Skid Road and Third Avenue. From there he turned left and walked down Third to where it met Washington Street, and crossed over into Chinatown.

The mark that Jewell had copied down when the attendant had pointed it out to him that same morning vaguely resembled a square with a single slash running through it top to bottom, at a slight left-to-right angle. Seattle had five Chinese-operated laundries, all of them on the block at the heart of Chinatown.

It was the work of another twenty minutes to show this design to the owners of the first four out of the five of these establishments. Nothing but blank stares and muttered, "No Englee."

Jewell had begun to wonder whether he had really just embarked on a fool's errand when he entered the last Chinese laundry on the block; the southeastern most one, sitting as it did on the corner of Third and Jackson.

The unmistakable odors of lye and bleach assailed his nostrils as he opened the door. The place was small, hot, and clean, the boards along the top of the walls and the entire ceiling turned a dull gray by who knew how many thousands of gusts of bleach-riddled water vapor. Stacks of neatly folded clothes lined shelving that ran the length of the back wall. A large cast iron pot, water bubbling in it, sat in one corner surrounded by piles of multicolored clothing.

According to the clerk, a slightly built Chinese youth barely five feet tall, a man named Louie Chong owned the establishment. He had gone on a long journey to someplace called "Gwongdong." The clerk professed no idea when Louie Chong could be expected back in town.

Jewell flashed his Treasury badge. "What's your name?"

"Me?" the boy piped in a prepubescent voice. He couldn't be older than fourteen.

"You."

The boy pointed at his own chest. "Louie Gon."

Chinese put the family name first, Jewell thought. *This is a relative. A younger brother, a nephew, a cousin, or a—*

"Son," the boy said as if reading his mind. "Louie Gon." He pointed at himself again. "Son . . ." he paused as if searching for the right word, "to Louie Chong." Then again, more sure of himself, putting the words together: "Me Louie Gon. Me son Louie Chong."

Having gotten that out of the way, Jewell held up his sketch of the laundry symbol he'd seen at the morgue that morning. "You know this mark?"

The boy leaned forward and squinted. His bone structure was finer than that of most Chinamen. His features were different too; not as flat as those of most Chinese, with a pointed chin. His hair, shorn at the sides and front, like that of most of the Chinese Jewell had seen, was glossy black and tightly wound into a long braid that ran down his back and out of sight. The youth's clothes were an odd mix of East and West. He wore gray woolen trousers and a black silk, Oriental-cut shirt. No customary black cloth slippers on his feet, though. Heavy, square-toed brogans completed his wardrobe.

The youth straightened up with a jerk, recognition crossing his baby face. Mouth hanging open, head shaking in the negative, he backed away from the long wooden counter that separated them.

"What's the matter?"

The boy shrugged. "No see that mark before."

"Have you a mark ledger?"

Another head-shake. "Keep all marks here." He tapped the side of his head. "Nothing written down. We busy. No time flip through big book."

"I'll need to satisfy myself as to that," Jewell said, making his way to the end of the long counter.

The youth blocked his path. "We no have book!" he repeated, voice rising into a near squeak. "Louie Chong no like customer behind counter! Him beat Louie Gon for letting you back here!"

"And what do you think the Treasury Man will do if you don't?" Appalled at the regrettable necessity of using strongarm tactics with a member of the community he was trying to help, Jewell continued, "Now stand aside and allow me to have a look around, short-leg."

The boy turned and fled. Before Jewell could react, he had flung open a cupboard on the room's back wall, snatching up exactly the sort of long leather-bound book Jewell had just been asking about. Recovering from the shock of the youth's unexpected move, Jewell sprang after him, catching the fellow by his braid just two steps shy of the backdoor.

The boy gave a squawk and began to flail his arms and legs about wildly, shouting in frantic, high-pitched Cantonese. Jewell hauled him round so he could look him in the face. "Listen to me." Exasperation lent a further edge to his tone. "A man is dead. You savvy 'dead'?"

The boy tried to bite him for an answer. They struggled further. Jewell got between the youth and the backdoor. No sooner had the two of them faced off than a gong sounded loudly somewhere within Jewell's head, lights cascaded in a thousand glorious colors before his eyes, and then the world went black.

An hour later Jewell's ears still rang, and a knot had begun to rise on the back of his head. By the time he'd regained his senses there in Louie Chong's laundry, the little Chinaman and whoever had hit him on the head were gone.

So was the ledger over which they'd struggled.

Porter was unmoved when Jewell reported his lack of progress to him. "Told you it was a waste of time," he said. Then he'd suggested Jewell go see Chin Gee Hee. "If he can't help you locate those two, no one in Seattle can."

Chin Gee Hee was the best labor wrangler in Seattle, and a leading member of the remaining Chinese community. A resident of the territory for over twenty years, Chin had come to Seattle a decade previously, bringing a wife over from China and starting a family upon their arrival.

On that terrible day when most of the Chinese in Seattle had been rounded up and forced down to the docks in preparation for deportation, Chin's family had been among them. It was a testament to the amount of respect he commanded among Seattle's old guard that he had been able to talk his way into both staying and keeping his family in town. No question, Chin Gee Hee had pull, and not just with City Hall, but within the Chinese community as well. Rumor had it that he was also the eyes and ears of the Chinese Consulate down in San Francisco.

If you were Chinese and you wanted to work, Chin was the man to see. If you were white and wanted to hire Chinese labor, Chin was also the man to see.

He ran his business out of a brand-new building on the southwest corner of Washington Street and Second Avenue. Jewell found him there, seated at a roll-top desk pressed into a cramped spot along the back wall of the single-room structure. It took some doing to arrange to speak to Chin, because the place was alive with Chinese; customers and tradesmen, Chin's employees and white contractors seeking labor.

In his mid-forties and a bit above average height for a Chinaman, Chin had thinning hair, a ready smile, and was dressed in rough Western work clothes, complete with square-toed, heavy-soled boots. No braid, no shaven head, no silk clothing. With a battered broad-brimmed hat perched on the back of his head, he looked the part of the prosperous Western businessman he was.

"Always happy to help honored Treasury Man," he said with a disarming grin after reading the note of introduction that Porter had scribbled for Jewell. They shook hands, and Chin offered the younger man a seat.

Chin's open face clouded when Jewell mentioned his quest for information regarding a laundry owner named Louie Chong. "Louie Chong not good man," he said. "Hock tell me when I first come here, 'Stay clear Louie Chong.' Not easy to do. Louie Chong bad man, but good customer."

Jewell asked how to spell the name, and as he wrote it down, asked who Hock was.

"Business partner, Chin Chun Hock. We come from same village in Gwongdong."

Porter had mentioned nothing about a business partner. "Oh, I was under the impression that you owned this place," Jewell waved his hand to take in the entire building, "outright."

"I do. Hock old business partner. I once own twenty-five percent of his company, Wa Chong. He buy me out last year."

"May I ask why?"

"Many reason. Final and most important on his part, he no want to stay in employment business after riot in '86."

"And you?"

"Opium," Chin murmured. "Not write that down, not report that. Hock want to sell opium here. I want no part of that. We dissolve partnership; I start up Quong Tuck Company last year."

"And Hock knows Louie Chong well?"

"Better than me. Louie Chong come from our village too, but he older, I do not know him there. Those two know each other long time, though. Why you ask?"

Jewell told him about the body found washed up on Mercer Island, the laundry mark on the man's tunic, and his attempts to track the mark in Chinatown's laundries. He showed Chin the sketch he'd made of it.

The man's eyes widened. "Triad mark," he whispered.

"What is a triad?"

Chin placed a hand on Jewell's arm, looking around the shop, motioning for him to keep his voice down. "Criminals. Smuggle opium, girls, whatever you like. That mark the sign of the Red Dragon of Macau, very powerful triad."

"Why would anyone use such a symbol as a laundry mark?"

"No Chinaman who see that going to mess up order on shirt." Chin cracked a lopsided grin at his own wry joke. "Louie Chong work with them."

"He's a member?"

"No. He work with them, though. Louie Chong smuggle for them. Long time ago. No more. Now run laundry."

"Did you hear that he has gone to Gwongdong?"

Chin shrugged. "Porter tell you I know everything happen in Chinatown, eh? I do not. No hear about any trip for Louie Chong. Who tell you that?"

"His son."

"Son? Louie Chong have no son."

Jewell blinked, then recovered and said, "The boy who works in his shop. Calls himself Louie Gon."

"Ah. Louie Gon not son. Louie Gon *mui tsai*."

"What is . . . 'mooey jooey'?"

"*Mui tsai*."

"Mooey jai?"

Chin shook his head, smiled again, and said, "Louie Gon paper son. Son on paper. Only Chinese merchant and their son can go back and forth between Gold Mountain and China, so many merchant sell paper to other people they not know, saying, *This my son, represent me,* and that get new Chinamen into Gold Mountain."

Jewell frowned. "Well, he didn't want me to see the ledger where his boss kept track of laundry marks. Is it possible that the boy's killed him and gone into business for himself?"

Chin laughed. "Louie Gon? Oh, no. Louie special case. No kill anyone."

"He put up a pretty good fight with me when I asked to see that ledger."

Chin laughed again. "He get away from you?"

"Someone fetched me a pretty rough blow on the back of the head while we struggled. Dazed me for a bit. When I came to my senses, I was alone in the place. Mr. Porter suggested I see you about it."

Chin removed his hat and absently stroked the thinning hair on top of his head.

"Is Louie Chong a habitual user of opium?"

Chin nodded.

"So was our dead man. Had the stained fingertips and nails to prove it."

Chin considered that for a moment. Then he said, "All ten fingers stained?"

Jewell shook his head. "He was missing his right pinkie finger."

Chin nodded decisively and said, "You go home now."

"What? Surely you don't mean that. I have—"

"I see to this problem. I fix for you."

"What is your interest?"

"No more excuse for riot here," he said. "Seattle good city. My neighbor good neighbor. No talk of triad or *mui tsai*, Chinese murders done in local newspaper. I handle it. You let me. I bring you solution." Chin looked from Jewell to an ancient grandfather clock against the wall behind him. "After 5 now. You go home. I bring you everything tomorrow."

And just like that, the interview was over.

A game of whist with the other boarders at his rooming house hadn't helped the evening go by any more quickly for James Robbins Jewell. He'd passed a sleepless night in the unseasonable heat waiting for dawn and an answer to the question of whether or not Chin would keep his word.

The walk to the office the next morning was uneventful, as was the morning routine of unlocking the backdoor, then the front, drawing the blinds, and looking over his desk for any pressing correspondence or other sort of paperwork in need of his immediate attention. It was only when Jewell sat down and happened to glance in the direction of the cell that took up one corner of the large room that he realized he was not alone.

An unkempt, bearded white man, black-haired and dull-eyed, half-sat, half-slumped against the opposite wall. He looked neither right, nor left, and took no notice of Jewell, not even when he attempted to speak to him. He was dressed in a ragged Chinese silk tunic and corduroy workmen's trousers, with Chinese slippers on his feet. His fingernails bore the telltale signs of frequent opium use.

"Who are you?" Jewell asked.

The man ignored him.

"Why are you in the cage?"

The man kept silent, his blank stare unchanging.

A double-folded and sealed note with the word *Porter* typewritten on it lay on the floor in front of the cell. As Jewell stooped to pick it up, he muttered, "If this is from Chin, why is it addressed to my boss, not to me?" It was 8:30. Over the next half hour Jewell considered breaking the seal at least once per minute.

"Ran afoul of a *mui tsai*, did you?" Porter said when he'd finished reading the note. It was five minutes past 9.

"According to Mr. Chin Gee Hee, I did."

"You've done nice work on this, boy. Nice work, indeed. Perhaps I've misjudged you."

"I fail to see how I've done anything of the kind. If this 'mooey jai' killed our Chinaman, then who is the fellow in the cage? Why does he resist any attempt at communication?"

"The fellow in the cage is the killer of our man, and that man is without doubt Louie Chong. The *mui tsai* played no part in this except that of victim, poor thing."

"But then why did this 'paper son' of Louie Chong's fight me so hard to keep me from that ledger?"

"Paper son?"

"Yes, the 'mooey jai,' that's how Mr. Chin translated the name: called him a 'paper son' in English. Claimed it was a reference to some false identification scheme running rampant through China."

"A *mui tsai*," Porter said, "is not a son of any kind. The phrase *mui tsai* in Cantonese means 'slave girl'."

Jewell's jaw dropped. It all suddenly made sense. The slight build, the odd cast of the boy's features, the piping voice.

Porter went back to perusing Chin's letter. "Chin's old partner Chin Chun Hock runs an opium den in the basement of his establishment. The bulls know about it. As long as they get their cut, they turn a blind eye to it, shrug it off as being part of the degenerate Oriental culture. Time was when part and parcel of that den was a brothel stocked with Cantonese girls brought over here by the triads. Chin bought their freedom as part of his deal to leave Hock with the lion's share of the profits from their partnership. But Louie Chong had pull with the triad, and he'd already bought one of the girls to keep for himself. He passed her off as a boy working in his laundry. You can imagine how else he used her. It was common knowledge among the Chinese. I told you that their notions of charity are not the same as ours."

"So why did this fellow," Jewell motioned with his head in the direction of the cell and its occupant, "kill Louie Chong and dump him in Lake Washington?"

"Who can say? Some sense of chivalry, perhaps?"

"I doubt that. Look at the poor wretch. He's an opium fiend if ever there was one. And where is the girl?"

"She's gone. Chin didn't mention what's become of her, but I have no doubt that she's not to be found within the limits of King County this morning."

Jewell sat thinking for a moment. Porter watched him intently. At length Jewell said, "I didn't see any of it."

Porter shifted his bulk in the Sears, Roebuck, and Co. chair. "You knew which questions to ask, just not which answers to listen for. But you've shown promise I didn't think you had in you. On the other hand," he said as he reached for his pocket watch and began to wind it, "Chin did tell you everything you needed to know in that single conversation. You've come a long way in three months, but if you're going to be *the* Treasury Man in these parts, you've still got quite a ways to go before you're ready."

"Yes sir. Apparently I have much to learn," Jewell said, chastened.

"Just remember this: it's also possible to go too far, to be too good at your job. It's a tricky, tricky balance. Don't go far enough and you can't understand them and you won't get anything constructive done. Don't get the work done and you risk losing your position. Go too far and you risk much more. There's a lot more at work in Chinatown than meets the eye."

"How do you mean?"

Porter motioned with a broad hand past Jewell's shoulder in the direction of the cell and the wretch who occupied it, the man turned completely inward, focused on the wreckage of a last opium dream.

"That," he said glumly, "was once Sebastian Clute."

THE MAGNOLIA BLUFF

BY SKYE MOODY

Magnolia

I

Before his star rose Skippy Smathers worked the carney circuit. He always played the dwarf clown. At thirteen he joined Carneytown Circus and right off the bat they made him a solo act. He'd been clowning in that show ten years when one night on a slippery tightrope Mel the Diminutive Man stepped into his life. The way it happened was some kind of kismet.

It happened under the big top in Walla Walla, Washington. Walking the highwire, Skippy lost balance and toppled off, tumbling for a chaotic eternity, pitching and falling until finally he landed with a broadside bounce in the mesh safety net. It wasn't the first time Skippy had plunged from a highwire, but this mishap, more topsy-turvy than most, jarred his nerves. Floundering in the net webbing, panic-stricken, Skippy's fear paralyzed him while the crowd roared: "Go back up! Sissy clown! Go back up!"

He wore a costume of baby clothes, a frilly bonnet, a grease-pencil baby face. The crowd saw an overgrown infant, not a twenty-three-year-old terrified dwarf. Jeers and hisses rained down. But he wouldn't go back up there. Couldn't. He sat in the net bawling as the crowd booed the frightened clown-baby.

"Booooo." "Sissy Pants!" "Dumb midget!" "Booooo!"

In the wings, Mel the Diminutive Man heard the rude

din. Grabbing a long baton Mel stepped onto the tightrope, regal in his leotard and tights, a natural born star. The spotlight swung to the tightrope, the crowd naturally rolled their eyes up to the sleek, pixie-like man stepping into the glare. Balancing his weight with the long baton Mel performed slow pirouettes along the tightrope, distracting the audience, while in the net below Skippy foundered in fear's lap. Somewhere a drummer tickled cymbals, adding to the tension as Mel the Diminutive Man captivated the awestruck crowd.

No longer the focal point, Skippy gradually recovered his nerves, scrambled over to the ladder, up the tightrope, and set a seasoned foot on the taut line. One cautiously arched step after another he moved toward this dark stranger, this apparition, this highwire angel offering his tiny hand. A breathless moment later, Skippy touched that hand to thundering applause.

Mel grinned at Skippy and quipped, "Way to go, sport."

Mel's first brush with an audience earned him a standing ovation, but he reacted with scorn and revulsion. After all these years of inventing Mel the Diminutive Man, he had squandered his debut on this claptrap crowd.

II

It was 1973. Mel was twenty-one and had been living off Ma all these years because she insisted her pixie was too delicate for work. When Ma died of exhaustion Mel worried about what would become of him, but not for long. Under Ma's mattress Mel discovered a fortune in nickels and dimes and quarters that she had squirreled away over the years of hard labor. Her accumulated pocket change would have choked a Coinstar.

Mel fled their rat-infested Yesler Terrace housing project,

bought a spanking new Cadillac convertible, and floated over the Magnolia Bridge into the Village, where he parked in front of Leon's Shoe Repair, ignoring the gawking Magnolians—Mel was probably the first dwarf to ever set foot in the neighborhood—and crossed McGraw Street to Magnolia Real Estate, where he and his bank balance were greeted with equanimity and a firm handshake to seal the transfer of a Magnolia Bluff house deed for cold cash.

Signing and initialing each contract clause Mel noted the bigotry: *Property transfer and residency are restricted to Caucasians.* Forgetting his own place in society, Mel signed it. Had Ma been above ground, she would have slapped him silly. Mel reasoned it was her fault, anyway, her making him rich.

Mel moved into the prettiest house Dahl ever built on Magnolia Bluff, whose namesake cliff plunged shamelessly into the crotch of Elliott Bay, ogled by the hoary Olympics Brothers, envied by eyeballing tourists from the Space Needle's observatory. To keep him company he replaced Ma with orchids. Certainly his snooty neighbors had no interest in fostering friendship. In fact, they actually shunned him, as if a dwarf neighbor was something to be ashamed of. They would cross the boulevard to avoid him. They never invited him to their fancy estates, and whenever Mel attempted neighborly gestures they would recoil, stammer incoherently, and flee. Except for Joy. His neighbor Joy was the only Magnolian with the guts to befriend a dwarf.

Joy lived in another Dahl house with a city view you'd slit your throat for if you had the bucks to buy it. A regular-sized lady, Joy had jazzed hair and a perfect figure in 1973, was still young and nubile and freshly divorced from Hubby #1. Mel misinterpreted Joy's neighborly gestures. Thought Joy had the hots for him. So he made a pass and she slapped him so hard he spun across her living room like a child's top spinner. Even so, they would remain friends through the years. Most of them anyway.

When Mel complained to Joy about the way the other neighbors treated him, Joy said, "Hey, quit your whining. You wouldn't have lasted five minutes on the Bluff back in the glory days." And she told him how it was growing up in the early Magnolia days, back in the '50s and '60s when the rich discovered God's Chosen Neighborhood.

Over the Magnolia Bridge in those glory days journeyed famous architects and interior designers to build and embellish fine estates for their feathered clientele, Mrs. Danforth Pierce-Arrow, Mel's next door neighbor, now in her dotage, being one, and Mrs. Neil Robbins being another. The Robbins were Jewish. Jews—even Catholics, as long as they could afford to—were permitted to own homes on Magnolia Bluff, although generally speaking Protestants were preferred. And no colored people, no, no. Magnolians, said Joy, feared and loathed diversity, but back in those days they didn't call them bigots. Just rich.

On many a day, Joy told Mel, Mrs. Danforth Pierce-Arrow, who's Episcopal? And Mrs. Robbins, being a Jewess? They would come into the Magnolia Pharmacy at the same time. Maybe nearly collide at the prescription counter? Never exchanged more than a polite nod. Joy saw this all the time growing up in Magnolia.

Mel remarked, "At least they recognized the other's living presence. Whenever I come upon Mrs. Pierce-Arrow or Mrs. Robbins they just tilt their noses and pretend they don't see me. Mel, the Invisible Man."

"Will you ever get over all this self-pitying?" said Joy.

Joy. A regular-sized person who'd grown up in luxury and privilege. How could Joy ever empathize? But she was still reminiscing on the good old days:

Over the Magnolia Bridge came the serving classes, housemaids in crisp uniforms overlain with thin cloth coats, shivering alone at bus stops in darkness on winter nights, snow drifting up to their bare knees before a bus agreed to stop. And the Carnation milkman who always entered homes through the *Deliveries* door or the *Housestaff Only* door, removing his boots before restocking, say, Mrs. Pierce-Arrow's fridge with glass bottles of milk topped by two inches of thick cream, along with fresh butter and eggs still warm from the nest. At Christmastime, Mrs. Pierce-Arrow would leave the milkman an envelope tucked discreetly into the fridge's egg section.

And over that glory bridge came roofers and plumbers and electricians to tweak the infrastructure, guaranteeing that all the Mr. and Mrs. Pierce-Arrows and Robbins and even the Catholic families with their unplanned children enjoyed the security and comfort of upper-class loos and hearths. Nothing like crime ever transpired on the Bluff, Joy told Mel, unless you counted when the Marvel family's colored maid was caught red-handed with Mrs. Marvel's sterling silver flatware, family heirlooms. The maid insisted she was carrying them into the kitchen for polishing. But Mrs. Marvel fired her on the spot. That was the biggest crime scandal on Magnolia Bluff in those early days, unless you counted three-year-old Dougie Marvel's appearing naked in teenaged Annie Quigley's bathroom. Annie, naked in the tub, screamed. And then the summer when little Kathleen Pierce-Arrow got caught playing touch tag with young Neil Robbins. Back then, that was about as criminal as things got.

And, too, the sacrosanct Magnolia Bridge delivered upper-class men like Joy's Husband #1 in sleek automobiles from their luxurious estates into the city's languishing heart, where they doctored and lawyered, ran their banks and visited their clubs, and wouldn't hesitate to drive right over the drunk Indian weaving against the stoplight.

"Back long ago?" said Joy. "What they call Magnolia now? It was an island. Separated from the mainland by a brackenishy slough. When the city's rich folk saw the potential out here, why, they filled in the slough and built the first bridge onto the island."

"Why did they name it Magnolia?"

Joy shrugged. "It was a mistake Captain Vancouver made back in history. See—"

"I'll bet Captain Vancouver hated midgets."

"Mel, how many times have I told you not to refer to yourself and others like you as midgets? You are a dwarf, a small person. You are not a little fly."

"I hate myself."

"Oh, stop whining. In my heart you're bigger than me."

In her regular-sized heart.

Then one day, less than a year after staking his claim in God's Chosen Neighborhood, Mel received a call from his banker. "Your account has five dollars left in it," said the banker. "You want us to apply that to your monthly fee?"

Having exhausted his inheritance on the house and big floater car, Mel needed to "work," a word only whispered by his neighbors. But he had no real training in any kind of work. Desperation unleashed a flash of genius. He invented Mel the Diminutive Man, learned the tightrope, and joined a traveling carney act. Joy told him, "One day, you'll be a star, Mel. In my heart, I know that."

Mel made his public debut in 1973 on that fateful evening in Walla Walla, Washington, when he rescued the famous carney dwarf Skippy Smathers from disgrace. And then Skippy Smathers rescued Mel from financial ruin, moving into Mel's house and paying monthly rent. Mel regained faith in his future.

When Mel introduced Joy to Skippy Smathers, he felt their instant chemistry. Joy broke Mel's heart the day she and Skippy wed, Mel standing as the best man. All along wondering to himself, *If Joy is okay with dwarfism, why did she choose Skippy over me? I've got more man in me than Skippy has in his little digit.* Meaning finger.

III

While Skippy mounted Joy's bounteous gifts, Mel spent three years solo, pampering exotic orchids in the solarium of his showcase home, waiting for his friends' marriage to fail. After the divorce, Mel and Skippy teamed up again, and this time they rode their dreams to Hollywood.

In Hollywood, Skippy's star skyrocketed, while Mel's career never took off. Skippy played the little man in every stage and film production where a dwarf counted, while Mel languished in his pal's burgeoning celebrity shadow.

Mel, destined to play the extra. Mel, destined to lose every casting call to Skippy. Destined, it seemed, to live off Skippy's earnings, while he propped up the star's fragile psyche. It wasn't a proud destiny, and Mel was a proud man. But destiny, like a fickle friend, can turn in the wink of an eye.

They never actually moved to Hollywood. Personally, Mel would have preferred moving from Seattle, fleeing God's Chosen Neighborhood. Mel wanted to live in Los Angeles, in that house next door to Jack Nicholson, the house he had always dreamed of owning. Overlooking Hollywood's glitz and glamour. That's where Mel knew he belonged. But Skippy balked at the idea. Skippy was afraid of Los Angeles. As if Los Angeles was a dwarf-eating monster. And Skippy always got his way.

Twenty years passed. Mrs. Pierce-Arrow got crushed by her dumbwaiter and her son Danforth III now occupied the Pierce-Arrow estate. Neil Robbins married Kathleen Pierce-Arrow, they placed Neil's parents in a luxury senior complex and now occupied the Robbins nest. Mrs. Marvel, a crotchety crone still lived in the Marvel estate and her servants came and went. Annie Marvel married, had a bunch of offspring, converted to lesbianism, and fled the Bluff.

As the century turned, the bigotry clause disappeared from real estate contracts but that didn't mean it disappeared from some Magnolians' deep-seated preferences. Persons of color and dwarfs received a friendly nod at Tully's but rarely got called over to join a table of fat cats. Nothing much had changed in God's Chosen Neighborhood.

IV

Mel was lounging on the patio chaise reading *Variety* when he heard "the Sound." The rubber butt of Skippy's walking cane thudding on flagstone made Mel cringe. Skippy had adopted the ornate cane as an iconic eccentricity. Thought it made him look debonair. Mel thought it looked ridiculous. A dwarf with a cane.

Mel glanced up. A blue PGA cap shaded Skippy's face but Mel could sense a sullen pout. Skippy's arms overflowed groceries, the cane poised to thud again. Sighing, Mel set *Variety* aside and went to help. Mel carried the groceries into the house, Skippy and his cane gimping along behind.

This limp was something new.

"What's wrong now?" Mel asked tiredly.

"Awful bad news," grumped the gimper, missing Mel's reference to the new limp. "If you really want to know." Skippy paused to emphasize the awfulness, then blurted, "No call back."

Mel clucked his tongue. "Tough luck, sport." He thought about bringing up the new limp, but why bother? Skippy would complain about it before long. Mel fed the groceries into the icebox while Skippy hung in the background, a broken shadow watching Mel work.

Stars don't put away groceries.

"Henry Chow's getting the part." The broken shadow spoke bitterly. "That's what Lana thinks. Like she was Henry's agent exclusively. Like she didn't even represent me. Talk about a two-faced, double-dealing opportunistic . . ."

When Mel didn't comment, Skippy limped into the breakfast nook and slid onto a sunstruck bench. Warm sunshine cut through a windowpane, washed the fine stubble on his babyface cheeks, refracting into tiny dots that danced along the wall. Skippy tried batting the dots away. When that failed, he flung his golf cap at them. It landed squarely on Mel's fresh orchid centerpiece. Mel's signature, Mel's pride. Skippy gazed disgustedly out the window.

Mel brought tall glasses and a pitcher of iced tea with frost dripping off it. When he poured, he didn't spill a drop, that's how fastidious he was. Skippy needn't have disturbed the flower arrangement, Mel thought. The least Skippy could do is pick the golf cap off the orchids, put things right. Where were Skippy's manners? Maybe stars don't need manners.

Skippy's tight lips blew light ripples across the iced tea's crown. He sipped, scowling, and said, "That role was tailor-made for me."

"M-hmm." Noncommittal.

Skippy persisted. "It doesn't compute. Henry's never played a clown before. This film's about an aging dwarf clown. Henry Chow doesn't know the first thing about playing a clown. I know clowning. I should have that part."

"Maybe they wanted an Asian."

"Oh, nothing's definite yet." Skippy sounded slightly hopeful. "It's just Lana's professional gut feeling that Henry's got it wrapped up. Anyway, if he gets the part, it's not because he's Asian."

"Then why?" Mel was only half listening. He wanted that golf cap removed from the orchid centerpiece, and he wanted Skippy to have the decency to do it. Was that asking too much?

"Because Henry's shorter than I am."

"That's not so. You're shorter than Henry. They probably wanted an Asian. You know how politically correct Hollywood is these days. Lana Lanai's the worst of the bunch."

Skippy was adamant. "Asian has nothing to do with it. If Henry gets this role, it's because he's shorter than I am. Now."

"What's that supposed to mean?"

"I'm growing, Mel."

The way Skippy said it, so serious, so . . . melodramatic, Mel couldn't help laughing. "Ha ha. That's bull."

Skippy reached across the table and touched Mel's sleeve. Lightly, to fix attention on what he was going to say.

"It's true. I've noticed it. You know it sometimes happens to a dwarf. Mid-life hormones get wacky. My hormones must have kicked up. I'm growing, Mel. Real fast."

Mel smirked.

Skippy insisted. "They noticed it. Must have. Or else

Henry Chow did and pointed it out to them. I wouldn't put it past him and I'm worried sick. This growth has happened over the last six weeks. Too fast. I'm fifty-three, for chrissake. It's not normal."

"But not unheard of in dwarfs. You said that."

Skippy passed a hand across his brow, reminding Mel of Tallulah Bankhead, then said, "Oh God, I'm scared. I'll never work again. And I bet you noticed it before. You must have noticed my limp. You did, didn't you?"

Mel nodded solemnly.

"Oh God, I'm finished."

Softly, Mel said, "What's the limp all about?"

Skippy had parked his cane on the doorknob. He retrieved it and walked back toward Mel. "See? When I use the cane, I limp. That's because I've grown. Just since I bought this cane two months ago. Cost me a bundle too, cherrywood with all this frippery on the handle. Now it's already too short for me. So I limp. If this keeps up, I'll soon be too tall for the good dwarf roles. I'll never get work again. Not even as an extra."

Something dark flickered in Mel's eyes, and Skippy instantly regretted his remark. "Geez, I'm sorry," he said. "I've been such a lucky son of a gun, and you always ending up an extra. All I meant was, my luck's changing. That's all I meant by that."

Mel laughed and grabbed Skippy's head like a football, wrestled it, ruffling the soft silver curls. "It's great," he chuckled, "just great. I like it. A growing dwarf. It's hilarious, really. You should try it out on Nick down at the Magic Castle."

A horrified thought struck Skippy then. He flung himself away from Mel. "You don't believe me," he cried. "You don't buy a word I said."

Mel stared. Skippy fled the room.

Sighing, Mel gently removed the blue golf cap from his orchids. Apparently stars have the right to ruin centerpieces. Mel took his iced tea outside and finished reading *Variety*.

That night Mel made frozen lime daiquiris with dark rum, placing a fresh orchid on top of one. He knocked on Skippy's door, heard a grunt, and went in. Wide awake, enveloped in darkness, Skippy sat stiffly upright on his canopied bed. Mel set down the daiquiris and jerked the heavy drapes aside. Moonlight poured into Skippy's cluttered, musty room. Skippy blinked, averted his eyes. Mel pushed a loud chintz chair up to the bed, climbed onto it, retrieved the daiquiri with the orchid, and held it out to Skippy. Skippy waved it away.

"C'mon, take it, sport. My peace offering."

Skippy sipped the frosty apology, licked his lips, and said, "I fell asleep for a while. I dreamed that Henry Chow died in an awful accident on the SLUT. They found his body floating in Lake Union, all covered with Satan's hoof prints. The train had derailed."

Mel aimed a remote control at the flat screen. Crazy colors flashed. Cacophony galloped into the room, riding a loud car chase across the high-def panel.

Mel muttered, "Henry Chow's an ass."

V

The next morning when Skippy woke, first thing he saw was the depressing saffron sky. He had no reason to get out of bed, so why was Mel rapping insistently on the bedroom door? Skippy sat up and yelled, "Go away! Don't bother me!"

The door opened a crack. Through the space came Mel's velvet voice. "Better get dressed, sport. We've got company."

It sounded like a warning. Grumbling, Skippy burrowed

into the sheets, but the scent of coffee brewing, of bacon broiling, eggs frying, wafted to his nostrils. Mel was so clever. He'd left the bedroom door slightly ajar so these delicious aromas would tempt Skippy. Sleep was impossible now. Skippy grumbled and rolled out of bed.

The table in the breakfast nook wore an aqua linen cloth and Mel had folded the napkins into swans. The good plates and Skippy's mother's sterling flatware were laid out. An artfully arranged fresh orchid centerpiece seemed too flamboyant. This table was celebrating something, Skippy thought, and then he saw Lana.

Perched on the bench, lumpy Lana sat at Skippy's place, and with one of Skippy's mother's forks she picked at Mel's home cooking. Mel stood on a stool by the stove flipping fried eggs. When Lana saw Skippy, she called out cheerily, "Surprise, surprise!"

"I don't like it," grumbled Skippy. "I don't like surprises at breakfast."

Mel smiled. "Why, Skippy, you're up! Good, good. Lana's got some great news."

Lana flicked her wrist, dangling her bejeweled fingers. "Come, sweetie. Sit, sit."

Begrudgingly, Skippy took a seat at the table. Mel waltzed over and poured Skippy coffee, then danced back to the stove.

"What's this all about?" Skippy demanded.

"All about you, sport," Mel bowed deferentially. "Your Eminence," he crowed.

"Stop clowning! Stop it this minute. Can't you see I'm out of sorts?" Skippy waved an arm at Lana. "You're the last person on the planet I care to see right now. What are you doing here anyway? I didn't invite you." He shot a furious glance at Mel.

Through the rudeness, Lana said, "Don't you want to hear the news, honeybunch?"

"Hey, don't call me that. I'm your gravy train. Why don't you just call me Gravy Train. Anyway, I've already heard the news from Henry Chow," barked Skippy. "I know he's got the part."

A prickly grin crossed Lana's face and for a moment Skippy thought that Lana Lanai might actually possess nerve endings. Still, when she picked up her coffee cup, watching Skippy over the brim, he didn't like the expression on her face.

Draining the bacon grease, Mel sang, "Tell-l-l him-m-m, La-an-a-a."

"You got the part."

Skippy stared, not daring to believe his ears. Lana scooted over and embraced him. She may as well have embraced a cigar store Indian.

Mel sang, "Skippy Smather-r-r-s starrrrring in . . . . *Standing Ta-a-all.*"

Skippy stammered, "Is . . . is it . . . is it for real?"

"Hey, would we pull your leg?" Mel grinned devilishly.

Lana purred, "It's not exactly on the dotted line yet, but I spoke with a production assistant this morning who overheard the producers talking. They were discussing you, raving about your great talent, your charisma, your magical screen qualities, your b.o.a."

Box office appeal.

Skippy batted his hand at her. "I know, I know, I know." She didn't have to dote. He despised doting.

Mel arranged breakfast on the table, climbed into his chair, and said, "Hey, I'll bet they didn't even notice. I mean, about the growing spurt."

Skippy felt his stomach churn. He jumped off his chair and fled.

The following afternoon, in Lana Lanai's Hollywood office, the star paced anxiously. His walking cane made dull thudding sounds against the plush carpet. Mel sat on a long couch leafing through *Vanity Fair*, trying to ignore Skippy's irritating third footfall. You'd think by now he'd have learned how to walk with that stupid cane. Across the room at the desk, Herself held court.

Two slick-buff film producers leaned over Lana's chaotic desktop, their Mont Blancs poised over contracts. Mel wanted to snicker out loud. They were all alike, diminishing youth, Bosley hairlines, faceless personas consumed with star envy, converting their filthy riches into control—power—over the gifted artist. Exploiting the artist. Growing rich off the artist's sweat, the artist's inherent talents. Sure, they'd invest in a dwarf's box office appeal, but would they take him out to dinner? Anyway, who remembers a producer's name in the credits? It was all Mel could do to contain his loathing.

Skippy limped over to Lana, stood on tiptoe, and whispered into her jaded ear. Lana nodded tiredly and waved him away. Skippy retreated. Lana smiled antiseptically at the producers.

"There's just one more detail," she said. "The understudy is to be Mel Rose. That is, should anything happen to Skippy. Which is totally a nonissue."

The men with remarkable hair glanced up in unison, and in unison they said, "We don't have understudies."

"In this case, you'll have Mel Rose. Or no Skippy Smathers."

The producers gaped. One said to Lana, "You're kidding," and Mel heard derision.

Lana snickered in a way Mel didn't like. "Otherwise, gentlemen, Skippy won't sign."

The producers huddled, conferring in earnest whispers.

Finally, one said to Lana, "We'd counted on Henry Chow. If anything happened to our star, we'd made Chow our second choice. Everyone's seen it that way. Skippy or Henry in the lead. Of course, we might find a bit role for Rose."

Lana shook her head and studied her acrylic nails.

"Consider our position," argued one producer. "We need really, really great talent in this role. We need a really, really brilliant actor."

Mel really, really hated them.

Lana didn't budge. "It's Mel or no deal."

Eventually Lana got her way. She usually did. She knew how. When all the contracts had been revised and initialed and signed, all the insincere handshakes wrung, Lana flung open her office doors to the entertainment media. Bee swarms made less commotion. The Hollywood press doted over Skippy. Fawned over him. Even the producers pawed Skippy now, and Mel noticed one of them pawing Lana. Totally ignored, Mel buried his face in the *Vanity Fair* and waited for it all to blow over.

On the way to the airport, in Lana's limo, Skippy and Mel were sharing a split of champagne when Mel heard Skippy mutter, "God, I'm terrified."

"He's not that bad," replied Mel, referring to the limo driver.

"I mean something else. Don't pretend you haven't noticed."

Mel said, "Lord help us, what now?"

"My limp. Getting worse all the time."

"Translation, please." Mel rolled extra brut around in his mouth.

"I'm still growing. I've completely outgrown my cane."

"Tsk. Then buy another," retorted an exasperated Mel. "Better still, give it up. It's so phony."

"You still don't believe me." Darkly.

"Hey, Skipper, would you just quit all this obsessing? You got the role, didn't you? If you want to worry about something then worry about the first day of shooting. There's something to obsess over."

Skippy stared out the window. "I went to see a doctor. About the growing."

"And?"

"Got as far as the reception desk and panicked. Ran out of there."

"Good Lord have mercy."

"What if they notice?"

"I'm telling you, it's not that noticeable yet. You've still got some time before it'll really stand out."

"Then you have noticed it."

Mel sighed. "Maybe a little. But it's too slight to get worked up over. Hey, sport, settle down. Look out there. That's Hollywood, baby, and it's all yours."

The thorny subject was not raised again until the first week of shooting, when Skippy came home for a visit, limping up the drive. As usual, Mel was lounging on the chaise reading *Variety*. When Skippy got close enough, Mel saw the deep frown. He put down the magazine and went to fetch Skippy's luggage.

Mel grabbed the suitcase out of Skippy's limp hand. "Now what?"

Skippy leaned hard on his cane. "They've got the Little People's Chorus in the scene we shot today? You know Ruby Lee, the lead singer? I ran into Ruby on the set and she commented on how I seem different since she last saw me. I asked, 'Different how?' Ruby Lee said I looked taller. Then this afternoon Lana visited the set. Said she'd noticed I was growing.

Just like Ruby Lee. Lana said if I didn't stop growing, the producers would drop me. I don't know if the director—"

"Autry noticed it too."

Skippy missed that it wasn't a question but a statement. He said, "According to Lana, Autry told her they can't be re-making costumes every five minutes, and besides, he said, an overgrown dwarf's no good to anyone. Lana says that includes her. Those were her exact words. Then, in a flash, I had this vision of my future. They notice me growing even taller. They drop me from the film. I can't get work. No one wants me anymore. All along, they only wanted me for my size. Lana's right. No one will hire an overgrown dwarf. Not in this business. I'm through, Mel. My career is finished."

Mel put a hand on Skippy's shoulder and said, "Lana called about ten minutes ago. I'm afraid she had some very bad news."

Skippy turned pale. "Autry?"

Mel nodded gravely. "There was an escape clause. Something about a change in your appearance being grounds for nullifying the contract." Mel sighed.

Skippy began sobbing.

Mel said, "What you need, sport, is a cocktail. Now, come on inside, let me fix you a daiquiri. And if it's any comfort, we already have enough stashed away for retirement. The world is not coming to an end."

Skippy turned and ran out of the driveway. He ran all the way to Joy's house. Joy met him in the front yard. A hose in Joy's hand sprayed water on her geranium bed. Joy's long feet were bare and her hair had new extensions. She leaned down and kissed Skippy's cheek, and the first thing she said was, "Skips, are you wearing those platform shoes again?"

"What makes you say that?"

Joy wrinkled her nose, looked him up and down. "You seem taller." She stood beside him and compared Skippy's height to hers. "Yep," she declared finally. "You're growing, Skips."

Skippy cursed and, pushing Joy aside, stormed into her house, raided the liquor cabinet, and locked the gin and himself in her bedroom. Joy heard the door slam and the lock snap into place.

At 10 p.m., Joy finally managed to convince Skippy through the barricades that under no circumstances would she spend the night on her own living room couch. Skippy unlocked the door. Once inside, Joy cleverly displayed her still-considerable charms and Skippy soon succumbed. Just for old time's sake. Around midnight, loud voices in the foyer interrupted them. Joy lit a cigarette and said, "Amy's got a new tattoo."

"So?"

Joy drew on the cigarette, watched it burn. "It's on her tush," she murmured, but Skippy wasn't listening. His bright eyes darted in the semidarkness, faster and faster, until Joy quipped, "Skips, you're plotting again. I can tell."

That night, Skippy Smathers hung himself from the chandelier in his bedroom.

VI

On opening night, Mel the Diminutive Man played the lead in *Standing Tall*, played it deftly, with brilliance and flair. Critics praised Mel's grace in the face of losing his friend, Mel's courage in walking the Great White Way for Skippy Smathers. In the wink of an eye and at long last, Mel's star skyrocketed.

He was in the backseat of a limo, coming home from the airport. He was alone because, besides the late Skippy Smathers, he didn't have any friends. Not the kind you'd want to be seen with in public anyway, with all the Hollywood kleig lights on full blast. Mel was drinking the whole split by himself and basking in his celebrity when suddenly, for no reason at all, he thought of Skippy's walking cane.

The house in God's Chosen Neighborhood seemed inadequate, pathetic, really, no place for a meteoric star like Mel. At long last he would move to L.A. Maybe snap up that cool house he'd always coveted on Mulholland Drive. The orchids would love it.

The limo's headlights washed the patio. A car was parked in the driveway. Mel paid off the limo service and walked up the drive. Joy Smathers greeted him.

Joy was lounging on the patio chaise, reading a newspaper. When she saw Mel, she looked up and smiled. "Mel, you're home. I've been waiting for you." Joy stood up, folded the newspaper, and tucked it neatly under her arm.

Mel stared.

Joy's smile twitched. "Why, Mel, aren't you glad to see me?"

"What's the meaning of this?"

"I wanted you to know."

"What? Know what?"

"I figured out how you whittled Skippy's walking cane down little by little. To make him think he was growing. When all the time his cane was getting shorter. It fooled everyone. Even me. You figured that sooner or later, what with Skippy's fragile psyche, it would drive him over the edge. Sooner or later Skippy would despair, maybe commit suicide. That was your plan, wasn't it, Mel?"

"What are you . . . ?"

As if suddenly inspired, Joy blurted, "Did you know that Captain Vancouver named Magnolia Bluff erroneously?"

Mel shook his head.

"Aren't you curious why he did?"

"No."

Ignoring him, Joy explained: "Captain Vancouver discovered this part of the world, you know. And he hated everything about it. Hated the rain and the fog and the Indians . . . I'll bet he hated dwarfs too."

"Make your point."

"Because Captain Vancouver mistook the bluff's madrona trees for magnolia trees." Joy broke into a wide smile. "It all comes down to wood, doesn't it, Mel?"

Mel placed a hand to his forehead.

"This might interest the media," said Joy. "Or the gossip columnists. I mean, about these cherrywood shavings I found in your orchid plants. Oh, I almost forgot to mention . . ."

"Can it, Joy."

Joy shuffled around, a tap dancer at heart, then froze. "To be frank, Mel, it mortifies me to catch you doing something so despicable."

Sweat bathed Mel's brow.

Joy said, "See, I took the rubber cup off the bottom of Skippy's cane. And I saw. It's locked up in a safe place now. I mean Skips's cane. Or what's left of it. See, I figured out what happened underneath that little rubber cup—"

Mel came at Joy, but swift Joy produced another talisman that drew him up short: the *Seattle Times*, tomorrow's early edition. Joy had folded the front page to emphasize a small headline: *Second Autopsy Reveals Star Dwarf Smathers Was Growing.*

Skippy's photograph accompanied the story.

Joy touched Mel's sleeve. Lightly, to fix attention on what she was going to say. From her regular-sized heart.

"If only you'd been patient, Mel. If only you hadn't whittled down his cane. See, I talked to Skippy's doctor and figured it all out. You didn't believe him, but something had gone wacky with his pituitary gland. It sometimes happens to a dwarf, you know. So the tightrope had already been greased." Joy smiled ever so gently. "You didn't need to push him." Joy stretched to her full height, reached down, and plucked Mel's house keys from his trembling hand.

"Come," said the woman in control of Mel's destiny, "let's go indoors and decide on a price for this sweet little Dahl house. I think we should put an offer on the Pierce-Arrow estate, don't you?"

SHERLOCK'S OPERA

BY LOU KEMP

Waterfront

I t was a quixotic message carved into the side of one of his cows that drew Sherlock Holmes from his farm in Sussex, England to Seattle. The cow tended to move during the carving, so I had removed its head. The carving read: *Jacob Moriarity.*

I'd rigged the cow to explode upon examination, but having faith in Mr. Holmes, I knew he'd not only survive, but would eventually dissect the cow to find a somewhat wet edition of the *Seattle Daily News.*

Of the several newsagents I had perused in America, the *Seattle Daily News* possessed the most colorful attention to lurid details.

Within the pages there appeared pictures of bewildered policemen and well-to-do couples dressed in morbidity and curiosity. The over-bright exposures of the corpses provided a nice touch. Given both the allusions to the supernatural and the country's fascination with Ouija boards and charlatans, I thought the piece more than worthy.

Confederate Colonel Seeks Revenge!
Seattle police are urging the good citizens of the city to stay indoors after dark. A killer, with a more voracious appetite than this writer's Aunt Cecile, has been dining, quite literally, on the citizens of Seattle. No one is saying so officially,

*but several witnesses report seeing a ghostly figure, dressed
in full Confederate uniform, fleeing the alleyway behind
John McMaster's store on Oak. A partly devoured body
was found there the next morning by Oliver Prindle in his
disreputable milk wagon. On the evening of February 4,
a similar occurrence was reported, nearly a mile away on
1st Street behind the livery stables. Again, the Confederate ghost was observed hiding like a dog in the shadows.
The body found there wasn't whole either; it was missing
both legs! From what your trusty reporter has discovered,
similar murders occurred earlier in the year. But we, The
Public, were not informed of these heinous crimes by our
city policemen.*

What do you suppose Mr. Sherlock Holmes did after dry-
ing off the article and reading it? I imagine he clamped his
teeth around his pipe stem, nearly biting it in two. Coarse
language would have been on the tip of his tongue, but being
the Victorian gentleman, I assume he refrained. The name
Moriarity was enough to ruin his digestion for days. Not to
mention the cow's.

But to business. Within a day, he would have used his
dunces at Scotland Yard to gather information on the Seattle
killings. He would have heard of the useless efforts to catch
the killer. How many policemen would enjoy chasing fanatical
ghosts? One in ten? Three in fifty?

Certainly within the next two days he assembled various
disguises, acquired a quantity of cocaine for the road, and
headed off to the docks in Liverpool. Once there, he would
have boarded a ship bound for New York. He doubtless inquired about recent departures for America, and then spent
an inordinate amount of time in his cabin pouring over the

manifests of other ships. He also would have brought along all his files on John Moriarity, his arch enemy. To be sure: in some dark and filthy corner of his mind he could admit to himself his crimes! He had pushed my brother over the Reichenbach Falls to his death (it was *not* suicide, Mr. Holmes!).

The celebrated sleuth would then have turned his attention to the other family members.

Would there be a photograph of me? Perhaps the American authorities in Boston (that hellhole) could find one. But the best likeness could be found in Moriarity's effects, if Sherlock Holmes cared to investigate. He would hear of my early genius (a doctor by the age of twenty) and the jealous comments concerning my experiments. The mystery of my public disappearance should tantalize him like the scent of an unseen wisp of tobacco.

Finally, on a stormy day in March 1889, the afternoon train steamed into the station on Railroad Avenue, bearing confidence men, Bible-thumping preachers, prostitutes, and Mr. Sherlock Holmes.

I almost missed him. For years, I had been aware of his finesse at disguise and mimicry. Once, I'd seen him masquerade as a woman, albeit a rotund woman. And I'd of course heard of his famous frolic of impersonating a dance hall performer. Sometimes I wish I'd spent a more active role in tracking the man. But back to the story—I will try to avoid further digressions.

Propped against the wall just to the right of the ticket counter, I held the *Daily News* in front of my face. Like one of the casualties of the recent Indian wars of the West, I appeared to be missing a leg and the will to live. Occasionally I would groan to demonstrate my pain. A tin cup before me awaited donations.

Thin slits in the paper, between an advertisement for Murberger's Hair Oil and an anatomically incorrect article on gout, allowed me to track Mr. Holmes as he meticulously made his way across the crowded boards toward the street. My, what an impressive disguise. I whistled an aria under my breath, ascending and descending in minor keys. Celebration, celebration! The cymbals clamored and the violins rejoiced. My prey passed by so close, I could have gripped his ankle. While the music whispered within me, I admired his disguise.

In a bushy white wig and matching Mark Twain eyebrows, Holmes shuffled along tapping a gold-tipped cane from side to side. He peered through thick spectacles as if examining the ground for ants.

Music, sweet music. There, he has bought a newspaper.

I crawled around the corner of the building. To the consternation of several prim citizens, I reversed my coat and put both legs into their respective pant legs, then hurried to the street. Following Mr. Sherlock Holmes to his new lodgings would be exquisite. I brought him here, after all.

As I strode by, Holmes tucked the newspaper under his arm. The headline blared: *Prohibitionist Mary Jones Cartright Latest Cannibal Victim!*

Holmes hailed a cab. I faded into the crowd and watched until his carriage rounded the next corner.

Would he read of last evening first? A most logical killing it was.

Insanity and music. How many times have I heard that refrain?

Music is a rainbow of color born of undeniable honesty. Have you ever bathed in a melody that caressed your senses until your skin tingled and you forgot to breathe? The music would release you, each tone fluttering, alive. The notes would bow, complimenting each other, joining in a blood tie of temporary harmony. In playful ecstasy or destructively lyrical, the notes have substance. Whenever the music demands, I obey.

It rained heavily that night, drenching me in anticipation. The raindrops fell like bullets in a fast staccato, drowning out the boulevard traffic. But in the alley behind the Orpheum Theatre, the music could still be heard.

Minor keys bled aloud, speaking of human misery. Each time the notes would tremble and wail, I felt their pain, always connecting, never holding.

The air held a winter chill that seemed alive in its own right. I leaned against the dirty wall and waited. Steam rose from the heating grates. Rats with hot eyes scurried for dry places while the blues wallowed in the darkness, asking me to stop the pain.

The woman entered the alley like a cat sniffing cream. Her steps hesitant, she drew closer. When she saw me, the caution vanished. Mary Jones Cartright, angel to the downtrodden, had spent years working with the whores and demented relics of the war. The music lamented with impatience. Soon, she stood before me smelling faintly of roses.

Without a word, I obeyed, thrusting the knife upwards, carefully avoiding the kidneys and liver. Drink had never passed her pristine lips.

Into the dark passages the music rushed, sinuously sliding and scheming, violating the walls of reason.

I heard a saxophone bleat from a saloon across the street.

Yes, I accept applause.

The next morning dawned blurry, like peering through a veil of snow that would never melt. I wallowed in the luxury of knowing that time had conspired to bring my emotions and desires to this day. If I knew my brother's nemesis, he would be awake. Heavens! He might even be afoot already.

I arrived too late at the Tate Hotel. A tall man in a disreputable tweed coat and reeking of pipe tobacco had hailed a carriage not five minutes ago. Holmes had assumed his natural appearance, although the doorman did not know it as such.

"Which direction did he go?" I asked, with a coin visible between my fingers.

The doorman snatched it away, flipping it into the air. "You mean the hop-head old Limey? He told the cabbie to take him to the Orpheum."

Ah. I dropped an extra coin between his shoes and disappeared.

From the other side of the brick wall, I could see the top of Orpheum's sign. With peeling paint and broken windows, the theater looked as frayed as an elderly dance hall queen in the light of early morning. I lay still, able to hear quite clearly the conversation from the other side of the wall.

". . . Certainly I did, Mr. Holmes. The chief heard from the mayor too. Bless his heart."

Sounds of footsteps, then a match scratched the bricks and lit. The smell of sulfur is pleasant in the morning.

"Sergeant Gordon?" Holmes asked. The man must have nodded, because he continued, "In the envelope in your pocket, you'll read of my credentials. You'll also read why we are most likely not dealing with a cannibal." His voice turned disdainful. "No matter how romantic the thought."

"I've read them," came Gordon's grudging reply.

A cockroach crawled from an empty tin in the refuse at my feet. When it reached the ground, I plucked it like a blueberry.

Did you know their legs tickle and wiggle all the way down?

Holmes's voice sounded dry as he continued: "Moriarity is dead. But his brother is not. Jacob Moriarity is a highly trained scientist. He has lived in Seattle for years. Are you aware of that, sergeant?"

"Humph. I'll take yer word for it. We've never collared him for anything."

I could imagine Holmes's shrug as he answered, "I doubt that he will give you a chance. He is . . . By the way, would you be so kind as to ask your men not to trample the area leading to the doorway there?"

"Why?"

"Footprints."

I smiled and the music soared. Holmes was taking the bait perfectly.

Gordon grumbled, "Maybe so. I'm not so convinced that tells you anything."

"Tell me about the victims. Specifically their backgrounds," Holmes requested.

In the pause that followed, I could hear the traffic from the street, the squeaking wheels of the carts, and clop of horses' hooves.

"What are you doing there, Mr. Holmes?" Gordon asked.

"Examining the body. The other victims?" Holmes prompted.

"Well," Gordon hesitated, or perhaps he was just observing the great detective. Either way, it was a careful moment before he spoke. "There's been two college boys. One local, strong as an ox. Captain of the track team—"

"If I remember correctly, his legs were missing?" Holmes interrupted.

"They were, and half his ass too."

"Ah ha!" Holmes exclaimed quietly. I could barely hear him as he said, "Give me that bag, would you?"

"Here. What is it?"

"A clue," Holmes replied, probably to Gordon's consternation. Holmes added, "It's half of a pay bill from Fisher's Butcher Shop." He grunted. "Where is that establishment located?"

"Southwest of here, over by the docks."

"Interesting," Holmes murmured.

Gordon retorted, "I am sure it is to you, Mr. Holmes." After a moment, he added, "I'm more interested in where our fool photographer has got to." I heard Gordon walk up the alley a few steps, then return in time to hear Holmes's remark.

"No matter. The body speaks, as it were, from the grave."

"Pardon me?"

"Observe," Holmes said. "No, don't block the light . . . There."

"All I see is where an animal tore this woman's guts out."

"It was not an animal. Look under this flap," Holmes instructed. "Do you see the precise cuts? The liver and kidneys were removed. Surgically."

"Son of a bitch," Sergeant Gordon murmured.

"Perhaps," Holmes commented.

I felt a brief flash of rage. Then the music soared once more; a beautiful distraction to dispel the anger.

Holmes continued: "He used something to tear the flesh and other organs, camouflaging the ones he removed."

"I can see that now," Gordon replied. "Like what you dig with in the garden?"

"Possibly. Hand me that bag, would you?"

"Never saw anyone really use a magnifying glass," Gordon said. "What do you see?"

"Particles of rust. Excellent observation, sir. This could have been done by a garden claw," Holmes said. "Now, I'll hold back the flesh. The tweezers are in my pocket . . . Ah. Thank you."

Silence. Then I heard them get to their feet.

"Satisfactory," Holmes announced. "I want to go over the ground here. Would you be so good as to ask your men to obtain dirt samples from along the alley and the other side of this wall? Have them beware of footprints. I would like to know if he entered the alley any other way than from the street."

I had deliberately dropped the other half of the pay bill from Fisher's where I hoped a bleary-eyed copper would find it.

Following clues like a bloodhound with blinders, Sherlock Holmes entered the docks later that day.

I followed him, driving a coal cart and blending in with the neighborhood roughs. By the time he approached old Wayland Billings, chief gossip and drunk of the neighborhood, I had urged my nag into a trot and arrived before him.

Shoveling coal down the shoot next to Billings's shack, I bent my ear to their conversation. Doubtless, the owners of the residence next to Billings would feel fortunate at their unexpected windfall.

"Good afternoon, my dear sir," Holmes addressed the disgusting form of Billings as if he were the mayor.

Billings grunted at him and scratched his privates.

A fine dusting of snow blurred the scene between us as Holmes removed a pint from his pocket. "No matter the afternoon, if we can warm it up, eh?" He offered the rye to Billings. Faster than he could blink, old Billings guzzled half of it. Then he cast a doubtful eye on the detective. I resumed shoveling coal as the sweat on my face froze in the air.

"What wassit you wanted?"

Holmes wheeled to point a long finger at Fisher's Butcher Shop. "By chance, have you seen a man of short stature, who drags his left leg, enter that establishment? He would weigh approximately 130 pounds and be somewhat, ah . . . ill kept."

I watched Holmes. He observed Billings like he would an insect in one of his experiments. When the rye had trickled down Billings's neck and his Adam's apple bobbed for the fourth time, Holmes said, "Well, sir?" Billings just returned the stare as the detective continued, "The man I seek most likely wears a blue watch cap and habitually eats fish and chips. Do you know of such a man?" Of course Billings did. He knew who gave him enough pennies for an evening's happiness. But it appeared I had underestimated his loyalty.

"What do you want him for?" Billings drawled with a glint of avarice in his eye.

Holmes nodded. "A good question, he . . ."

Billings caught sight of me over Holmes's shoulder. He didn't flinch under my gaze, though I could see a tick begin to flutter under his left eye.

"Don't know him!" Billings shouted. "Get out of my way." He shuffled down the street, casting persecuted glances over his shoulder at Holmes. Perhaps he did so at both of us, since I stood just beyond the detective and behind the coal cart.

Holmes waited until Billings rounded the corner, sidestepping two policemen and an irritated horse, before following him.

"Ah. Come in, Mr. Holmes," I called. The music flitted quietly with anticipation.

The basement door had creaked. Sitting as quiet as death, while the day turned to night, I knew each sound intimately. Moonlight filtered down from high windows like a mist, illuminating the room. Recently slaughtered cow carcasses hung in row after row, the ribboned fat glowing in the moonlight while the blood dripped crimson to the straw on the floor. The door opened another scant inch. I saw a shadow beyond it.

"Please, come in," I said. I'd waited so long for this moment. Was it not fitting I should fork his queen while checkmating him? Yes. Logic dictates not just a move, but a reward.

A thin hand gripped the door and it swung open. With the light behind him, I could not see his features . . . Something seemed odd. He was of the expected height, yet . . . there was something amiss. He seemed to have an enormous development of the frontal lobes. Familiarity . . .

As he started down the stairs, the moonlight struck him fully. The music trembled in my ears.

I couldn't believe it. I blinked again. In an instant, confusion turned to rage and the music roared.

"NO!" I shouted. The bastard. The ultimate bastard!

Holmes had assumed his final disguise, that of my dead brother Moriarity. From the dandified brocade vest, to the wire-rimmed spectacles, curled wig, and penciled brows, he *was* Moriarity. He affected his walk. He even swung his head from side to the side in the same reptilian fashion.

"Jacob?" Holmes asked. "Is that you?" The music intensified. He *sounded* like him. "Oh, brother dear? Come out where I can see you."

I covered my ears. *He can't do this.* The music grew angrier.

"Jacob?" Holmes repeated. He gained the basement floor. "Weren't you expecting me?" He sounded reproachful.

Rage shook me. I lifted the revolver and drew a bead on

Holmes's back. But he turned, and even though he couldn't see me, he smiled. It was my brother's smile.

"I heard a click, perhaps from a revolver?" Holmes teased. "Would you shoot *me*, Jacob?"

The pain inside my head competed with the storm of music. It became a cacophony, screaming down without harmony, without pity. I tried to hold the gun, yet even with both hands, it wobbled.

Holmes stooped and came up with a lantern. He sat it on the butcher table. I heard the scratch of a match. The light hurt my eyes, and I backed further into the shadows. Holmes kicked at the bloodstained straw at his feet.

"My, this place is filthy. I'm surprised at you, Jacob. You are a scientist, not a carver of meat," Holmes scolded.

I watched him investigate the tables, the drainage pipes, and then the trash bins. He seemed as unconcerned as a fawn that I would shoot him.

The music complained of cowardice.

"But you are a scientist, aren't you, Jacob?" Holmes said. He'd reached a long ice box with many compartments that lined the back wall. I heard him wiggle the lock on one of the clamps. "Locked? My, my. Dear brother. What is inside?" Holmes inquired.

He waited a moment, and then began a stroll down the aisle near me. Circling closer.

"Body parts? Am I not correct?" Holmes queried. "Why, I wonder," he mused as he fastidiously ducked under a carcass and sauntered toward me. The lantern in his hand swung with his walk. One second he was a faceless enemy in shadow. The next, he was Moriarity. Music, sweet music.

I raised the gun.

The music moaned. I wavered, and then lowered the gun.

The pain deep in my head throbbed and with it the vision of my brother turned dim. Then the music returned with a plaintive vengeance, bleating furiously.

I could not think, so I retreated behind the butcher tables.

"There you are!" Like we were playing a childhood game, Holmes gave a triumphant shout and trotted forward.

I raised the pistol and fired. The shot went wide and plowed into the carcass beside his ear. The impact blew the haunch apart, splattering him in raw flesh.

"Stand back!" I shouted.

Holmes wiped gore from his face and said, "Why, dear brother?" He took another step forward.

Close up, I still couldn't believe the likeness. From the color of his eyes, to the way he pursed his lips, he was John Moriarity.

The music quivered inside me. Could it be?

"John?" I whispered.

Holmes threw back his head and laughed.

The music exploded and I grabbed my forehead.

"Why did you murder those people?" he asked. Through my fingers, I could see Holmes as he inched closer. The revolver felt hot in my hand. "You took the best of what they had. Strong legs, artistic hands, healthy organs. Why?"

I couldn't hear him above the music anymore. His lips moved. He was my brother.

"You're building a man, aren't you? A perfect man," Holmes stated.

Involuntarily, I glanced at the ice box and then fixed a stare upon him. The music slowed. It quieted, waiting. Gentle notes calmed me. This was what I wanted, had planned for. Breathe and victory is mine. I could see clearly again.

"Yes," I answered, pleased that my voice did not quiver. "A perfect man."

"And you brought me here because . . . ?" Laughter erupted from me. I could not stop it.

The release started in my gut and built up inside of me until tears streamed down my face. Through it I screamed at him, "You're the genius! Your celebrated *brain* has brought you here! What do you *think* I want?"

Holmes frowned. I saw a flash of uncertainty cross his face. The music pulsed like a heartbeat within me. It was time.

Deliberately, I lifted the pistol and fired. The smoke blinded me. I fired again.

In his haste, Holmes dropped the lantern. The straw around us caught, then burst into flames.

"Damnation!" I screamed.

In an instant, the room was ablaze. From below, the flames licked the carcasses, scorching them until they looked like disembodied and grotesque ghosts. Smoke billowed everywhere. As the music skittered and fragmented, I turned toward the ice box, then back toward the stairs—then back again toward the ice box. I stumbled through the black smoke. Under my hands, the ice box sweated in the intense heat. Fumbling, fumbling, finally I had the first compartment unlocked, when I heard Holmes's voice in my ear.

"Come along, Jacob. I can't let you burn in your own hell," he intoned.

As I struggled, he threw me over his shoulder and hastened for the stairs. When I looked back, the music solidified, taking form.

Holmes cried, "If you die, Jacob, it will be at the gallows!" He tightened his grip on my legs as he dashed through the conflagration, pausing only to vault over burning debris.

As he ran up the stairs, I looked again for my brother.

In the flames, I saw the music building, bleeding in colors up the walls. John Moriarity stood in the flames, wearing his secret smile.

He held a baton. Conducting, of course.

The mournful notes dripped like rain, hissing into the fire and lamenting my name.

FOOD FOR THOUGHT

BY G.M. FORD

Pioneer Square

T he address turned out to be one of those Oriental rug shops down in Pioneer Square, one of those joints that, depending upon which banner hung in the window at the time, had either lost its lease, gone bankrupt, suffered smoke and water damage, or was just now in the process of retiring from the business . . . for the past twenty-five years or so.

A broken bell sounded as I used my knee to separate the warped door from the frame. The door came loose, shaking in my hand like a palsy patient as I looked around the place. Awash with piles of brightly colored rugs, folded back, strewn this way and that, the space smelled of dust and desperation. Movement at the back of the room lifted my eyes.

He was a short little guy, bald as an egg and shaped like one, seated at an ancient desk, up to his elbows in paperwork; he glanced up, immediately made me as a noncustomer, and went back to his paper shuffling. I ambled along the central aisle.

"You Malloy?" he asked, without looking at me.

I said I was. He sat back in the chair. His hard little eyes ran over me like ants.

"You don't look like a private eye."

"It's a cross to bear."

He considered the matter for a long moment before heaving himself to his feet and retracing my steps back to the front door, where he flicked the lock, flipped the sign to read CLOSED, and pulled the shade to the bottom of the glass panel. He fished a mottled handkerchief from his pants pocket and wiped his hands as he waddled back my way. I held my ground. He walked around me.

"I've got a problem," he said.

"That's what you said on the phone."

He dabbed at his wet lips with the hankie. I looked away.

"My wife's trying to poison me."

I shrugged. "Eat out."

"I'm serious."

"So am I."

He repocketed the hankie.

"I need her to stop."

"I don't do muscle work."

He laughed.

"What's so funny?" I asked.

"You'll see."

"Probably not," I said.

Somebody tried the front door, gave it a frustrated rattle, and stalked off.

He sensed I was losing interest and reached into his other pants pocket.

He waved a wad of cash, two full inches of greenbacks, bundled both ways by a red rubber band. "I've got $2,500 here for somebody can get her to stop."

I tried to stay calm. Twenty-five hundred would solve a lot of my present problems . . . food and rent for instance. "Why me?" I asked.

"They say you're a hard guy."

"They who?"

"Fella I know."

I thought it over. "How do you know she's trying to poison you."

"My doctor says so. He says she's been trying to poison me little by little over the past few months." He let his hands fall to his side with a slap. "Some kind of algicide he thinks."

My eyes followed the wad as he dropped it on the desk. "Call the cops."

"I can't. She's my wife."

"Get a divorce."

"I can't."

I made a rude noise with my lips. "Sure you can." I waved a hand in the air. "Even if you needed cause . . . which you don't anymore . . . I'm pretty sure poisoning would qualify as irreconcilable differences."

He made a face. "I'm orthodox. My religion doesn't allow for divorce." He caught me ogling the money. "All you gotta do is get her to stop." He made the Boys Scouts' honor sign, which really made me nervous. "My friend says you can be very persuasive."

"Not to mention this is a community property state."

His face went bland and blank as a cabbage. "Not to mention," he said.

"And all I've got to do is get her to stop."

"That's it."

I held out my hand. We each cast a glance at the wad on the desk.

"Later," he said. "After I'm—"

"Now," I countered. "I don't want to have to come back here."

"And if you can't pull it off?"

"Your buddy was right. I can be very persuasive."

He hesitated, took stock of me again, and then picked up the money, bounced it twice in his palm, and dropped it onto the desktop. He of little faith.

"Come see me when you get it done," he said, and went back to the paperwork.

The icy rain marched across the pavement like ranks of silver soldiers. I stood in the doorway of a used furniture joint directly across the street from the address he'd given me. I fondled my pocket imagining the wad of bills weighing heavy on my hip and smiled as wide as a guy who was two months behind on his rent could manage. It was a sandwich joint, half a dozen tables and a stand-up counter, big saltwater fish tank along the north wall. The Gnu Deli Delhi. Cute. Real cute.

I'd made a quick pass an hour ago. The place was jammed. The sign on the door said they were only open for breakfast and lunch and closed at 3. I'd decided to wait it out. It was 3:10 and the place had cleared except for the pair of girls who'd been working the counter.

The sight of the girls shrugging themselves into their raincoats sent me hustling across the rain-slick street. Halfway across, squinting through the hiss and mist of afternoon traffic, I saw her for the first time, coming out from what must have been an office somewhere behind the counter, big ring of keys in her right hand, holding the door open long enough for the girls to slip out and my toe to slip in.

She looked me over like a lunch menu. "You want that foot to go home with the other one, you'll move it."

We were nose to nose through the crack in the door, which made her over six feet tall. Big and brassy, showing a half acre of bony chest and a thick tangle of red hair held at bay by an enormous tortoise shell clip. Hard as I tried, I couldn't work up a picture of them as a couple.

"I need to have a word with you."

She leaned against the door. My shoe started to fold.

"Whatever you're selling . . ."

"Your husband sent me."

It was hard to describe the way her lips moved, somewhere between a smile and a sneer . . . a snile maybe. She eased off on the door. "Get out of here."

"He's been missing you," I tried.

"You know what my husband's missing?"

"What's that?"

She smirked. "A stepladder and delusions of grandeur."

"He says you're trying to poison him."

She eased off on the door. My shoe unfolded. "What if I am?"

Took me a second to recover my jaw. "You're not even gonna deny it?"

"Why should I? The world would be a better place without that little worm."

She turned and walked back into the restaurant, leaving me standing in the doorway as the steady rain beat itself to death on the awning. I stepped inside and closed the door behind me.

She skirted the counter and made her way back by the meat slicer. "I asked him for a *get*." She switched the slicer on. "He laughed in my face." She could tell I was confused. "A *get*'s an orthodox Jewish divorce."

"So? *Get* going. *Get* lost. *Get* down the road. No need to kill the guy."

"And give up everything? My business . . . my children . . . my standing in the community." She waved the whole idea off. "Not a chance. I'd be an outcast, a pariah." She shook her head slowly. I opened my mouth but she cut me off. "If I was trying to kill that maggot, he'd be long dead."

She pulled what appeared to be a roast beef from the refrigerated display case and plopped it down onto the slicer. I watched as she made an adjustment and began to slice.

"He says you've been feeding him an algicide or something."

She glanced up at the big fish tank and smiled. "I was just trying to get his attention." She returned the meat to the case. "I figured a couple of days in the can might help him see his way clear." She produced a block of cheese, separated several slices. "Besides . . ." she said, gesturing at the tank, "the fish don't seem to mind that stuff at all."

"So you figured . . ."

She took a bite from the sandwich and grinned again. "I figured what was good for pond scum was probably good for my husband."

I took a deep breath. "All he wants you to do is stop."

She lifted an enormous knife from the counter.

"Fat chance," she said around a mouthful. She waved the blade as she spoke. "What he wants . . . Mr. . . . ."

"Malloy," I said.

"What he wants, Mr. Malloy, is for me to come back and take care of him . . ." she sliced air with the scimitar, "clean the house . . . take care of the kids . . ."

I started to speak, but she cut me off again. "And what you want . . . Mr. Malloy, is that 2,500 bucks he offers every damn fool he can get to come out here and bother me."

I felt the color rising in my cheeks. I started to protest.

"So what's your story, Mr. Malloy? How did he talk you into this fool's errand?"

I'd have objected but I was busy asking myself the same question.

"You behind on your alimony payments? You need to pay your lawyer?" Her voice began to rise. "Or did you just go to school on the short bus?"

My mouth moved but nothing came out.

She held up a restraining hand . . . went right to unctuous. "Here I am being rude," she said. "Eating in front of guests. Can I make you a little something. A nice brisket sandwich or something? A little coleslaw maybe?"

My stomach did a series of back flips. "I'll pass," I replied.

Her face said that was what she figured. "You go back and tell that bottom feeder that either I get my *get* or he can spend the rest of his life sleeping on the couch with one eye open and eating take-out Chinese."

She used the remains of the sandwich to point the way out. "Now take yourself back out of here. I'm going to close up."

I opened my mouth again, but once more she beat me to the punch. "You tell him . . . you tell him . . . either I get my *get* or I'm going to spend the rest of my life making his existence as miserable as humanly possible." She swallowed the remainder of the sandwich and then licked her fingers and showed her teeth. "Till death do us part."

"Listen . . ." I stammered.

She picked up the knife and started back around the counter. I reached behind me and took hold of the door handle. "Easy now," I whispered.

"Easy my ass," she spat. She came forward, holding the knife low, making a sawing motion as she moved my way. Parts of me contracted like a dying star. I pulled open the door. She kept coming. I stepped outside and closed the door. Rain drummed the awning.

She locked the door with a smile. I'd seen that smile before. On the Discovery Channel. *Shark Week*. The neon *OPEN* sign went out.

He was still at the desk with the roll of bills at his elbow. He waited until I picked up the money to look at me. His facial features seemed to be having a meeting in the middle of his face. "You did it?" he asked.

The wad was warm in my hand. I shook my head, removed the rubber bands, and peeled off two hundred bucks.

"I'm taking two hundred for my per diem and for the aggravation."

"Guess you weren't as hard a guy as they said."

"If I had to go against her every day, I'd be in the storm door and aluminum siding business."

"So what is it I get for my two hundred bucks?" he asked.

I pocketed the bills. "Let me see if I've got this straight," I said as I wrapped the rubber bands around the pile of money. "You're not giving her a *get* . . . no matter what. Is that right?"

"You're a quick study, you are."

I cleared my throat. "And you plan on staying married to that woman and living in the same house with her."

He nodded.

"Well then . . . I guess what you get for your two hundred bucks is a piece of advice."

"Such as?"

"If . . . you know . . . sometime in the future . . . you think maybe she's trying to slip you something . . . a little more of that algicide or something . . ."

"Yeah?"

I dropped the wad onto the desk. It bounced.

"Take the poison," I said, and headed for the door.

ABOUT THE CONTRIBUTORS

KATHLEEN ALCALÁ is the author of a story collection, *Mrs. Vargas and the Dead Naturalist*; three novels set in nineteenth-century Mexico: *Spirits of the Ordinary*, *The Flower in the Skull*, and *Treasures in Heaven*; and a collection of essays, *The Desert Remembers My Name*. A cofounder of and contributing editor to the *Raven Chronicles*, Alcalá has been a writer in residence at Seattle University and the University of New Mexico. She teaches in the Northwest Institute of Literary Arts on Whidbey Island.

CURT COLBERT is the author of the Jake Rossiter & Miss Jenkins mysteries, a series of hardboiled, private detective novels set in 1940s Seattle. The first book, *Rat City*, was nominated for a Shamus Award in 2001. A Seattle native, Colbert is also a poet and an avid history buff. He is currently finishing the fourth book in the series, *Nowhere Town*, as well as working on a present-day novel, *All Along the Watchtower*, featuring Rossiter's son Matt as a Seattle-based PI.

R. BARRI FLOWERS is a best-selling, award-winning author of more than forty books, including the thrillers *State's Evidence, Persuasive Evidence,* and *Justice Served*. He is the editor of the American Crime Writers League's mystery anthology *Murder Past, Murder Present* and the recipient of the prestigious Wall of Fame Award from Michigan State University. He has appeared on the Biography Channel and Investigation Discovery. He lives in the Pacific Northwest.

G.M. FORD is the author of the six-book Leo Waterman series, which has been nominated for Shamus, Anthony, and Lefty awards. He also writes another series based on the disgraced reporter Frank Corso, and he recently completed his first nonseries novel, *Nameless Night*. Ford lives and works by the shores of the Pacific Ocean, and is a former creative writing instructor. He is married to mystery author Skye Moody.

PATRICIA HARRINGTON is a Derringer Award winner and her work has appeared in *Woman's Day* and *Mysterical-E*. The author's first mystery novel, *Death Stalks the Khmer*, had the distinction of being used as supplemental reading in university social work and intercultural communication classes.

THOMAS P. HOPP lived his earliest years in a West Seattle housing project. He draws on his European and Native American heritage to explore diverse themes in fiction. He studied molecular biology at the University of Washington, earned a PhD in biochemistry at Cornell Medical College in New York City, and helped found the biotechnology company, Immunex Corporation. His latest medical thriller is *The Jihad Virus*.

LOU KEMP'S writing has appeared in *Eldritch Tales, Black October,* and *Pirate Writings,* as well as several anthologies. One of her short stories received an honorable mention in *The Year's Best Fantasy and Horror 2005* edited by Ellen Datlow. She has just completed a novel, *Farm Hall.*

Rob Rose Studio

BHARTI KIRCHNER writes novels, cookbooks, essays, short stories, and magazine articles. She is the author of eight books, including four critically acclaimed novels. Her first novel, *Shiva Dancing,* was chosen by *Seattle Weekly* as one of the top eighteen books by Seattle authors in the last twenty-five years. Bharti's work has been translated into German, Dutch, Spanish, Thai, and other languages. Her story in this volume, "Promised Tulips," is an excerpt from a novel-in-progress.

John Vanee

ROBERT LOPRESTI is enjoying his third decade in western Washington. His more than thirty published short stories include a Derringer Award winner and an Anthony Award nominee. His first novel, *Such a Killing Crime,* was published in 2005.

Gene Frogge

STEPHAN MAGCOSTA has worked as a contributing writer for the *Stranger* and guest film curator at the University of Washington's Henry Art Gallery. He has read commentary on NPR and his writing has appeared in *La Voz,* the *Raven Chronicles,* and on numerous websites. He recently finished writing his first novel, *Surrounded by Grey,* an Aztec noir set in Seattle and pre-Colombian Mexico.

Rosanne Olson

SKYE MOODY is the award-winning author of seven books of fiction, three books of nonfiction, several short stories, and a five-year newspaper column about New Orleans' French Quarter for the *Times-Picayune*. Her latest nonfiction book, *Washed Up: The Curious Journeys of Flotsam and Jetsam*, was a "Washington Reads" selection in 2008. She has been a poet in residence at Tulane University and writer in residence at Seattle University. Moody is married to thriller writer G.M. Ford.

PAUL S. PIPER is a librarian at Western Washington University in Bellingham. His work has appeared in various literary journals, including the *Bellingham Review, Manoa, Sulfur,* and *CutBank*. Piper has four published books of poetry, and his writing has appeared in the books *The New Montana Story, Tribute to Orpheus,* and *America Zen*. He also coedited the books *Father Nature* and *X-Stories: The Personal Side of Fragile X Syndrome*.

BRIAN THORNTON'S short fiction short fiction has appeared in *Alfred Hitchcock's Mystery Magazine, Shred of Evidence,* and *Bullet Magazine*. He is also the author of several books of nonfiction, including *101 Things You Didn't Know about Lincoln,* and recently had a piece on Ross MacDonald published in the anthology *A Hell of a Woman: An Anthology of Female Noir*. A native Washingtonian, he lives in the Seattle area, and is Northwest Regional Chapter President for the Mystery Writers of America.

SIMON WOOD is the Anthony Award–winning author of *Working Stiffs, Accidents Waiting to Happen, Paying the Piper,* and *We All Fall Down*. A California transplant from England, he is a former racecar driver and a licensed pilot. He has published more than 150 short stories and articles. His stories have been included in "Best of" anthologies and he's a frequent contributor to *Writer's Digest*. For more information, visit www.simonwood.net.

Also available from the Akashic Books Noir Series

PORTLAND NOIR
edited by Kevin Sampsell
280 pages, trade paperback original, $15.95

Brand-new stories by: Gigi Little, Justin Hocking, Chris A. Bolton, Jess Walter, Monica Drake, Jamie S. Rich (illustrated by Joëlle Jones), Dan DeWeese, Zoe Trope, Luciana Lopez, Karen Karbo, Bill Cameron, Ariel Gore, Floyd Skloot, Megan Kruse, Kimberly Warner-Cohen, and Jonathan Selwood.

Violent crime, petty mischief, and personal tragedy run through these mysterious tales that career through this cloudy, wet city. *Portland Noir* is sure to both charm and frighten readers familiar with this northwest hub and intrigue those who have never traveled to this proudly weird city.

SAN FRANCISCO NOIR
edited by Peter Maravelis
292 pages, trade paperback original, $15.95

Brand-new stories by: Domenic Stansberry, Barry Gifford, Eddie Muller, Robert Mailer Anderson, Michelle Tea, Peter Plate, Kate Braverman, David Corbett, Alejandro Murguía, Sin Soracco, Alvin Lu, Jon Longhi, Will Christopher Baer, Jim Nesbit, and David Henry Sterry.

"Haunting and often surprisingly poignant, these accounts of death, love, and all things pulp fiction will lead you into unexpected corners of a city known to steal people's hearts." —*7x7* magazine

LOS ANGELES NOIR
edited by Denise Hamilton
360 pages, trade paperback original, $15.95
*A *Los Angeles Times* best seller and winner of an Edgar Award.

Brand-new stories by: Michael Connelly, Janet Fitch, Susan Straight, Héctor Tobar, Patt Morrison, Robert Ferrigno, Neal Pollack, Gary Phillips, Christopher Rice, Naomi Hirahara, Jim Pascoe, Scott Phillips, Diana Wagman, Lienna Silver, Brian Ascalon Roley, Emory Holmes II, and Denise Hamilton.

"Akashic is making an argument about the universality of noir; it's sort of flattering, really, and *Los Angeles Noir,* arriving at last, is a kaleidoscopic collection filled with the ethos of noir pioneers Raymond Chandler and James M. Cain."
—*Los Angeles Times Book Review*

BROOKLYN NOIR
edited by Tim McLoughlin
350 pages, trade paperback original, $15.95
*Winner of Shamus Award, Anthony Award, Robert L. Fish Memorial Award; finalist for Edgar Award, Pushcart Prize.

Brand-new stories by: Pete Hamill, Arthur Nersesian, Ellen Miller, Nelson George, Nicole Blackman, Sidney Offit, Ken Bruen, and others.

"*Brooklyn Noir* is such a stunningly perfect combination that you can't believe you haven't read an anthology like this before. But trust me—you haven't . . . The writing is flat-out superb, filled with lines that will sing in your head for a long time to come."
—Laura Lippman, winner of the Edgar, Agatha, and Shamus awards

D.C. NOIR
edited by George Pelecanos
304 pages, trade paperback original, $15.95

Brand-new stories by: George Pelecanos, Laura Lippman, James Grady, Kenji Jasper, Jim Beane, Ruben Castaneda, Robert Wisdom, James Patton, Norman Kelley, Jennifer Howard, Jim Fusilli, Richard Currey, Lester Irby, Quintin Peterson, Robert Andrews, and David Slater.

"Fans of the [noir] genre will find solid writing, palpable tension, and surprise endings to keep them reading."
—*Washington Post*

CHICAGO NOIR
edited by Neal Pollack
252 pages, trade paperback original, $14.95

Brand-new stories by: Neal Pollack, Achy Obejas, Alexai Galaviz-Budziszewski, Adam Langer, Joe Meno, Peter Orner, Kevin Guilfoile, Bayo Ojikutu, M.K. Meyers, Todd Dills, Daniel Buckman, and others.

"*Chicago Noir* is a legitimate heir to the noble literary tradition of the greatest city in America. Nelson Algren and James Farrell would be proud."
—Stephen Elliott, author of *Happy Baby*